RECKLESS CURVES

Drive Me Wild

BRONWEN EVANS

RECKLESS CURVES
DRIVE ME WILD—Bad Boy Autos

Published By Bronwen Evans March 2020

Copy Editor: Leigh Kaye
Cover: Les

Reckless Curves...

*From **USA Today** Bestselling Author, Bronwen Evans, comes her latest sexy contemporary romance! A secret baby, best friend's little sister romance set in Bad Boy Autos.*

Thomas (Tom) Lorde's morning couldn't get any worse. One call changes everything. Apparently he's a dad. *He* should be on the phone to his lawyer. He wouldn't put it past a woman—any woman—to lie to get at his hard earned money. His mother trapped his father into marriage and then left them both for deeper pockets. But when the news is delivered from between the sweet lips of Kendra Black, his best friend's out of bounds little sister, and his one major 'fucking' mistake, he knows he's screwed and that she's not lying.

Kendra Black knew contacting Tom would be a mistake. Three years ago, he'd made it very clear he had no feelings for her. He slept with her and then flew to Europe without a backward glance. However, he left more than a broken heart behind. He might not want her, but now that's he's back in California, her son, their son, Connor (Con) Black, deserves to know his father. What she hadn't expected was Tom's old-fashioned lap of honor.

He wants to marry her. Why couldn't he simply be a weekend dad like her father? She can't deny the physical attraction is still there. *He* might be okay with a marriage based on hot, raw, animalistic sex and only sex, but she wants more. She deserves a man who loves her and she refuses to wave the checked flag until he gives her his heart.

This book is for those who have overcome.
Overcome their past mistakes.
Their upbringing.
Or anything that causes us to struggle and improve ourselves every single day.
We live and learn.
And of course LOVE.

Prologue

os Angeles, Four Years Ago
Kendra slowly eased off the pedal as she sped down Hollywood Boulevard, least she speed her way into a ticket. She wanted nothing to kill her buzz today.

She was driving like her brother Marcus Black drove on the race circuit. *Speed kills you idiot.* She laughed out loud. She was on a natural high from her successful meeting this afternoon and she knew it. Finally, she understood why her brother craved speeding around a race-track—the adrenalin. The feeling was addictive.

Even with the negativity from her parents, she'd gone ahead and auditioned as a backup singer for James Tan, the latest boy singing sensation's California tour.

Her father was pushing her to go to law school mainly because her brother had walked away from university to become a formula one racing car driver. There had to be at least one lawyer in the family, and as the only other child, she drew the short straw. Law bored her silly. And life was too short to be bored. She should know.

She relived the audition in her head and a shiver of joy raced through her. No one had believed she could do it. But she hadn't spent most of her teenage years combating and beating cancer without learning that in life you had to fight to reach your dreams.

She had much bigger plans than going to university and sitting in an office for the rest of her life. Music had always been the love of her life—well—the second love of her life. Unfortunately, the first love of her life, Thomas (Tom) Lorde spent most of his time pretending she didn't exist.

Tom was her brother's best friend and head mechanic on the racing circuit which meant he spent most of the year in Europe, with Marcus, racing. It was almost as if Tom relished his job just because it took him far away from her.

When he was here, they flirted all the time but, damn it, he would not cross that brotherly, best friend line. *Yet!*

The light up ahead was turning green, so she didn't even slow down as she drove to Porter's bar, where she was meeting Stella to celebrate her audition. Her best friend was more excited than her at her signing and was already lining up for an introduction to James.

She pushed down the fear churning in her stomach at having to tell her father, but what he didn't know couldn't hurt him. Maybe he didn't have to know. She could still go to University and sing. *Music isn't a career. Only 1% make a living...* She pushed away the darkness of her father's disapproval ringing in her head. She had one year to prove that she could make music a career, just like Marcus had done with driving. Perhaps then, her father wouldn't shout the roof off when she told him she was dropping out to sing full time.

For some reason, her father was much tougher on her than he'd been on Marcus. Tougher on her for two reasons, probably because there were no other children after her. And he'd watched her beat cancer and now seemed to think he had to watch her every minute of the day. Worse still, her father had visions of her carrying on in the family law firm as if she'd beaten cancer just to fulfill this role.

She reached across the passenger seat and patted her bright pink Alexander McQueen The Story tote bag with her fake ID safe inside. Tonight, of all nights, nothing would stop her getting into Porters, the hippest club on the boulevard. She had plans for this evening. Special plans. It was her day and she would make it her night too.

Marcus and his racing buddies would be drinking at the club, and there was one person in particular she'd set her sights on. Hell, it was her birthday after all—twenty today. She glanced in the rearview mirror and smiled. She'd just signed her first paying music contract and tonight she could do anything, and what she wanted to do was Thomas Lorde.

Her body shivered. It must really be her night she laughed, as she found a park near to the bar, and when she flashed her ID at the bouncer, he simply waved her through. *If only everything in life was this easy.* She of all people knew how tough life could be. She'd spent years battling leukemia and had been given the all clear four years ago. Pride saw her straighten and walk tall. She wasn't a quitter; she was a fighter, and as she stared across the bar at Thomas, Tom to his friends, that fighting spirit rose to engulf her.

He'll be mine tonight.

As Kendra made her way toward her friend, she noticed guys glancing her way with appreciative looks on their faces, fantastic for her confidence. Except there was only one guy she wanted glancing at her with such a look on his face. She mentally willed him to turn around, her eyes spearing him, and wow she was on fire, because he looked over his shoulder and watched her every move as she drew near.

For once, his eyes didn't look away. Her outfit was working its magic. His eyes flared with heat as he took in her skimpy pink halter top resting just above her 'fit like a glove' white Capri jeans, showing off her Californian tan. Her pink stilettos made her legs look as if they went on forever, and she wore her long black hair loose. It had taken her almost a year to grow her hair back after her chemo, and she hadn't cut it since.

"You work it girl," Stella said when Kendra reached their table just behind where Marcus and Tom stood at the bar. She hadn't taken her eyes from Tom, and he certainly hadn't taken his eyes off her either.

This was the night… she could feel it in her bones.

Giddy with excitement, she took a seat facing Tom and lifted a shot Stella had waiting for her. "Here's to your first music contract," Stella exclaimed, clanking their glasses together as they downed their shots quickly.

The hit of alcohol didn't stir her as much as Tom's sexy grin.

For once Tom wasn't hanging off Marcus's every word. His mouth hung open watching her as if he wanted to eat her all up. *Fine with me.*

Tom's smoky gray eyes held her hostage. He was drop-the-fuck-dead gorgeous with scruffy, shoulder length surfer blond hair framing a GQ model face. He had that hint of danger about him, as if life hadn't been easy. Yet his clothes screamed money. He was tall and had powerful arms. She briefly closed her eyes, remembering the huge eagle tattoo on his chest. Having a swimming pool at your home did have some advantages. She'd seen just about every inch of his perfect body.

Stella leaned over and whispered, "You did it, girl. You've got Tom's attention. How about I ensure Marcus's attention is elsewhere?"

"Did I ever tell you how much I love you," Kendra said to her friend as she picked up another shot and drank it. And still Tom was watching.

She didn't really even notice Stella leave the table to distract Marcus, but Tom must have, because he sauntered toward where she sat as if he knew she loved looking at him.

"You look different tonight," he said as he took the chair Stella had vacated.

"I'm celebrating." At his raised eyebrow she added, "Today I signed to be a backup singer for James Tan."

His grin widened. "Way to go. I knew you could do anything you set your mind to."

She wanted to hug him just for those words. At sixteen, when she'd been declared in remission, he'd been the one to tell her. That you shouldn't let anyone stop you from reaching for your dreams. He'd never treated her as the sickly, weak, fragile girl most people saw when they looked at her.

He signaled for the waitress. "A bottle of your finest champagne."

She couldn't help herself. "Aren't you scared Marcus might see us talking?"

"Even he won't mind me helping you celebrate such a milestone. Besides, he looks as if his mind is elsewhere."

She tore her gaze from Tom and looked at her handsome brother. Yip, Stella was working her magic. Her best friend could make guys beg for just a smile, and it appeared Marcus was no different.

"I'm waiting for Marcus to see you are here and wonder how you got into the bar." Her face heated. "I suspect with you looking like that the bouncer didn't really look at the ID very closely," Tom added with a naughty grin on his lips.

"Are you going to tell on me?"

He leaned closer. "I'd be stupid to do that. I'd rather ask for a reward for not ruining your evening."

This time it was her turn for her lips to form a naughty grin. "Reward?"

Tom winked. "A kiss should seal these lips."

They'd flirted like this hundreds of times before. Tonight, she would not back down. "For the kiss I want to give you, you most definitely want your lips unsealed."

Tom threw a glance over his shoulder. She followed his gaze and saw Marcus was no longer standing there. Nor was Stella.

"I like how you think," and he took her chin between his fingers and slowly lowered his lips to hers.

OMG, he's finally going to kiss me. She held her breath.

When his lips touched Kendra's, her whole body caught fire. She moved closer, lifting her hand into his hair, bringing them closer so their chests touched. He deepened the kiss, slowly parting her lips, before driving his tongue into her mouth, sweeping and swirling his tongue with hers. She'd never experienced a kiss like it. She'd dreamed of kisses from Tom… reality blew her imaginings out of the water. His kiss was filled with such passion, if she'd been standing her legs wouldn't have held her up. She put her whole self into returning fire with fire, showing him what was in her heart.

When they parted, she knew one kiss would never be enough.

"Be mine for tonight. Only tonight, that's all I have," he breathed in her ear.

She couldn't talk, speechless with victory. She merely nodded.

"Let's get out of here," and with her hand swallowed by his very large one, they left the bar.

This was her night.

*This was **their** night.*

Chapter One

L os Angeles, *four years later....*
      "Yo, Tom! Catherine's working late and told me to
      tell you you've got company in reception, dude."
Tom pushed himself out from under the car he was replacing
the muffler on and stood. No client would come to the auto shop
this late. Bad Boy Autos clientele were too wealthy to hang
around what was essentially a chop shop, be it a high-end
chrome and glass garage on Sunset Boulevard filled with
Maserati's, Ferrari's, and Porsche's'. Tom loved customizing the
dream machines as he called them and was thankful their rich
clients were prepared to pay handsomely for their services.

   "Did Catherine say who it was, Zip?" Catherine Beckett was
the office manager, accountant, and the gorgeous face of the
company. She was also a partner in the firm. She handled the
money. She had a brain like Einstein, but she also dazzled the
clients with legs that appeared to never end. Cat had a body that
could rival any in a Playboy spread, and a face that had men
looking at her rather than their cars.

   Zip Chang, the mechanic they'd hired last month, just
grinned. "She's hot, I'll tell you that, but then every woman who

turns up here looking for you is hot. You have a type when it comes to women, smokin' hot. Envy, man."

He shook his head at Zip's words. Shoot him. He liked hot women, what man didn't, but he never led them on. Never promised more than he could give. But when they were with him, he treated them like princesses.

He hoped it wasn't Trina, or was her name Katrina, from the other night. While he loved women, a lot of women, he didn't do love—one on one. Ever. Life had shown him that love meant loss. Relationships between men and women were doomed to fail, and the fallout wasn't worth the risk.

"Just tell me who she is."

Zip laughed harder. "You'll see. Just go see her and I'll finish up."

"Taylor wants another 1000 horsepower under his bonnet so we need two more mufflers on the right. Thanks, Zip."

Tom wiped his hands on a rag and headed towards the plush reception area of Bad Boy Autos. Dealing in high-end cars didn't feel like a job, but one side of the job he hated was the glitz and glamor that went with the clientele they procured. Men and women who spent more on a car than some people spent on their houses. Maserati, Porsche, and Mercedes. With his lowly background, he'd never been comfortable around money, even though he now had plenty of his own.

For over five years he'd been the number one mechanic on the formula one racing circuit and he'd earned plenty. A share of the drivers prize money and a salary that was seven digits, coupled with a great investment advisor, meant he never had to worry about money again. Six months ago he'd invested in Bad Boy Autos with his best friend Marcus Black, the formula one race car driver who's back was so badly injured in a crash eighteen months ago that he could no longer drive professionally.

Catherine waved at him through the glass partition and pointed to the luxury reception area. She often worked late in the office to keep on top of the invoicing. They'd offered to get her some help, but she preferred to keep control of everything. Control freak, he supposed. But they'd be lost without her.

He hoped whoever this woman was, she would be a pleasant diversion from the crap day he'd had. His dad had come through the surgery and was doing well so far. Tom had stayed at the hospital a lot longer than he'd intended since his brother Sam had guilted him into hanging around until Vincent had returned to the recovery room. He was still angry with Sam. Tom didn't owe his father anything. Not after the upbringing he'd had.

He knew coming back to LA was a risk. The European circuit meant he didn't have to see his father or revisit his childhood. He'd been back barely a month before his past came calling. His father needed a new liver. No surprises there. He'd drunk himself to the point of death, also the excuse he now used as to why he'd been so shitty to his kids.

This morning Tom had come directly to work from the hospital, and on top of a lack of sleep, had found out that one of their parts suppliers had mucked up an order. It had put them behind schedule for the day, which was why he was still working at eight o'clock this evening, dead on his feet. Zip had volunteered to stay to help, and Tom had been happy to give him the overtime.

The smile on his lips died as soon as he saw Marcus's sister, Kendra Black, standing by the counter. She was still a princess, and he was most definitely still the bad boy from the wrong side of the tracks. She was more beautiful than ever with her long, sleek black hair, olive-green eyes, and the sweetest, softest lips he'd ever kissed.

Even after all this time, he still remembered the way she'd felt against his mouth, his skin, and the sounds of pleasure that had come from between them. Reining in his libido, he walked closer.

"Kendra. Zip said that someone was here to see me, but I think you must want Marcus—"

Her eyes glittered like green glass. "No. I've come to see you."

Tom's eyebrows rose and a prickle of unease slid up his spine. Normally Kendra Black avoided him, and he was relieved. It hurt just looking at her. He still wanted her as much as he ever had, but she was still Marcus's little sister and still off limits, especially now she had a kid and now he was in business with her brother. Marcus was still feral over the fact Kendra protected the man who'd done this to her. Tom had even offered to help Marcus kick this guy's ass when they learned the truth. How dare this guy treat Kendra like this, let alone a little boy? He'd only seen Connor a few times, but he was the spitting image of Kendra with jet-black hair.

He thanked God every day Marcus never learned of his one big fuckin' mistake. Tom had known to stay well clear of Marcus's little sister. It was the bro code, but that was fuckin' hard to do when she'd pursued him as if he was her favorite treat. Finally, four years ago, on a break from the racing circuit, he'd ultimately given in to his desire. She was a beauty, and though he had promised to leave her alone, he couldn't. But really, when had he ever adhered to the rules?

From the minute of their first meeting by the pool, when she was still jailbait, Kendra let him know she was up for a taste of him. He deserved a medal for his resistance. He'd steered well clear of her until that fateful night four years later.

It helped that he spent most of the year in Europe on the racing circuit. But the down season was the hardest, and it finally got him into trouble.

The night he'd caved in to his burning need to taste her, she'd just turned twenty, and instead of remembering Marcus's warnings, he had slept with Kendra. The exotic memory was burned into his brain. He should regret that amazing night, but he didn't. He blamed it on her birthday party and her asking for a personal present—a kiss from him. It was the best night of his life. He'd told himself dinner and dancing, nothing more—she deserved way better than him, anyway. But that first kiss ignited something in them both, and it wasn't long before they moved to his hotel and melted into one another's arms, wanting way more than kisses. He still wanted more, couldn't get her out of his mind even all these years later.

But happy families were not for him. He didn't have any plans to be involved in a relationship. In his experience people let you down. Marriages never lasted, and you simply ended up hating each other, just like his parent's had.

"We need to talk," she said, looking at him coolly. Her voice coated him like a honey glaze. Kendra had a sweet tone with a slight rasp that turned him on. But there was an edge to her comment that made him concerned.

"Has something happened to Marcus?"

"The world does not start and end with my brother. No, this is about you and me."

"Kendra, babe, there is no you and me," he said looking around wishing she'd keep her voice down. Catherine was watching with interest. "Aside from friends I mean, or is that what you mean?"

"Friends, really? Okay, the past you and me then. Or have you forgotten our one night together, perhaps you have, as it has been awhile… almost four years ago."

Forget? That night burned in his memory.

When he said nothing, her eyes narrowed. "I suppose it's hard to keep track with all the women who throw themselves at you. Let me refresh your memory. You screwed me once and then tore out of there afterwards like your ass was on fire!"

Tom remembered everything. He especially remembered back further, eight years ago, to the day when he'd first met Marcus and laid eyes on his little sister, Kendra.

Marcus had caught him eyeing Kendra up — his recently recovered little sister who'd been sick with leukemia, though you'd never know it by looking at her now. Marcus had made it crystal clear back then that his sister was off limits, especially as they both had man-whore reputations. He'd vowed to his best friend he'd keep his zipper up around her. That vow had ripped to shreds when four years ago he'd been weak, and he'd given into temptation, betraying Marcus and totally screwing up with Kendra.

Tom forced his attention back to the present and shook his head. "That night was a mistake. I think we both agree about that. Why bring it up now?"

He was further startled when her jaw clenched and she banged a pretty fist down on the counter.

"A mistake? Well, some mistakes have consequences and it's about time you faced up to yours whether you like it or not."

Her breasts rose and fell under her black tank top, making it hard for Tom to think with his brain instead of where his blood had flowed. Shit. Only two minutes in her presence and he was ready to back her up against the wall and...

"I don't know what you mean," Tom said. "I only left that night because I had an early flight out. I had to get back to Prague and the racing circuit—" Tom stopped short of saying anymore because of what came to mind. He vividly remembered the condom incident too, something that may have propelled him out the door. They'd talked about it, but she assured him she couldn't get pregnant.

"That's it? Surely you remember our conversation about the condom breaking?" Kendra hurled at him. "Maybe that's why you left that night, but what about after? You never answered my calls, emails, nothing! You never even tried to contact me."

Tom hid his guilt behind a stony expression. He felt bad about not staying in touch, but he always figured she'd let him know through Marcus if there was a problem. Besides, Marcus would never approve of him hooking up with his sister, so staying in contact was a bad idea all the way around. "Look, it was just one night, all turned out good, right? And I warned you I wasn't into relationships." He shrugged, feeling like the gum on the bottom of his shoe. "I wasn't trying to hurt your feelings, but I figured that a clean break was best so I ignored your messages and emails. Maybe that wasn't the right thing to do, but I've been back in America for almost a year. How was I to know that you're still pissed about it?"

She came closer, and the enticing scent she wore hit him like a ton of bricks. Heat roared through his body and he cursed the fact she still affected him so strongly. The instant arousal took Tom completely off-guard, and he staggered back a step.

"You think I'm still pissed about you not wanting more, more between us? You're even more conceited than I thought. Think for a moment. Why might I have been chasing after you so hard?"

Tom's second sense rose to the surface like it had back in the day whenever his drunken father was around. His insides clenched, fearing the worse. "What are you implying?"

Her eyes never left his. "What kind of man ignores a woman's pleas?"

"Pleas?" But spots danced behind his eyes. It was as if his body knew what she was about to say, but his mind could not grasp the implication.

"What kind of man knocks up his best friend's sister and doesn't even want to acknowledge his son's existence but is happy to go into business with her brother?"

Her hissed statement was like a sucker punch to the groin, and Tom couldn't move. "What?" he asked softly.

"You got me pregnant and left me to face it all alone," Kendra said, tears shimmering in her eyes. "I begged and begged you to come be with me, to help me, but you wouldn't. Obviously, you wanted nothing to do with me or Connor."

A buzzing started in Tom's brain, and he shook his head to clear it. "Connor? What the hell are you saying, Kendra?"

"Like you don't know! It was in the emails I sent you!"

"No! I *don't* know!" Tom shot back. Shit, he'd received her calls and emails but never *listened or read* them... he couldn't, he missed her too much and he didn't want to fuck up both their lives. He was just beginning to taste success and Marcus would've killed him for sleeping with his little sister, destroying both their chances to make it big. Why bother to cause that pain for something that would never last. Once Kendra got to know the real him, she'd leave anyway. Princesses always got their prince, not the frog.

Kendra said, "You're Connor's father! I told you in all those emails I sent!"

Tom could barely get his words out. "What? No, I'm not. Emails?"

She searched Tom's face as if looking for any sign of deception. "Did you get my emails?"

Tom nodded, I guess now was as good as time as any to confess. "I got them, but I never opened them. I deleted your voicemails before I listened to them." He knew if he'd opened even one, he'd be tempted to contact her and that wasn't an option with the racing team on the cusp of victory. He couldn't let anything destroy Marcus's chance. He'd also promised Marcus he'd stay away from Kendra—but if he'd known... He looked at the hurt on her face and knew she spoke the truth. Finally, he understood why Kendra had refused to reveal the baby's father to her brother.

Fuck. It was to protect him.

Guilt hit hard and fast. "You should've come and told me in person as soon as I moved back to LA."

"I thought you already knew and had decided you didn't want us."

He ground his teeth. If Kendra had been a man, he'd have punched her for implying he'd treat any woman, let alone a child that way. Did she even know him at all? How could she? He'd never let her get that close. "I didn't know."

Kendra folded her arms. "Really?"

Tom's expression tightened. The hits kept coming. "I can prove it to you." Striding around behind the counter, he went to the computer. "Come here."

* * *

Kendra followed him and stopped by his side. She watched him bring up his email account and log in. His hands were greasy, but that didn't dim her sudden desire to feel them on her body. She'd loved the way his calloused palms had satisfyingly scraped along her thighs, while he'd held her down so he could pleasure her with his tongue.

Tom was right, he'd been in LA awhile now and she should have told him he was Connor's father, but she'd hoped he would've come to her by now. That he wanted to come to her. Not that she expected him to be a dad, but he could pay his fair share.

Connor deserved to be protected and financially secure. She knew Marcus would always look out for Connor, but her son deserved to have one living parent in his life.

She jerked back to the present when he turned the computer monitor and pointed at an email folder with her name on it. "See that? I put all of your emails in here, but never opened them." He clicked on the folder, and a list of over twenty emails lined the screen. Every single one of them was still in bold, and they were in chronological order.

Kendra looked at all the unopened emails and then into Tom's eyes. She couldn't hold his gaze for long, though, because she didn't want him to see the tears that threatened. *He hadn't known!*

She *should* have confronted him sooner, but pride had gotten in her way. She would not beg to have him in their lives. But today when Marianne, a fellow cancer survivor, had shared her terrible news, Kendra's world became very black and white. Marianne's cancer was back, and it was terminal. Marianne had been in remission as long as Kendra. What would happen to Connor if her cancer came back? Her little boy deserved to know and love, at least one living parent.

Lowering her eyes, Kendra said, "Let's go somewhere and talk about this."

She walked to the door. Relief sparked when she heard Tom following her. Anxiety gnawed at her insides as she led him over to her powder blue Honda Odyssey van.

"I can't believe that Marcus is letting you drive this piece of shit," Tom remarked.

Kendra's chin rose. "Marcus has always been there for me. I won't let him buy me something else. I depend on him too much as it is. It's hard to make a car payment on what I make, but I manage… most of the time."

She'd dropped out of law school as soon as she knew she was pregnant. When her father refused to support her unless she named the father, she'd turned to teaching music and doing backup vocals, mainly for new singers wanting demo tapes. She got by; proud she could do it on her own—mostly on her own. Marcus helped when she couldn't make ends meet, but Tom didn't need to know that.

Guilt and anger flitted across Tom's chiseled face as she watched him look down at her, and Kendra's lungs refused to expand for a few moments. He'd been downright sexy when they'd been younger, but he'd matured, he'd become even more devastating.

She'd liked when he wore his hair long, but the close-cropped, almost military style cut he now sported made him look edgy and even more dangerous. The black, Bad Boy Autos T-shirt molded his well-defined, muscular body. A tattoo peeked out from under the left sleeve, but she couldn't make out what it was in the dark. It must be new, because she'd memorized every tattoo on his body that one night.

"You want to explain to me what's going on in that head of yours?" he asked.

The unsure, perplexed look on his face softened her heart a bit. "You really didn't know, did you?"

"No. And I sure as hell would have helped if I'd known. I've even met Connor. He looks nothing like me." He stood looking down at her.

"You haven't looked hard enough then, or spent enough time with him."

"Why did you wait so long to confront me then? Is it because you're not sure he's mine? Weren't you seeing a guy in your father's law firm at the time? Marcus is sure he's the father. He even let all the tires down on the dick's Audi one night and refused to work on his car once too."

"When you meet Connor, you'll know."

"Now. I want to meet my son now!"

"He's asleep. Let's go somewhere and talk about this situation."

He gave a curt nod before looking across at Catherine. "We'll go to my place. No one will bug us there. Just give me a minute while I let Zip know I'm leaving."

Kendra swallowed the panic at the thought of being alone with Tom at his house, but they couldn't talk at her place since her neighbor was watching Connor there. "Okay. I'll follow you."

He nodded again and walked back into the office. She watched him have a quick chat with Catherine, and then he disappeared into the work area.

In her head, Kendra went over the sum she'd come to for child support. It was fair, and it was an amount Tom could easily afford. He'd had a very successful career on the racing circuit.

She wasn't greedy. She just needed enough money to ensure care of Connor. What she really wanted was for Tom to want to know his son, especially if the worst should happen to her. Her health—touch wood—at this point was good, although she had to be realistic. That could change in the blink of an eye. Like it had for Marianne.

About five minutes later a whistle pierced the air signaling he was ready to go, and she watched as Tom strode over to a red Mustang while she got in her van. She started it and tried to get her racing heartbeat under control. Tom had never lied to her. Even if he'd known something would hurt her feelings, he'd always been honest with her. She believed his story of not opening the emails.

A horn beeped, and Kendra saw Tom's car now faced the road. She put the van in gear and trailed after him as he pulled out and sped away. As she followed him, she pondered the fact that all her emails to him were still unopened, and she wondered why he hadn't bothered to read them.

Why did she wait so long? It just never occurred to her he'd never even looked at the communication she'd sent him.

Had he just not considered them important enough? No, that couldn't be right. You didn't keep emails unless they meant something to you. You deleted them and forgot about them. But Tom hadn't just kept them; he'd put them in a special folder. Why would he do that?

Had she been more than just a quick lay to him? Kendra squashed the tiny seed of hope that tried to sprout in her heart. *No way I'm going down that road again,* she thought as she kept Tom's taillights in sight.

Chapter Two

Tom gripped the steering wheel so hard it was a wonder he didn't snap it right off the steering column. His brain was going a hundred miles an hour as he tried to wrap his mind around this bombshell; he was a father. He did not doubt that Kendra spoke the truth, but perhaps it might pay to get a DNA test just to be sure. If Conner was his flesh and blood, why had she waited so long to tell him? She should have been right up in his face as soon as he'd arrived back in LA. He'd been here for months, she'd had plenty of opportunity.

He glanced in the rearview mirror to ensure Kendra was still following him. *Kendra.* The mother of his child. Over the whole drive to his house, he tried to solve the puzzle of their past, but he didn't have all the pieces. He'd have to get more information from her.

When he pulled into his driveway, he quickly killed the engine and got out as Kendra parked beside him. Standing against his car, he watched as she gathered her things, and when her legs swung around after she'd opened the door, his physical response was immediate. He'd never gotten this woman out of his head.

"This way." He directed her, watching those long legs as she brushed by.

They walked in silence to the front door and as he unlocked it, turning off the alarm, he felt a sense of pride for his accomplishments in life, now mingled with remorse for not knowing his son and his mother. Life sure throws you curveballs. He'd dealt with plenty in his life, and he'd learned that these struggles gave you strength through either accepting or overcoming them. "You want a drink? I have iced tea, water, or soda."

"No beer? I could use a beer," Kendra replied.

"I don't drink so I don't have it in the house, sorry," Tom said, flicking on the living room light.

"Since when?" she asked.

"Since I found out that my dad pickled his liver. Haven't drunk liquor in three years." Addiction was hereditary, and he was already too much like his father. He would never end up a sad, sorry excuse of a man whose wife left him for a man with deeper pockets and who was sober. He didn't blame his mother for leaving. But he'd never forgive his mother for leaving and not taking him with her. Why had she left him behind?

He shook away the insecurities caused by his childhood, remembering the day he'd heard about his father's liver. It was the last day he drank. It had been tough, but he was nothing like his father and never would be.

Tom motioned towards the ugly gray couch against the far wall. "Have a seat."

Kendra's gaze roamed around the room, and her expression told him she hated the place. The distaste on her beautiful face made him laugh.

"Pretty ugly, huh?"

Kendra's mouth curve upwards. "Yeah. Why do you live here when you're rich?"

Tom said, "I bought it for the land. I'm going to tear this down and rebuild. I've always wanted to design my house and I want a large garage to play in." He wanted to show the world he'd made it. He'd escaped to the right side of the tracks.

"Men and their cars… " She stared outside. "It will be a huge house." She eyed him incredulously. "For one man?"

He shrugged. Something deep within him wanted a big house. "I have nieces and nephews."

She nodded and perched on the right end of the couch, so Tom took the left, the anger that had been building the whole drive home barely under control.

He'd earned a fortune working in formula one and when Marcus had suggested the concept of Bad Boy Autos he jumped at the idea. He would be the head mechanic and oversee the team, while Marcus would take on operations, marketing, and finance. Plus, it was the famous formula one world driver's champion, Marcus Black's name that would draw most of the clients. The perfect fit.

Their first year was looking extremely profitable.

Yet Kendra seemed to struggle financially, and he hated that.

"So, I'm responsible for you dropping out of law school and the estrangement with your father. Marcus kept me informed about your life when he learned you were pregnant. You really know how to hammer a guy. I have a son I don't know, and you've waited all this time to tell me. All you had to do was tell Marcus and I would have learned the truth about those emails and phone calls."

He watched as Kendra breathed deeply before replying. "I would have dropped out of law school at some point, anyway. I only went to school because father couldn't get Marcus to go. He wanted one of his children to take over the family law firm. Getting pregnant was a blessing. It gave me the courage to stand up to my father."

"Your father, like mine, is a bit of a bastard." At least they had that in common.

"My father is a control freak, and while I have little respect for the man, he made sure I got the best treatment when I was battling cancer. I can't forget that."

Tom considered her words. "I think you have a lot of your father in you. You're stubborn, and you also seemed to like controlling things. You could have told me as soon as I set foot in LA. I don't know if I can ever forgive you for not telling me I had a son sooner. I know I'll never forgive myself for not reading your emails or taking your calls."

Again, she was quietly considering his words, and then said, "Hindsight is a wonderful thing. I thought you didn't want us, and I worried about your business with Marcus. But you are right. I should have done this ages ago. Connor should have come first, not you or Marcus."

Turning to her, some anger he held deep in his gut died. "Okay, start at the beginning, Kendra. And what I really want to know is why you didn't tell me the minute I arrived back in LA."

Connor was already three years old, and he'd missed his baby's early years. How did he forgive that? He swallowed back his anger, knowing part of this was his fault. He should have responded when she'd contacted him years ago. He knew Marcus's warning about his sister was merely an excuse. When he was younger, he was not willing to have a steady relationship. After the disaster of his parent's marriage, he definitely didn't want to go down that track at any speed. He'd planned to conquer the formula racing circuit with Marcus. It had been his dream for so long. *Their dream.* A dream that would prove he could rise above his upbringing and get away from his father.

And he'd succeeded.

So he could not blame her entirely....

"Kendra?" he prompted.

She was playing with a small hole in her jeans. Tom still thought it was ridiculous how ripped pants were fashionable, but Kendra was concentrating on pulling them apart just as she started talking. "I haven't had a lot of experience with men. You're the second man I ever slept with. I hadn't been with anyone for about four months before we slept together. I found out I was pregnant around seven weeks later. I called and emailed you right away, but you didn't answer. I kept trying, but I never heard from you. So, after Dad threw me out, I had Connor by myself. My friend Stella helped me too."

"What about your mum?"

Kendra scoffed. "She does whatever Dad says and he forbade her to see me."

"You could have told Marcus. He would have let me know immediately." With his fists, Tom thought darkly.

"I didn't want to drag Marcus in to this. At the time he had a real chance of winning the formula one driver's world title that year. His first ever chance. I knew if I told him it would tear you two apart and destroy the team. I could not do that to him. Thank God I didn't, as bloody Jason Colter ended his career not a year later. It had been Marcus's one and only chance."

Tom's gut clenched. He couldn't deny Marcus's only shot at winning the title could've been ruined if all hell had broken loose over Kendra being pregnant... by him. "A part of me understands, but the other part, the part that has missed out on my son's first three years is pissed. What about after his accident? You could have told me then."

"Marcus crashed. You were his head mechanic, and Marcus always said only you could feel the car like he could. I thought you'd be blaming yourself for the car spinning out and I couldn't intensify everything with blurting out you were a father too."

She had a point. He had wondered if the crash was his fault, and he'd not left Marcus's side until he came out of ICU, but a replay showed Jason Colter had clipped Marcus's car. "But once he was better.... You could have told him then. He could have got hold of me and told me. I would have—"

"What would you have done? Come home? I don't think so. The circuit was your world as much as it was Marcus's. By then I was coping okay on my own, and I didn't want to be the one to bring Marcus's world crashing down around him. I still don't."

He closed his mouth, unable to deny that racing cars *had* been his world—both their worlds. "I don't know what I would have done, but now we will never know. You decided for me."

She looked like she might cry. "I did what I thought was right at the time. And when you came home… I assumed you had read the emails and didn't want to know your son. I must admit, I've never pictured you as a family sort of guy."

Kendra rubbed her palms down her thighs, and he remembered the way her fingers felt on his skin. "I'm sorry but... Thinking you were rejecting us made me hesitate to confront you. Rejection is difficult to take."

Tom's jaw clenched. "So, you let your parents disown you and kick you out so you didn't screw things up for me? Even after you thought I didn't give a shit that I got you pregnant?"

Kendra sat back a little on the couch. "What would you have done if you'd known about Connor?" She held up a silencing finger and answered her own question. "You would've come back and tried to be a family, which would've been a disaster. Neither of us was ready for that. That's what. And you would've wound up hating me for keeping you from reaching your dreams."

Tom propped his right ankle up on his left knee. "Hell, we're older and supposed to be wiser. Sometimes dreams change, Kendra. I mean, look at Marcus. He can't race anymore since he hurt his back in the crash, so he's making a different dream come true. So am I. It wasn't as much fun out on the circuit without Marcus, and we'd always talked about opening our own custom shop. It was the right time to make the move for a lot of reasons."

Kendra shook her head. "You deciding, on your own, is far different from being forced to come back to LA because you found out you got a one-night stand pregnant and that you had a kid."

"I never thought of you as a one-night stand." He could feel a muscle in his jaw jump as his right fist clenched. "What if I hadn't come back? Were you ever going to tell me, or were you going to keep my son from me forever? What made you tell me now?"

A look of such fear and sadness swept her beautiful face that for one terrifying moment he thought her cancer had returned. The idea of her being sick again made his insides churn and all thought of blame vanished.

She sighed. "Don't look like that, I'm not sick. But my friend was in remission with me and now she's sick, and it's terminal. What if that happens to me? I owe it to Connor that he has at least one parent in his life."

Tom's mouth dried as the idea she could get ill again after being well for so long, hit him like an out-of-control car. "It won't happen to you."

She gave him a sad smile. "I hope not, but there are no certainties in life."

"So what do we do now? I want to get to know my son. I want to be in his life." He watched her for any signs she would stop him. "And I'll have to tell Marcus."

Chapter Three

E ven though her first instinct was to snap 'no' at him, Kendra remained calm. "Don't tell Marcus, not yet. You and I have too much to sort out first. Marcus being the overprotective, angry big brother won't help our situation."

Ever since her scare with cancer, Marcus had been overprotective. She'd just been told she was in remission, and at sixteen her world was glowing with promise. She remembered the first time she'd laid eyes on Tom. Marcus had seen the attraction too and didn't like it. She remembered the scene like it was only yesterday…

S he'd stood on the terrace in her parent's back garden, lifting her face to the sun. Six months in remission and she was in love with the world once more. Excitement engulfed her. Who would have believed at sixteen she had a life ahead of her once again, filled with endless possibilities? Determined to decide for herself what she wanted to do with her second chance at life, she now jumped out of bed each morning to greet the world.

She wanted to take risks and face her fears. After all, she'd faced the *biggest fear anyone should have to face and kicked its ass. The world was there for her, and she wanted to conquer it.*

"Come inside, Kendra, you'll catch cold."

Her smile faded. "Mother, it's 82 degrees out here. Besides, Stella's coming over soon."

"Lovely. I like Stella. She was a true friend while you fought the cancer. She was always there for you. She'll ensure you don't overdo it."

She grinned. There her mother was sadly mistaken. Stella would take Kendra's side. She always had and always would.

"Let's wait for Stella in the kitchen with a nice cup of tea."

"I want a walk in the garden."

While she tried to argue through the open French doors, Kendra walked down the steps into the garden until she couldn't hear her mother any longer. She thought she heard her older brother talking with someone by the pool. At twenty, Marcus had just been hired to drive his first formula two race car with Honda. They'd thought so highly of his skill they had given him his own head mechanic, a guy around his age, Thomas Lorde. Mom told her Tom was staying the weekend too, but she'd yet to meet him.

Kendra looked over her shoulder, ensuring her mother wasn't chasing after her with a coat, and followed the sound of her brother's voice to see what he and his friend were up to. As she rounded the corner of the garden, she could hear they were lounging around the pool.

It was as if an invisible wall blocked her way as she stopped short, her mouth gaping open and her body flooding with heat. A near naked bronzed Norse God with fair hair, which at the moment because of her chemo was longer than her dark locks, was standing under the outdoor shower five feet from where she stood. He hadn't seen her, thank god, because she imagined she probably looked like a dork right now with a woolen jersey on in this temperature, so she drunk in his broad shoulders, strong thighs, and ripped stomach. But what made her mouth water was the tattoo of an eagle in flight covering seventy percent of his chest. It must have hurt a great deal getting inked like that. She under-

stood how painful needles could be! It was truly a work of art. Every time his pecs moved, the bird looked as if it was soaring.

"Are you going to swim or merely stand there staring?"

She started, heat invading her cheeks at being caught ogling him. His voice was gravelly and fluid, like rain falling on a tin roof.

"My mother would freak if I got in the pool." She pulled her eyes away from his chest to watch a drop of water slide down his crooked nose. "I've been ill and my mother insists I don't overexert myself." Why'd she have to say that? She hated people knowing about her illness. They looked at her differently, before escaping as fast as they could, as if she could pass her cancer on to them.

He turned off the shower and walked towards her, water running down over his body and she'd never wanted to let her fingers follow that flow on any boy—man—before.

"I'm Tom, your—"

"I know who you are. I'm Kendra—"

"I know who you are," he said with a sexy smile. He stopped before her with a genuine look of puzzlement on his face. "Marcus told me you'd beaten the cancer."

"I have. Six months clear. I'm in remission."

He eyed her up and down. "You look pretty healthy to me."

"I am," she said proudly. And she was proud. It had been a tough few years of constant trips into doctors' offices and hospitals. Being kept in isolation, prodded, poisoned with chemo… She'd lost contact with her friends and a few were hard to connect with again, some people didn't know how to interact with you when you were ill, when really all you wanted them to do was treat you like you were normal for a little part of each day, so you could forget that there was something eating away inside you. Luckily, she'd had Stella.

"So, what's stopping you? If you want to swim get in." When she hesitated, he moved so close droplets of water dripped on her clothes. "Swim or don't swim I don't care, but if I had ever let anyone prevent me from doing what I wanted to do, I would not be going with your brother to race in Europe." His attention swung to the pool house as

Marcus emerged with two beers in his hand. "Marcus tells me you're a fighter, Kendra. Don't let anyone or anything hold you back."

Marcus must have told him about her illness and also told him how overbearing her parents were. "I can't blame my family for caring too much."

"No. You can't. And you shouldn't. But you can blame yourself for letting them decide for you."

With that, he sauntered off to grab his beer.

Kendra looked at the water and let the anger build. Who the heck did he think he was? It wasn't as if she asked his opinion. But with a shiver, she knew Thomas was right. This was her life, and she'd fought hard to keep it, given everything she had gone through. And even now she knew the odds were still strong that she might have to fight the disease all over again.

Fight. And that's truly what it was. The pain had been beyond bearable, and emotional, she wasn't even sure if she would make it… it had been hard to keep her spirits up.

But she wasn't a quitter.

It was a tough pill to swallow as a teenager. To learn that life was a constant battle. Six months ago she'd been tired, but now… now she was ready to fight for what she wanted.

She wanted her hard-won life on her terms.

She turned and looked at her brother and his hot, oh, so hot, new friend.

She might not know what she wanted to do with the rest of her life, but right now she knew what she wanted—and he was sitting on a lounge chair ten feet from her.

I t had taken her four long years to wear Tom's resistance down. The night of her twentieth birthday, the day she'd signed to sing for James Tan.

What a night that had been. More so because he'd given her Connor. A child that she never thought she'd have after her chemo. She would never regret her son or the night that created him.

Tom cleared his throat. "Are you okay?"

"Just reminiscing. It's so strange sitting here."

"I wish I'd been in Connor's life earlier. Look, it's obvious you need help financially, but I won't just be a silent partner who only contributes money. I want to be in my son's life."

She looked into his eyes and knew if she had to do it all over again, she would. "That's good." She should be happy, right? It's what she wanted—didn't she? Yes, but it would also mean he was in her life too. "Why does everything have to be so complicated?"

"It's not complicated at all. I'm Connor's father and I have just as much right to see him, to be with him, as you."

He sounded so angry, and yet he was the one who'd ignored her when she'd tried to let him know. For the past three years, he'd probably never even given her or Connor a second thought. She wasn't the villain here. "We'll work out child support and a visitation schedule." Even though having him in her life regularly would send her world spinning, he deserved to be in her son's life. She would have to act as if seeing him every day did not send her pulse racing. Worse still, she would have to watch him with his revolving door. She assumed he still maintained a rotation of women. She'd just have to hide how much she wished he wanted her the way she *still* wanted him.

His presence was wreaking havoc on her hormones, but Kendra held her reactions in check. Something she'd become an expert at. She'd gotten used to being half in heat every time she was around him, and it seemed like that hadn't changed. But, just to be safe, she'd better leave. Besides, she had to get home to relieve Mrs. Bailey from across the hall, since the elderly woman liked to go to bed by ten.

This had been an impulsive decision to talk with him, but her friend's situation brought several 'what ifs' to light and she needed answers. She needed space to sort through what confronting Tom had set in motion. She'd half expected him to be happy to simply dish out money. She'd never even considered he'd want to be in Connor's life—she'd hoped, but wasn't certain, given he'd had no contact with him for three years.

She wanted to raise Connor with a father in his life. She'd always wanted Tom to be there for Connor, but she'd doubted that would ever happen, so to see her dream coming to fruition was scary. Dreams always seem so easy, it's the reality that makes you think twice. Makes you question everything.

She stood because it was time to leave. She needed to consider a lot of things, emotionally and logistically, like how was this dual parenting thing going to work. "We'll talk more about this when I have more time. I have to get home."

Tom rose and ran a hand over his hair, making her want to do the same. *Was it soft like she remembered from four years ago?* Kendra needed to get out of there.

"So, that's it?" he asked. "You drop a major bombshell on me and then run away? That's not fair, to any of us."

"Fair? Don't talk to me about fair. Is it fair I had Connor all on my own? That I had cancer—OMG, life isn't fair. I don't have time to argue. I have to relieve the babysitter. Anyway, I need some space to think." Kendra said, briskly making a move towards the door.

But Tom shot quickly past her and blocked her departure. "Think fast then because I'm not waiting too long to see my son. I've missed out on so much already."

His eyes had darkened with the force of his emotions, and his supple mouth had thinned into a hard line. She wanted to kiss him until it softened again and let him devour her mouth. As if sensing her reaction, he reached out and ran a finger over her cheek.

"Please, stay. You can't just drop this on me. I need to know— I need to know about my son. I have paid little attention to Connor before. Can I see a picture of him at least?"

His touch sent desire coursing through her, making her

breathing quicken. She had to get out of there before he saw that even after everything, she still wanted him. "I—I'll text you one or you can see him on my Instagram account, KendraB. I'm so sorry. I didn't think this 'revealing the truth situation' through. I guess the news of my friend's cancer returning sent me here on an impulse, it's not every day you tell a man he's a father. But Mrs. Bailey could only stay with Connor for a little while. I promise that we'll talk soon, just not now."

Tom's gaze bored into hers. "Why would you tell me when you only had a bit of time? Are you punishing me?"

"No. No. Not at all. I just didn't think you'd even care. I thought you knew all along and I was simply going to ask you to face up to your financial obligations." Kendra couldn't look away as tears stung her eyes. "It hadn't occurred to me you didn't know about Connor, or what this would mean for you. If I'd known, I would have told you differently. And made sure we had more time." She gulped back a sob. "I really am sorry."

Her words, or maybe her tears, made him flinch, and he quickly moved out of her way. Kendra yanked the door open and walked from the house to her car. She refused to look at him as she backed out of the driveway and then sped away into the night.

Chapter Four

I t was a second night without sleep. Tom was still awake when the sky outside his eastern bedroom window lightened.

He'd spent the night studying Kendra's Instagram account, looking at all the pictures of his son, and trying to come to grips knowing that he was a father. He'd also mentally whipped himself for not reading at least one of Kendra's emails or listening to a single voicemail.

What an asshole he'd been back then. So consumed with the racing circuit, just to prove to his drunken excuse for a father, and everyone who'd never believed in him, that he could be a success. And for what? He'd learned he didn't care what anyone else thought, only what he thought of himself and those he cared about.

And he'd cared about Kendra. He'd been just too scared to stay and face the turmoil that having a relationship with her would have caused. He'd face it now though because he was older and wiser. He had a son! As soon as he got to Bad Boy Autos today, he would read every single email.

However, he felt like a complete wanker because Kendra

went through having Connor all on her own... the self-loathing became suffocating and he threw the sheet off.

He was thankful that she'd had help from Marcus, and from the photos on her Instagram account, her best friend, Stella, but still... He was the father and he should've been the one in the delivery room. Tom thought he'd never be a father. He'd never wanted to marry and play house. He supposed he was lucky he hadn't fathered other kids given his history. He loved women. Plural. Or he loved the release and pleasure they could give him without the usual emotional entanglements. He was always upfront with the ladies who shared his bed. Nothing long-term. His family experience taught him nothing long-term ever lasted, anyway.

When he was twelve, his mother had walked out on them. Left without a word. He could understand her leaving his drunken father, but she left him and his brother, Sam. Left them with an abusive drunk. That's when he'd first suspected he wasn't loveable. There was something deep within him that put up barriers, making it so difficult for anyone to care for him. Or was it he was too scared to let anyone close? Losing his mother had done a number on him. He kept everyone, even Sam, at arms-length. He would never experience the pain of loss again. But now he had a son, and the wall around his heart was fracturing. He very much wanted to love his son and be the father he'd never had.

He turned off the alarm since he was already up and went to the bathroom. Looking in the mirror over the sink, he studied his reflection and thought about Connor. He'd only briefly seen the kid a few times. Did he look like him? The photos showed that he had Kendra's dark hair, but Tom wanted to see him up close, to hold him, and love him.

One of the decisions Tom had come to during the long, sleepless night was that Kendra and Connor's lives were about to change. He would not let his son grow up without a family. Without a loving family. There was only one problem—he laughed out loud—only one problem—yeah, right. How the hell was he going to give his son a loving family? He didn't know what one looked like.

An hour later, arriving at Bad Boy Autos, instead of going straight to the pit to work on the cars he loved, he found himself at his computer.

With shaking hands he opened the folder holding all of Kendra's emails, and for one second his finger hovered over the mouse, before he finally pushed the pad. With a small click, the first email opened.

Hi Tom
Sorry to bother you, I know you're busy, and we said it was just that one night—awesome night BTW—but you haven't returned my phone calls and it's imperative I talk to you. Please, please, can you ring me as soon as you read this?
Your friend, Kendra

Tom clicked to the next email, and then the next, while his stomach clenched against the churning pain. Each email from Kendra became more and more desperate, pleading for him to ring her. But it was the final email that saw a tear slide down his face, and his entire world exploded in mind-numbing pain.

Tom
I guess I don't need you to ring me. It's obvious you don't want to have anything to do with me or the baby I'm carrying—your baby in case the many emails I have sent haven't made that clear.

I'm writing to let you know that I'm keeping my baby and I won't be asking you for anything ever again.

I won't be revealing to anyone who the father is. And that's not for your sake, but for Marcus's. He loves you like a brother and this would destroy him and his chance of winning the driver's championship.

I don't know how you can live with yourself. You're obviously not the man I thought you were. My baby and I are better off without you. Have a nice life.

BTW, it's a boy.

Kendra.

S lowly he closed his computer and rose. He brushed the tears from his face, and his mouth firmed. He had many regrets in his life, but this one almost had him reaching for a bottle of Jack Daniels, until he remembered what Kendra had written—'*not the man I thought you were*'.

She might have been right back then, but now he had changed. He had someone worth fighting for—a son and a woman he could love. He'd prove he was the man she thought he was before he'd walked out of her life.

If she'd give him a second chance.

Chapter Five

Connor bopped Kendra on the forehead with a small stuffed giraffe as she put his little cammo sneakers on while he sat on the couch. They and the matching cammo outfit had been a present from Marcus for Connor's birthday. He'd said he'd had to make sure she wasn't always going to dress him in sissy cartoon character clothes. Then he'd laughed and left the room when she'd glared at him.

Marcus might be a tad overprotective, but one thing she knew for certain, he loved his nephew and would do anything for Connor.

Kendra shook her head at the memory. Marcus might not want kids himself, but he took his role as Connor's uncle very seriously. Since he'd quit the racing circuit and opened Bad Boy Autos with Tom, Marcus came to visit a lot. When she'd had cancer, he never left her bedside, even when all his friends and girlfriends were out having fun. He virtually willed her to live. She owed him a lot. He was the best brother she could ever hope for.

She frowned as she finished with Connor's shoes. Marcus hated where she lived. That gut curling feeling hit her stomach as it did whenever she disappointed Marcus. She felt his disapproval of her home even though he didn't mention it. He didn't need to.

It was in his green eyes when he looked around her small living room with the watermarks on the ceiling. Both of them had grown up with money, living in Beverly Hills where Marcus still lived. And where Tom lived. She was a long way from Beverly hills now. She heard it in his voice whenever he said goodbye. The short phrase of "take care, sis" was filled with such reproach that she almost winced when he said it. She was the first to admit this was not the affluent area where she'd grown up, but she took pride in the fact she had a roof over her head paid for by money she earned from her music career.

"Mama, dink," Connor said, bopping her with the toy again.

Kendra smiled and tickled him under the chin. "Thirsty, huh?"

Connor nodded and kicked his feet a little.

"Okay. Let's go get a drink, little man."

She helped Connor off the couch and watched him trot out to the kitchen on his little legs. Love for the adorable toddler filled her as she followed him. A knock on the door had her changing direction to answer it.

"Who is it?" she called out while watching Connor, who was standing in the middle of the kitchen staring at her with a frown.

"Mama! Dink!"

"Okay, my little man. I'll be right there," she said. "Who is it?"

"It's Tom."

Kendra's pulse leaped at hearing his voice. What was he doing here? She wasn't ready for this. But the revelation last night meant no turning back. So because Connor was here, he would finally meet his father. This was all happening so fast that her head spun. "I thought we would set up a time to talk?"

"Mama!" Connor wailed and stomped his foot.

Kendra suddenly felt as cranky as Connor was acting. She unlocked the door and opened it. "Come in."

She barely looked at Tom before hurrying to the kitchen to stop Conner's pounding on the fridge.

Connor looked up at her with a furrowed brow when she took his wrist. "Mama, dink."

"I know, baby, but you have to wait for mama. Back up so I can get the door open," she said.

Connor turned around so fast that he almost fell over. Looking up, Kendra saw what had startled him. Tom stood just inside the kitchen, staring at Connor, who stared right back. But they weren't the only ones staring.

Tom's long, muscular form captured Kendra's attention. The way his black work T-shirt stretched across his broad chest made her mouth go dry. Following the V of his torso down to his narrow hips, Kendra flushed as the images of the sculpted muscles that lay beneath his clothes flitted through her mind. Why did Tom have such power over her emotions?

Connor threw up his hand and hollered, "Hi!"

Tom's expression instantly lightened and a big smile spread over his face. His eyes shone as he squatted down. "Hi, Connor."

Connor tapped his chest. "Me, Connor." He walked over to Tom and patted his thigh. "Me, Connor." The likeness struck her anew. How Marcus hadn't seen it… She swallowed back the emotions and the protective mother instinct to push Tom away— Connor was hers.

Tom said, "You sure are." Tom couldn't take his eyes off him —their son. "He's adorable, Kendra."

Kendra smiled proudly. "I know."

Connor patted Tom's thigh once more. "Me, Connor."

Tom looked questioningly at Kendra. "Why does he keep saying that?"

"He wants to know who you are," Kendra replied.

Tom rolled his eyes. "I should've figured that out. I'm your—"

"No!"

Both Connor and Tom looked at Kendra in surprise at her loud tone.

Kendra met Tom's gaze. "That's not how to do this. Connor picks things up fast and we have some things to work out first. If he hears you called that, he'll repeat it. I'm not ready for anyone to know yet, especially Marcus. So, for now, you're just Tom."

Tom's expression darkened and he looked like he would argue. Then he glanced at Connor, pointed at his chest, and said, "I'm Tom."

Kendra sighed in relief. "Thank you."

Tom greeted his boy, "It's nice to meet you, Connor."

Emotions collided in Kendra's heart as she watched the father and son. Anger at Tom for not reading her emails or listening to her voicemails cloaked the meeting with sadness. Three wasted years. But the picture of them together filled her with happiness that the two were finally meeting. Connor deserved to know his father. It looked like Tom wanted that too, but what would that mean for them all?

Connor smiled. "Hi, Tom." He looked up at Kendra. "Mama, dis Tom."

Kendra laughed. "Yes, Con. I know who he is."

There was no forgetting the man she'd loved for so long. He always filled her dreams and he was never far from her mind. After all, he was her first love. And their night together had given her Connor. She could never regret that.

Tom ruffled Connor's hair and stood up. "I came over to meet Connor and to talk about what we're going to do about the situation. I'm not waiting any longer to be in my kid's life."

Kendra took a deep breath, walked over to the refrigerator and opened it. The cold air felt heavenly on her flushed cheeks, and she wanted to crawl right inside the appliance. She located a bottle of apple juice and concentrated on pouring some into a sippy cup so she didn't have to look at Tom.

"Here, Con." She handed it to him.

Connor took the sippy cup, drank a few swallows and then

ran into the living room, leaving Kendra alone with Tom. She propped a hip against the counter and crossed her arms over her chest.

"Well, I guess the first thing is setting up child support and visitation through the court," she said. "I think supervised visits would be best at first until you're more used to taking care of Connor. Then we could do every other weekend and figure out who gets him on each of the vacations."

"You've got this all figured out and we haven't even talked." Tom moved closer and Kendra was forced to tilt her head back to meet his eyes.

"No, Kendra. I will not drop him off and pick him up like a damn suitcase. He deserves better than that. Connor needs a full-time dad, not a part-time father."

Kendra's eyes widened as fear constricted her chest. "You're going for full custody? Oh, hell, no! I'll fight you on this and I'll win, Tom."

Fortunately, Tom shook his head, assuaging her concerns, "Whoa, I will not sue you for custody, Kendra. That's the last thing I want to do. I'd never separate Connor from his mother. I thought that we could work this out privately."

"What do you mean, privately?" she asked. "I want it to be legal. Just in case… I want to know Connor is taken care of."

"I'll never stop taking care of him—or you." He stepped even nearer and Tom's aftershave teased her senses. "I want it to be legal, too, but I was thinking of something more old-fashioned."

Kendra fought down the effect he was having on her body. "More old-fashioned? What are you talking about?"

That determined look she knew so well settled on his face. "Connor needs both of us full-time. I want to give him the kind of life he deserves and I know that you do, too."

She couldn't figure out what Tom was driving at. "Well, of course, I do, but—"

"Kendra, let's get married."

Kendra shook her head. Did he just say married? Her eyes

locked on his and goddamn, he was serious. He didn't blink, didn't utter a sound. So she did the only thing she could to lighten the mood. She laughed.

He stepped back as if someone had slapped him when she burst into laughter and put a hand to her chest. His proposal made her shiver, like a bucket of cold water poured over her head. Never had she imagined he would propose.

"This is no laughing matter." Irritated, she watched him cross his arms over his chest and cock his head while her laughter subsided. She supposed she better hear him out, but there was nothing short of 'I love you and want you both in my life' that would even make his proposal remotely acceptable.

"Old fashioned all right and completely ridiculous. So many people make marriage a joke because they enter into it for all the wrong reasons. There is only one reason to marry—and that's for love. Marrying me, just because of Connor is not fair on me, or him, or you. How can a marriage based on a child satisfy any of us?"

More than anything, she wanted love. How could she marry a man, who, until yesterday, barely acknowledged she was alive? Her parent's marriage was cold and empty, her mother a shell of her former self from simply being another of her father's possessions. She wondered if the pair had ever loved each other or that it was just too convenient—like a marriage between Tom and Kendra would be now.

"I can offer you and Connor a better life." He glanced around her tiny apartment; his mouth firming as if to say, 'look at this shit hole', and as if she wasn't doing the best she could. "You can't enjoy living like this. I'm surprised Marcus hasn't insisted you move from this part of town."

Kendra stopped laughing at his comment and she wanted to hit him. He was pissing her off now, just as Connor rushed into the kitchen. He giggled as he clung to one of her jean-clad legs. "Mama, what funny?"

Even though it was clear he was still irritated, Tom couldn't resist their son, and a smile tugged on the corners of his mouth as he watched Connor laugh too. Connor looked so much like Tom, Kendra thought as the little boy giggled with them, without knowing what was funny. A pang of regret ran through her, quickly chased by guilt. She should have tried harder to tell Tom about Connor.

The other fact hanging over her was she should have told Marcus. He would have sorted everything out, but it would have ruined his chance of winning the drivers' championship. Tom had only learned about Connor on his return stateside last year after Marcus's crash. When she'd been so concerned with her brother's injuries, she'd taken Connor to the hospital. Tom hadn't even asked who the boy's father was, and since he hadn't read the emails, it obviously never occurred to him he was Connor's dad.

He arched an eyebrow at Kendra as she sobered.

"You're not laughing," she said.

"No, I'm not."

She put a hand on Connor's head. "You're joking, right? Please tell me you're joking."

"I'm deadly serious," Tom said. "Connor needs a real home, Kendra. I want to be in his life every day, not just on weekends. We could make this work."

Sorrow sparked in her gut, but she kept her voice mild. "No. I'm not marrying you, Tom. Having a child together is not the basis of a successful marriage. Love, friendship, mutual respect, those things count. We really don't know each other at all anymore. We have both grown and changed. If you think I'd marry you just because of Connor..." She took a step back. "No way. Not happening."

· · ·

That went about as well as Tom thought it would. But what had he expected? Deep inside he knew Kendra was right. He didn't want to put his boy through a divorce, because if he did this, if he committed to Kendra, it was for forever.

But they barely knew each other anymore. Except he knew he still wanted her. Just being this close made his body burn.

She was hot. His reputation screamed that he'd thought a lot of women were hot. Marriage meant sleeping with no one but Kendra. Could he handle that?

He ran his gaze over her body and those long legs that he'd love to feel wrapped around him once more and decided it would not be a sacrifice. The night he'd shared with Kendra four years ago, still played like a movie in his head. He'd often woken up hard and needy, jerking off to the memory of her touch, her kisses, her tight…

They could make this work.

He sighed. Pushing wouldn't accomplish his goal. *Just like her brother. Stubborn as hell.* But maybe he could coax her. "Kendra, I know that it's not the perfect situation, but we could make a marriage work. There is no question that we still desire each other. It would solve your financial problems, too. Just think about it."

Her delicate nostrils flared, reminding him of a spirited horse. She gave a big sigh and hugged Connor. "This is not the time or place for this conversation. I have a piano lesson to give in fifteen minutes—I teach piano, by the way. I think you need to take a day or two to think about what you just said. I'm pretty sure you'll change your mind. You never struck me as the one-woman kind, and I won't have a marriage of convenience."

Tom gave her his best disarming smile, the kind that used to make her blush. "You're right, we really don't know each other —yet. Just so you know, I'd never cheat on my wife. I'll go for now." He squatted down again in front of Connor. "Hey, little man. I have to go, but I'll see you real soon, okay?"

Connor cocked his head a little. "You go bye-byes?"

Tom smiled. "Yeah. Me go bye-byes."

"'Kay." Connor held his arms out to Tom. "Give hugs."

Tom had hugged his niece and nephews dozens of times, but enfolding his own son in his embrace for the first time was such a profound experience it brought tears to his eyes. Knowing this solid little life in his arms was his flesh and blood made the floor beneath his feet tilt. His life was crashing and pounding around him, but he'd give his life for this wee boy. Love hit him like a cannon ball in the chest and he could barely breathe.

And he'd missed three years already. He was not about to lose more. Nor was he going to play fair. He played to win. And he wanted his son with him, and that meant Kendra too.

He hugged Connor close for a few moments until Connor squirmed. Tom loosened his hold on the toddler, but took his face in his hands. "You be good for Mommy, okay?"

Connor's smile was the sweetest thing Tom had ever seen. "'Kay. Bye."

Tom rode the wave of love as he stared into his son's eyes, not wanting to leave. He wanted to stay and get to know Connor. He wanted to make up for the time he'd missed. The feeling made him even more determined to marry Kendra so they could finally be a family. It was the perfect opportunity to get what he didn't deserve with no one pointing that out.

How someone so small could change a determined bachelors mind he really didn't know, but he knew what he felt and he felt he wanted to be part of this family.

He kissed Connor's forehead and stood up. "See ya, buddy." He smiled at Kendra. "I'll call you later to arrange a time when we can really talk about things."

"Fine. But Tom, you can't expect to simply walk into my— our," she patted Connor on the head, "lives and expect to run everything. I have been on my own with Connor for three years."

He bit back the words 'whose fault is that', because both of them were to blame. "Just promise me you won't dismiss the idea. We don't have to get married right away. We could date and see…"

She hesitated before nodding, then added, "But I'm not promising anything."

Tom gave her a last, direct stare, winked at Connor and left her apartment. Jogging down the stairs of the dilapidated apartment building, Tom smiled to himself as he thought about the sexy mother of his child.

He looked up and down the street and knew even if Kendra wouldn't marry him; she would not remain living in this neighborhood. He'd lived in a rough area and no child of his would go through what he went through, not when he had the money and space to give his son a fabulous and safe upbringing.

Tom remembered how often Marcus complained about Kendra's stubbornness to do things on her own. He could empathize with her need to be in control, given how her cancer had taken all the control from her. But this was about all their lives. He wanted a relationship with his son that was better than the one he had with his father. She would be tough to convince.

He'd grown up in a single-parent household and it sucked. When his mother had walked out, he'd felt torn between two people he loved the most in the world. One parent always lost. He didn't want to be the loser, but he wouldn't wish that on Kendra either.

He glanced at his watch. Speaking of fathers, he should pop by the hospital and see how dad was doing. It was hard to stay angry and bitter at the shell of the man who was lying in the hospital struggling after his liver transplant. Somehow it made Tom even angrier that he couldn't go on hating his father.

He swore Connor would never end up hating him. His son. He had a son.

He had wracked his brains all night trying to think of a better solution. How else could he have his son in his life in the way he wanted? He saw how kids got shoved from house to house, from parent to parent; and what would happen when Kendra met someone she wanted to marry? What if they wanted to take Connor out of state? Coldness swept over him. What kind of relationship would he have with his son then?

Yet, he'd be giving up his plan to never marry and risk ending up a part-time dad, anyway. The idea of a divorce scared him as much as losing a chance to know his son did. But the longing from his shitty childhood, that he'd always kept hidden deep inside, to belong to a happy family like most other kids, rose like an avenging dragon to fire him up. He longed to give his kid what he'd never had—a loving, perfect family—if they even existed? Maybe then he would lose his feeling of worthlessness.

If there was a better solution to give his boy the dream of the perfect family, he didn't know what it was. This was the only way that he could see a way ahead for him. He had to at least try.

Now all he needed to do was convince Kendra they should be a family. She wanted love. She had loved *him* once. And it had sent him fleeing. But not this time. Surely, he could make her fall in love with him again?

So he would fight for his son and try.

Chapter Six

Kendra had asked her best friend Stella Perry to pop over. She had grown up in the same neighborhood, Beverly Hills: a world away from where she lived now. She couldn't blame Stella for not understanding why she lived like this. Why would any sane person give up a life in high society? But she refused to let herself be under her father's thumb. He thought he could control her as he controlled her mother, but she would show him.

To be fair, she wasn't sure if she'd have gotten through the cancer if her father hadn't been their fighting with her and providing her with the best treatment money could buy, but once she'd recovered, he thought it meant he could control every facet of her life. That she owed him her life for helping to save it.

He'd tried to map out her future, even to the point of arranging a marriage to a lawyer in her firm.

"Forget college, my dear. Women raise the children and run the household so the men can earn the money."

For fuck's sake—really? In this day and age?

The day she'd told him she was pregnant and wouldn't reveal the father's name, he'd got so mad. She thought for a moment he might hit her. He disowned her when she refused his plan to marry her off by tricking the lawyer in his firm into thinking the baby was his. So she'd been on her own, with only Marcus and Stella helping her ever since.

Stella shifted Connor to her other hip. "I'm just saying. Marcus will not let you keep dodging his questions about Connor's father forever."

"Tell me something I don't know," Kendra said while putting on some coffee. "He rips my head off every time he comes to see me and Connor. He hates me living in this neighborhood."

At least Marcus still wanted her in his life. In contrast, her father was a wealthy, prominent lawyer and having a pregnant, unmarried daughter was damaging to his reputation. Her mother was so browbeaten by her father that she always took her father's side.

"I don't understand why you won't take Marcus up on his offer to set you up in a better neighborhood," Stella said.

"If I give in on that, he'll think he can run my life just like my father. Believe me, he's more like my father than he wants to admit."

"If you ask me, you both are," Stella took a seat in the chair by the window. "Why do you think you have to do all this on your own?"

How could she make her friend understand? For most of her life she'd been Marcus's quiet, shadow-like, sickly little sister. Mr. and Mrs. Black's little girl, whom everyone had needed to look after because she'd spent much of her childhood in the hospital battling her leukemia. She still hated how cancer had defined her.

She wanted to stand on her own two feet for a change, to prove to the world she wasn't as weak and helpless as they all thought her to be. No more pampering for her.

That's what had attracted her to Tom. He'd never treated her like some fragile vase that would shatter at the slightest touch. He'd never tried to protect her. He never thought of her as the sick girl. At their very first meeting he'd treated her like the survivor she was, daring her to push back and take a swim in the pool if she wanted to. Perhaps that is why she fell so hard for him.

Wanting to end the conversation, Kendra fell back on her usual excuse. "I don't expect you to understand, but I need to be independent."

Stella knew not to push her, but she said, "So, now that Tom knows about Connor, is he going to step up and help you out?"

"Tom's not just a wallet, you know. He's Connor's father. He popped by and met Connor today." She tried to act like it was no big deal. "Oh, and he suggested we try being a real family."

Stella choked on the sip of wine she'd just taken as she and Kendra sat in the living room later that night. "He said what?" she croaked.

Kendra crossed her arms and deepened her voice while giving Stella a hard look. "Let's get married, Kendra," she mimicked and cracked up. "I can't believe it. He's absolutely serious, though."

Stella sat her wineglass on the coffee table. "I certainly wasn't expecting him to react like that. He doesn't seem like the marrying kind."

Tom was a more casual sex kind of guy. Relationship was a foreign language.

Running a fingertip around the rim of her wineglass, Kendra said, "There's more to Tom than I suspected." She might still consider him a man-whore, but how many people knew he didn't drink? She suspected there was more to him than anyone knew, more than she knew. She understood that his shitty childhood probably tarnished his views on happy families. That's what scared her about his offer. Did he even know what he was doing?

Stella arched an eyebrow at her. "You could do worse. I mean, you still have the hots for him and he's a rich stud."

Kendra gaped at Stella for a moment. "What happened to you hating Tom and calling him a prick?"

Stella's shoulders lifted. "If he didn't know... He gets points for taking responsibility now he does. Are you sure that he didn't know?"

Bold lines of text rose in Kendra's mind. "Yeah. I'm sure. None of the emails were opened. He'd never read them." Why did he keep them?

"He's still an ass for not opening them or listening to your voicemails, but he's not quite as big a jerk as I thought," Stella said.

"No, he's not. Tom was never a jerk to me," Kendra said. "He was the one person who didn't sugar coat stuff or treat me like a fragile piece of china. I liked how honest he was with me."

"Even when he loved you and left you?"

"Sex is not love. The love word never crossed his lips." She could not blame him for that either. "You mean when I chased him so hard, he finally gave in? He never made me any promises, and I knew he was leaving the country the next day."

"I love how you constantly defend him. You're still in love with him."

Tears stung Kendra's eyes and she closed them. "Yeah. I fell in love with him the first time I saw him. God, he was so hot. He's even hotter now."

Stella's snicker made Kendra open her eyes. "Boy, you got it bad. I doubt he loves you. If he did, why has he ignored you this past year?"

"Oh, I'm pretty sure he doesn't. I think he's too scared to love anyone. I'm simply the mother of his child, who he wants in his life and this is the way to get his son." It was the ghost in the room when he'd suggested getting married. His proposal wasn't accompanied by a 'I love you' and Kendra wanted that. Wanted it badly. Her parents had a marriage not based on love and she refused to ever end up in a marriage where separate bedrooms were the norm and you lived separate lives too. The children usually suffered. It was far better to tell them the truth and live separately.

Her face must have said it all as Stella added, "Look, don't rush into anything, but maybe you should explore a relationship with Tom."

Kendra shook her head. "Is that so? If not for Connor... If he'd wanted me, he would have come for me by now. He's been in LA almost a year. I bet he's never even thought about me over the years. I was a one-night romp. I don't blame him for that. I chased him like crazy. I'm not about to repeat my performance." She paused. "Plus, you know his rep with the ladies. A different one every night. I don't think he's the marrying kind. What happens if he cheats on me? I'd leave and Connor would be heartbroken."

Stella waggled her eyebrows. "Keep him happy in bed and he won't want to cheat."

"You know that's not true." But her suggestive remark made Kendra laugh. "I can't believe you just said that. Yuck. You're encouraging me to get hitched to Tom after all the nasty things you said about him." Her smile died. "Besides, there is more to a relationship than sex. I want a partner, not just a bedmate."

"I'm not saying to jump right into it." Stella crossed her legs. "Just keep your mind open to the possibility that things could work between you. Try dating him, where is the harm in that?"

Kendra pondered Stella's statement as she looked her over. Stella's blonde hair was swept back on the sides and her fringe of bangs brushed her perfectly shaped dark blonde eyebrows. It was simple and stylish. Her outfit of satiny red blouse, knee-length gray skirt, and black high heels was smart and sexy.

Looking down at her black jeans, pink tank top, and black sandals, Kendra remembered the days when she'd dressed like Stella. That had been when she'd had the money to buy nice clothes and go to upscale hairdressers and spas. Now, all her money went to pay for bills, groceries, and whatever Connor needed. There wasn't room in her budget for expensive clothes. She still had some nice outfits from a few years ago, but she didn't have much occasion to wear them.

Her old clothes were not what she needed, except perhaps her sexy La Perla lingerie. Tom hadn't been able to resist her in the silky lace. But she wanted more than a man lusting after her. Could she make a man like Tom fall in love with her?

"How did your piano lessons go today?" Stella asked, changing the subject.

Grateful for the change of topic, Kendra started telling her about how funny little Amy Phillips had been. As she talked, Kendra tried to throw off her negative thoughts and be grateful for what she had.

It worked as long as Stella was there, but it wasn't long before she left, and loneliness settled over Kendra. Conner was in bed, and none of her other friends would brave her neighborhood at night. Sighing, Kendra poured more wine and settled on the couch with her laptop.

Logging onto Facebook, she saw that she had a new friend request and clicked on the notification icon. Her heart flipped over when she saw that it was from Tom. Why would he do that? Marcus would see that they'd become friends and wonder why. She hovered the pointer over the approve button, but couldn't bring herself to hit it. Instead, she clicked on the button to bring up a message box.

She mulled over what to say and then typed, "I can't believe you sent me a friend request. Are you crazy?" and sent the message.

It wasn't long before Tom sent a reply. *I've been called that. Are you going to accept it?*

Kendra pursed her lips in annoyance. *No! Marcus will see that we became friends.*

Tom: *Just set our relationship to private. No one will know. Besides, you know Marcus hardly gets on here.*

Kendra typed, "*Not true. He keeps in touch with his racing buddies. Besides, I won't take the chance. Someone else from the garage might see it and comment on it.*

Nothing came back for several moments, and she could almost feel his irritation coming through the Internet.

Tom: *What's your number?*

Kendra: *You don't have it?*

Tom: *Why would I have it? Marcus would never give it to me.*

He had a point. A couple, actually. Why would he need her number when he'd cut her out of his life? Plus, Marcus would want to know why Tom wanted it. Marcus would explode once he knew the truth, which she would not let happen until she'd made some decisions, and when she and Tom were sure about their future.

But how long would Tom keep their secret? He'd said that he wanted to marry her so they could give Connor a good life. Kendra knew he meant well, but getting married just for a child was a stupid idea. She had to make him see that, before the identity of Connor's father became public. They needed to be on the same page before that happened.

Kendra typed in her phone number and a few moments later, her phone rang. Getting a grip on her emotions, she answered it. "That was fast."

"I don't waste time. Want me to come over?"

Her hand tightened around the cellphone. "What for?"

"To talk."

"We're talking now."

His rough-timbered chuckle in her ear made goosebumps break out along her arms. "I'd rather talk in person."

Panic wormed its way into her blood. "No. Uh, not tonight. Connor wakes up sometimes and I don't want him to see you here. I have never had a man over." Damn, she hadn't meant to reveal that bit of news. Quickly she added, "I usually go to my dates house."

His voice deepened. "Then when?"

Kendra rubbed her forehead. Knowing how dogged Tom was when he was on a mission, she knew that she couldn't hold him off for long. She had to make him see reason and do it fast. Better to start right away.

"Tomorrow night. Come over around seven. I'll arrange for Connor to stay at Stella's."

"Okay," Tom said. "How's Connor?"

Kendra smiled, glad that he was interested. "He was one tired little man. My friend, Colleen Wilkins, watched him for me today since I had that piano lesson this morning and then I had to lay down some studio tracks this afternoon."

"I'm pleased to see you followed your passion and you are singing."

"Always." She could picture his smile.

"So, Colleen kept him busy, huh?"

Kendra closed her laptop and sat it on the coffee table. "Her four kids kept him very busy. She has twins who are only a little older than him."

"Four? Wow."

His amazed tone made her laugh. "Yeah. Her husband makes good money so they can afford them. Plus, she loves being a stay-home mom."

"And what about you? If you could be a stay-home mom, would you?"

"No. I love what I do, and I will build a career in the music business. I can be a good mother and still pursue my dreams," Kendra said. She loved writing songs and was surprised at how many she'd sold.

"How's that working out for you?"

Anger burned in her chest. "Don't you judge me, Tom! I'm doing the best I can. Connor is fed, clean, and has everything he needs. I make damn sure of that."

"Easy, Tiger. I know that you're a good mom. Marcus has said so frequently. It just can't be easy."

Despite her irritation, his use of the nickname he'd given her made Kendra smile a little. *Tiger.* She hated to admit she purred only for him. "I didn't do it by myself. I had Stella, and Marcus has stuck by me through it all."

His sigh came through the phone. "Don't you think I would've liked to have been included? I would've liked to have been there for Connor's birth and to help pick out a name. Everything, Kendra! You stole all of that from me."

"Well, if you'd only answered one damn voicemail or read one fricking email, you could've!" Kendra stood up, too mad to stay still. "You know what? This conversation is over. I'll see you tomorrow night."

Her hand trembled as she hit the end button and she tossed the phone onto the couch. She stomped over to the open living room window and raised the screen. Then she grabbed the bottle of wine and stepped out onto the fire escape.

She spent a lot of time out here once Connor was asleep at night, so she'd put a chair cushion and a small tropical plant on the landing. It was her little oasis and sparked her creativity. Song ideas often came to her out there as she looked at the sky and let her mind drift.

However, right then, no lyrics or melodies entered her mind. Closing her eyes, she leaned her head against the brick building and enjoyed the night breeze. It helped cool her simmering temper.

Part of the reason she'd gotten so upset was because Tom was right. She shouldn't have just assumed that he was a bastard. It was a safety mechanism. She could tell herself that she had tried to contact him and it was his choice not to be involved in their lives, without having to face his real reaction. Not having to face his rejection... All she'd had to do was tell Marcus and everyone would have known. Would she ever forgive herself for not doing that?

But it would have ruined their friendship and perhaps destroyed her brother's dream of winning formula one. And he'd won. It was to be his only win, as soon after he crashed his car and his career ended.

Only now she would have to tell Marcus anyway, and this time it could end the friendship and ruin their business. Would her brother blame Tom for leaving her alone all this time? It would be bad, she just knew it, and so would Tom.

She hoped they acted like adults regarding this situation, and she showed Marcus that they were not at each other's throats, that Marcus would understand too.

But knowing her brother she doubted it.

Chapter Seven

"Give that back!"

Tank, Zip's large Amstaff, had stolen his socket wrench, which Tom had just been about to use. Tom struggled against the huge dog's grip in vain. The brindle beast growled playfully and shook his head back and forth.

"Tank, drop!" Tom said.

His authoritative tone got through to the dog and Tank released the tool. He grumbled and then barked at Tom in disapproval. The booming sound blocked out the whine of air compressors and idling engines.

"Bad dog," Tom said, laughing. "You can't have my tools. You have plenty of toys. Play with them. Go get your chewy."

Tanks ears pricked forward at the word "chewy". He gave another woof and trotted off. Tom grinned as he wiped dog slobber off the socket wrench and leaned over the engine of the Maserati he was working on. A loud clanging reverberated throughout the garage, announcing the ringing of the pit area phone.

He set the wrench down, strode to the bench, and picked up the wall phone. "Catherine, can you take a message? I'm busy here."

"It's for you," and Catherine hung up.

"Tom Lorde, speaking." Silence met his greeting.

"Hello? Anyone there?"

"Hi, Tom. Is Marcus there? Please tell me he's there."

Tom's aggravation from the previous evening warred with concern over Kendra's slightly panicked tone. "He's not here, Kendra. He hasn't come in yet this morning. What's going on?"

"It's all right. I'll figure something out."

Tom's hand tightened on the phone. "Wait! Kendra, what's wrong?"

Connor started crying in the background.

Kendra's voice wavered a little. "I have a flat and I can't get Marcus on his cellphone. I've been out here for almost half an hour now. Connor is hungry and I have no more animal crackers or juice to give him. It's hot and—"

Concern overrode Tom's anger. "Why don't you change the tire?"

"I can't get the nuts undone. They're screwed on too tight."

"What?" Tom ran a hand over his face in frustration. Why hadn't Marcus loosened them? "Never mind. Where are you? I'll come get you guys."

"It's okay. I'll eventually get a hold of him," Kendra replied.

"Goddamn it, Kendra!" Tom forced himself to lower his voice. "Tell me where you are and I'll be right there."

Connor let loose with a squall and he heard Kendra sigh. "Okay. We're out on Route 12, about three miles past the Dream Cinema."

Tom was familiar with the old-fashioned drive-in movie theater. "What are you doing all the way out there?"

"I went to pick up a new keyboard that I've been making small payments on. The studio paid me yesterday, so I could pay it off," she said.

"Oh, I see." Tom grabbed his keys from the hook on the wall by the counter. "I'll be there in fifteen. Hang tight."

"Thanks, Tom."

"No problem. See ya soon."

Tom hung up. "Sully! Where are you?"

"Back here, boss!"

Tom followed his voice to the far side of the workshop to Sully's bay. At six-foot-four and weighing over two hundred pounds, Jake Sullivan towered over a lot of guys. Long, lean muscles, chiseled facial features, and ice-blue eyes gave him an air of danger.

He wore his long, silver hair in a ponytail and his square jaw was constantly shadowed with salt-and-pepper stubble. Sully was only in his early forties, but he'd gone prematurely gray when he'd been around thirty.

"Whatcha need?" he asked Tom.

"I have to go out. Don't touch the Maserati till I get back, okay?"

As third in command, Sully knew the business backwards and kept close tabs on what their other seven mechanics were working on. He was also the resident classics expert and catered to clients who wanted to restore their auto treasures from the past.

"Yeah, sure." Sully lowered the hood on a cream-and-black 1936 Ford F1 pickup truck. "Everything okay? You look kinda' worried."

"Kendra's stuck out on Rt. 12 with a flat tire, so I'm going to get her. She tried Marcus' cellphone, but he's not picking up."

Sully grunted. "Not surprised. He never remembers to charge the damn thing. I'll ream his ass out about it again."

Tom smiled. He and Marcus might be the bosses, but Sully didn't hesitate to call them on stuff. "You do that. I'll be back soon."

"Right. Tell Kendra I said hi and that I'm mad at her because she hasn't come to play pool lately," Sully said.

Sully's house was often a gathering spot for their crowd, and he had two pool tables set up in his huge finished basement. Tom thought it odd that he had never seen Kendra there. Had she not come if she knew he would be present? If so, what did that mean?

Sully stood looking at him strangely, so Tom nodded. "I will."

He jogged out to his Mustang, settled behind the wheel, and cranked the engine to life. As he turned the air conditioning on, he thought about how hot Kendra and Connor must be in the 90-plus degree weather. He threw the car into gear and pealed out of the parking lot, racing down the road to get to them as fast as possible.

Nearing the place where Kendra should be, several inky, meandering ribbons crisscrossed the asphalt. Looking ahead, he saw Kendra's blue van sitting at the end of the skid marks on the shoulder of the road. The tire must have blown. Relief flooded him because she'd been able to keep control of the van so it didn't flip or go off the road into the ditch. Marcus had taught her how to drive.

He pulled up behind them and cut the engine. Hopping out, he jogged over to the van and saw that Kendra had both front windows and the side door open to allow air to circulate. She emerged from the vehicle just as he reached the rear wheel.

"Thank God you're here," she said.

"Why isn't the van running, for the air-conditioning I mean?"

"Oh, that's been broken for a while. So can you hurry, it's hot as Hades out here!"

Her words didn't register with Tom because her appearance transfixed him. Even with sweaty, wilted hair she was gorgeous. Her white jean shorts showed off her toned thighs and calves to perfection. She filled out the ruby red tank top she wore like a model in a music video. Tom had traveled all over the world, but he knew that he'd never find another woman as beautiful as Kendra.

She waved her hand in his face. "The flat is on the other side," she said. "Rear tire."

Tom mentally shook himself. He'd been gawking at her like a horny teenager. "Hi. You guys okay? How's the little man?"

He was glad when Kendra didn't seem to notice his preoccupation with her.

"Yeah. We're all right. He's just really hot and hungry."

Tom looked inside the van at his son, who was almost asleep. "Take Connor to my car and sit in the air-con while I get this." Connor's black hair was as sweaty as Kendra's and his face was flushed.

He helped Kendra pick up Connor and his things as he slept, placing him in the cool, air-conditioned mustang, which Tom had left running. Though instead of joining their son, she followed him back to her car. Changing a tire was easy, but not when legs that he longed to have wrapped around him were in his line of sight.

"We'll get you out of here in just a few. I can't believe that Marcus didn't loosen the nuts for you," he said as he walked to the back of the van and opened the hatch. "I tell everyone to get them loosened so that this situation doesn't happen."

Kendra followed him. "I asked him to, but he must have been busy."

Tom stopped lifting the floor panel to stare at her. "You're kidding. He always fusses over you."

She lifted a shoulder. "True. He still thinks of me as a sick girl sometimes."

"That's bullshit. You've been healthy for a long time with no signs of relapse. Marcus told me that several times," Tom said. "He's an ass."

Kendra snorted. "Tell me something I don't know. Big brothers are a pain."

Tom pulled up the floor panel and saw that Kendra had a donut instead of a proper spare tire. Still, it would do the trick for now. Unfastening the donut, he lifted it out and leaned it against the back bumper. The space underneath the donut was empty.

"Where's the jack?" he asked.

"Isn't it there?" Kendra came to his side and looked down into the wheel-well. "What the hell?"

"I don't believe this. What the hell is wrong with him?" Tom started putting the donut back in place. "He doesn't loosen the nuts, doesn't make sure you have a jack and spare tire. I'm going to kill him."

Once he'd secured the donut in place, Tom replaced the floor panel and shut the hatch. Walking around to the passenger side, he saw that the jack wouldn't have done them any good.

"Your rim is bent all to hell. We will have to tow this to the garage," he said.

Kendra groaned and dropped her head into her hands. "How much is that going to cost?"

Tom gave her a sharp look. "Cost? Nothing. I'll take care of it."

Kendra raised her head. "No, no. Marcus can fix it."

It was hard, but Tom held his temper in check. "The only thing Marcus will fix is his broken nose because I will beat the crap out of him."

Her mouth curved upwards and her eyes lit up. "I'd like to see that."

Tom couldn't remember wanting to kiss a woman more than he did Kendra. Her luscious lips were so inviting that it took superhuman effort not to haul her against him and capture her mouth with his. "Don't tempt me. C'mon, you'll ride with me. The Mustang's backseat is big enough for his baby car seat."

"Really? How do you know?" she asked, following him around to the other side of the van.

"I've taken my niece and nephews a few times so that Sam and Tonya could go away for the weekend," Tom said. "Mikey still has to ride in a baby seat."

"You watch their kids?"

"Yeah."

He watched her climb into the back of the van to get

Connor's seat and had to curb his body's reaction at the sight of her perfectly shaped ass clearly outlined as the shorts pulled taut over it. Needing to divert his attention, Tom walked to his car and looked to Connor, who was fast asleep on the seat.

Tom reached in the car for his son. Connor never stirred as Tom settled him against his shoulder. Looking down at Connor, Tom still couldn't believe that the perfect little boy was his. A lump formed in his throat as potent love rose in him. Watching Kendra fasten the baby seat in his car, Tom became even more determined to bring her around to his way of thinking. He didn't know how yet, but he would. He wanted his son with him every day, and Kendra was the one woman who didn't make his body break-out in hives at the idea of marriage.

But right then, his priority was getting them home and then coming back for the van. And then he would have words with Marcus.

Chapter Eight

Kendra watched Tom's jaw clench as he downshifted and slowed down as the light ahead turned red. His anger was almost palpable in the car, hanging in the air like electricity during a thunderstorm. It unnerved and excited her at the same time.

The air conditioning felt heavenly after being stuck out in the sweltering heat for so long, but Tom had turned it way down so it wasn't such a shock to her and Connor's systems. While it cooled her skin, it did nothing to diminish the heat that burned inside as she noted the way the corded muscles in his forearm rolled as he shifted into second gear when traffic started moving again.

"You okay?" he asked for the fifth time.

She raised her eyes to his before he focused on the road again. "I'm fine. Why are you so mad?"

His hand tightened around the gearshift. "Marcus should've made sure that you could change a tire on your own by ensuring you had the right equipment and the nuts weren't too tight. What if it was an area out of cellphone coverage?"

Kendra thought his concern was sweet. "Tom, it's okay. Marcus is not my keeper. I've told him that over and over, so I can't expect him to be there as soon as I call. I hate the way he acts like the great protector."

"He hasn't in this case."

His statement confused her. "What do you mean?"

He glanced at her, his eyes almost topaz in the sunlight. "If he was really being protective, he'd make sure you could change a flat or learn how to fix minor problems. What if you'd gotten a flat at night when the shop was closed and your cellphone was dead? You'd have been a sitting duck. With my son in the car, too. Plus, he hasn't got his phone on. I don't call that being protective."

It shamed Kendra to realize that he was right. She prided herself on being as self-reliant as possible, but if her cellphone had been dead or no signal, she'd have had to hope that she'd be able to flag down someone nice to help her. In LA, that could be a dangerous thing to do.

"I always make sure it's charged before I leave the house," Kendra said.

Tom shook his head. "What if you are somewhere with no coverage?" Then he asked the question she'd been dreading. "How come you didn't run the air conditioner? At least for some of the time."

Kendra gnawed on her bottom lip and stayed silent.

Tom glanced at her. "Well?"

Might as well tell him. "The A/C died last week. It needs freezone."

Tom laughed and rubbed the back of his neck. "Freon. It needs Freon. How do you not know this stuff? You spent so much time around us."

"Cars are not my thing. Music is. Remember?" She wasn't about to tell him that she'd been too busy watching him for all the car-talk to sink in.

The angry look returned to his face. "Well, it's *going* to be your thing."

"Huh?"

"I'll teach you how to take care of simple repairs so that if you're ever in a tough spot like you were today, you can fix it at least good enough to get somewhere for help," Tom said.

Alarm shot through Kendra. "No, you're not. I don't want to learn."

Tom looked meaningfully back at Connor. "Not even for his sake?"

"That's not fair! A lot of women know little about the cars they drive," Kendra said.

Tom grunted. "They should. Especially the sister of a race car driver who is driving a hunk of shit!" He shifted again. "We will start with changing a tire and then I'll teach you how to check all your fluids. And I'll put together an emergency kit for you."

"Tom, all of that isn't really necessary," Kendra said.

They came to her apartment building, and Tom turned into the parking lot. He shut the engine off and turned to her. "You listen to me, Kendra. You *will* learn because I don't want you driving around not knowing what to do if you have an emergency. Your lives could depend on it. Do you understand me? Alternatively, you could let me buy you a new car that shouldn't have any mechanical troubles."

Granite couldn't have been any harder than his expression, but Kendra wasn't about to back down. "Perhaps it's time I looked at buying a new car myself. But don't you dare think you will start bossing me around, Tom? You can shove that idea right up your ass."

Why could the men in her life not realize how much it meant to her to live her life her way? To prove to her father that she could survive. They would never understand what it had been like to be helpless against the cancer. She could fight the disease, but she had no idea if she would win. It was important for her to have control. At the moment, letting Tom into her life made her feel as if the ground was moving under her feet. She was feeling overwhelmed, and her muscles tightened from the top of her head to her toes.

Her sassy statement apparently made Tom smile. He'd always admired her feisty attitude. She needed it when she was younger to fight the cancer. "Duly noted. I don't think anyone can force you to do anything, Tiger. But let's arrange a time for me to take you car shopping. I am the expert you know?"

Kendra gave a curt nod. "Don't rush me."

"If I help financially, as I should and have a right to, you could afford a new car."

Damn. That made sense. "Fine." She opened the door and got out. When she tilted the back of her seat forward, she saw that Connor was still asleep, tuckered out from the heat and stress. She released the safety straps and pulled him out of the child seat. He roused a little as she backed out of the car and settled him on her hip, but then went back to sleep.

Not realizing Tom was behind her, she bumped into him. "Oh, sorry."

Tom let his hand settle on her waist and leaned into her a little. "Feel free to back into me anytime."

His touch made breathing difficult for Kendra. She had to get away from him; he was making her feel things she was afraid to feel again. She chuckled and moved aside so he could get the baby seat out of the car. "Still charming the girls, I see."

When he flashed her that sexy smile, she melted. "Always."

It only took a moment for him to unhook the baby seat. He shut the door and hit the alarm button on his key fob as he looked around the neighborhood with disapproval. Kendra knew what he was thinking because it was the same look Marcus always got on his face when he was there.

"I can afford the rent here," she said.

Tom's eyebrows rose. "I didn't say anything."

Kendra turned away from him and started for the building. "You didn't have to."

* * *

Her anger was apparent in the tense way she held herself as she marched ahead of Tom. He hadn't meant to make her feel bad, but parking his valuable car in the derelict neighbor-hood made Tom uneasy. He hated them living in such a bad area of town, but there wasn't much he could do about it at the moment. Telling her to move was not the answer. She had to come to that decision herself. With his encouragement, of course. House hunting might be an idea. Women loved looking at homes. Appealing to her love for Connor by offering a large backyard would be a start. His house had a huge backyard.

Looking up at the dingy building that had once been white, Tom took in the peeling paint and dented pieces of siding. Two windows were cracked and apparently, the tenants had tried to fix them with duct tape. Tom shook his head as he followed Kendra inside.

He hated how much this reminded him of his upbringing.

He hadn't paid a whole lot of attention the day before, but the foyer and stairwells were just as depressing and in need of repair like the outside. There were cracks in the ugly yellow paint, and some stairs sagged. He also saw some nails sticking up from the wooden boards.

Someone will get hurt. Who the hell owns this place? They ought to be fined for not keeping stuff up to code. Tom put those thoughts out of his mind as he watched Kendra mount the stairs. His temper-ature rose as he watched her backside move, and he itched to fill his palms with her sweetly rounded flesh. He was glad when Connor woke up and provided a distraction.

Connor raised his head and looked at Tom over Kendra's shoulder. He raised a chubby little hand. "Hi, Tom!"

It amazed Tom that Connor remembered who he was after their brief meeting yesterday. He gave Connor a little wave. "Hi, buddy. You okay?"

Connor bobbed his head. "Mama, me hungee."

Kendra chuckled. "I know, honey. We're just about home and I'll make you your favorite, okay?"

"Geen beans! Yay!" Connor shouted.

Tom laughed as they reached the third floor. "Green beans are his favorite?"

Kendra set Connor on his feet. "Stay there." She fished her keys out of her purse. "Yeah. He loves fruits and veggies. It's a struggle to get him to eat meat most of the time."

That surprised Tom. "Really? Even hotdogs?"

Connor gave him a fierce look. "Hotdogs yucky."

"Well, all righty then," Tom responded. "No hotdogs for you. Can I eat them?"

Tom got a kick out of the way Connor's brow furrowed as he thought. He looked like Tom's brother Sam when he was thinking. It pleased Tom that Connor also took after his side of the family.

Kendra opened the door and Connor ran inside. "Geen beans!"

Tom shook his head. "The kid really loves his green beans." He followed Kendra into the living room and stopped when a hot breeze hit him. One window was open, the curtains fluttering in the breeze. "Did you leave that open?"

Kendra had followed Connor to the kitchen. "Yeah, for air," she called out to him.

"For air? The same piss-hot air outside?"

His eyebrows shot up when she charged out of the kitchen at him. "Watch your mouth around him! He picks up everything!"

"Okay, but where's your air conditioner? You're going to die of heat exhaustion," Tom shot back.

"There's an air conditioner in my room and I let it cool both our bedrooms. I block off the hallway with a curtain to keep the cold air back there." Kendra lifted her chin. "I can't afford to run two air conditioners. It'll make my electric bill go through the roof."

"Please let me help my son. Let's look for a new place for you both to live. I can afford the rent and no matter what happens between us, I have a right to provide for my son," Tom said quietly.

"It must be the heat making me so cranky." Kendra rubbed her temple. "I want to provide for Connor as much as you do. I guess I'm scared you can provide more than me."

Tom gritted his teeth for a moment. "This isn't a competition…" he broke off to make sure they were alone. "I'm his father and want to help him and you. You've had to do too much on your own as it is."

"Marcus has been helping too. He'll get suspicious if I suddenly move. He'll want to know where the money is coming from."

"Then perhaps we should inform Marcus of our situation before he works it out for himself, because I will not deny my son, nor deny him the things he needs in life because you're too scared or too ashamed of me."

Tom didn't care that Kendra had stiffened with fear and indignation. "You promised that you wouldn't say anything!"

"Wrong. I promised nothing. I just didn't tell Connor I'm his father, that's all."

Kendra glared at him. "I thought we agreed that we would work some things out before we went public with it."

"You just assumed that I'd agreed," Tom said.

Kendra threw up a hand. "So what? You're blackmailing me now?"

Tom sighed. God, she could be ornery. "I'd rather think of it as guiding you to the right decision. You either let me help you and my son, or I'll tell Marcus right away. I won't wait forever to tell people I'm Connor's father, but I'll hold off for a little while if you let me help financially. It will be a few weeks before we find a place and get you moved. We should have worked out the details by then. Do we have a deal?"

Kendra's gaze didn't flinch. "Fine."

"And you'll let me date you? You'll give a relationship with me a try?"

"I will as long as we don't tell Connor or anyone else, he's your son for at least one month."

Tom couldn't believe it. "A whole month? Why?"

Her emerald gaze turned diamond-hard. "Because I need to know that you really care about Connor. Prove it to me—and him. I don't want to be made to look a fool."

Her protectiveness made sense to Tom. He could understand why she'd doubt him, but waiting a whole month when he'd already lost so much time with Connor didn't sit well with him.

Her eyes narrowed. "Well?"

As he mulled it over. It might be beneficial to wait that long. If he proved his worthiness to Kendra, maybe he could persuade her to marry him. Maybe she would agree to be his wife before they had to tell Marcus. It might soften the blow. "All right. One month, but that's it."

She seemed to calm a bit with his agreement until Connor came running out of the kitchen.

"Mama, I peed," he happily announced. He'd taken off his T-shirt somewhere and stood in only his little jean shorts and pull-ups, which were now down around his ankles. "I pee-peed in da potty."

Kendra gasped, and they both ran to the kitchen, looking around the room they searched for the "potty" that Connor had used. It didn't take long to find it. In the corner by the refrigerator stood a small clay planter with a spider plant in it. A trail of yellow droplets led from it to the middle of the floor.

She put a hand on her forehead as Connor stood next to Tom. "He peed in the plant."

Tom looked at Connor, who smiled at him. "Well, I guess it looks like a potty to him. It's better than where my niece, Courtney, used to go in their old house."

Kendra looked at him. "Where did she go?"

Tom gave her a grin. "They had a forced hot air heating system. No one knows why, but she liked to pee down the heating vent in the living room. Smelled like hell when the heat ran."

Kendra tried to hide her smile. "What did they do? How did they get her to stop?"

Tom answered, "Moved to a place with no heating vents in the floor."

Laughter bubbled up from Kendra's throat and filled the kitchen. Tom joined her and even though he didn't understand the joke, Connor chimed in.

Kendra took Connor from him. "Come on, Squirt. You and Mommy need a bath."

Tom had to tease her and asked, "Need someone to wash your back?"

Kendra's jaw went slack at his comment, which had to mean the thought of getting hot and soapy with him was not a bad thing. "No, thanks. I think I can manage."

Tom chuckled. "Suit yourself."

Kendra gasped, startling them all. "Tom, we forgot my keyboard! It's in the back of the van. It will melt in this heat."

Tom put a hand on her shoulder and gave it a brief squeeze. "Don't worry. I'll go get your van and bring the keyboard when I come over tonight, okay? We can look at some apartments online and make a list of the ones we want to go see."

He loved that she shivered at his touch. "Okay."

Unable to resist the urge, Tom leaned closer and kissed her cheek. "See ya, then." He ruffled Connor's hair and kissed him, too. "See ya, buddy. No more peeing in plants, okay?"

Connor giggled. "'Kay. Bye, Tom."

Tom smiled and left the apartment, but not before noticing her longing gaze at him, before saying to her son, "Come on, honey. Let's go get cleaned up."

Chapter Nine

Tom parked the Mustang around the side of Bad Boy Autos and locked it. He took a couple of deep breaths as he walked to the office. It wouldn't do any good to immediately lose his cool with Marcus, but he would not put up with any shit, either.

Marcus stood behind the counter, doing something on the computer. He looked up and smiled. "Where have you been? Sully said that you had to leave for a while."

Tom shot a perplexed look at the shop as though he could see Sully through the wall. Why hadn't he told Marcus where he'd gone?

"Everything okay?"

Tom walked over and leaned his elbows on the counter. "It is now. Is your phone on?"

Marcus frowned and took his phone from his back pocket. He hit the home button a couple of times, but nothing happened. He sighed and swore. "Forgot to charge it. Why?"

"Well, your sister's van broken down on the side of the road out by the Dream Cinema. She called the shop for you, but you weren't here and you weren't answering your cellphone. So, I went to help her and Connor," Tom replied.

Marcus' eyes widened. "Are they okay? What happened?"

"Tire blew and Kendra couldn't get the nuts undone. Why is that, Marcus? The first thing you do is loosen them so women have the strength to change the tire if need be." His temper started rising.

"It's a secondhand van. I didn't think they would be that tight. Usually it's only new cars whose nuts have been machined tightened." Marcus smiled.

Tom's anger went from twenty to a hundred, and he banged a fist on the counter. "How the fuck is she going to get a hold of you when you can't even remember to charge your phone? How could you leave her helpless like that? Especially when she had Connor with her! It's a hundred degrees out, and they were out there for almost an hour. By the way her air conditioner is shot, so it was as hot as fuck. Ever hear of heat stroke?"

Marcus rounded the counter and came to stand toe-to-toe with Tom. "Stop yelling at me. Are they okay?"

He battled down his anger. This is how his father was. He would get angrier and angrier until the fists flew. Tom closed his eyes and battled the demons he'd inherited. He repeated in his head that he wasn't his father and he could and would control his temper. What if he lost his temper with Kendra or Connor? He would never forgive himself. At least he didn't drink, so hopefully he'd never make a drunken mistake and lash out in a fit of rage.

"Yeah, no thanks to you," Tom said.

A flicker of guilt crossed Marcus' face. "Thanks for taking care of them."

"I don't need your thanks. I need you to be accessible. What if we'd had an emergency at the shop?"

Marcus held up his hands. "Okay, okay! I'm sorry. I'll call Kendra later and apologize. Are we good?"

Tom brushed by him. "Not even close."

Marcus followed him into the shop. "What's that supposed to mean?"

Tom turned around and Marcus almost ran into him. "It means I will do what you should've done a long time ago."

Marcus's left eyebrow arched. "Oh, yeah? What's that?"

Tom put his hands on his hips. "I will fix her van, including getting the air-conditioning working, and then I'm teaching Kendra how to do other minor repairs. She should've been taught as a teenager. I just assumed that you had."

He moved away, but Marcus grabbed his shoulder. "Wait a second. I know you're mad, but don't get your nose out of joint too far. You're right. I should've taught her, but then cancer hit and we had more important things to focus on. I'll teach her now."

"No, you won't. You didn't do it before, so I'll do it," Tom said, shaking Marcus off. "I already told her I would."

"Why would you do that?" Marcus' eyes narrowed in suspicion. "What gives?"

Tom shook his head. "Nothing. I'm her friend and I want to make sure she can take care of her and the kid if they get stuck again, that's all."

"Why do you have to be the one to do it?" Marcus crossed his arms. "Besides, since we came home, you haven't hung out with her. Just the opposite, in fact. Now you want to suddenly be all buddy-buddy with her. Why?"

Tom stepped right up to Marcus. "Maybe because I've been honoring your order from all those years ago. Maybe I'm rethinking that."

Anger chased the surprised expression from Marcus' face, which was turning red. He raised a finger and seemed to struggle for words.

People rarely caught Marcus off guard, so it was amusing to Tom to watch Marcus fumble. Tom broke into a grin and then laughed while backing away. "Oh, man! You should've seen your face."

Marcus gave him an uncertain smile and then chuckled. "Ha ha. Very funny."

"I know it is." Only his promise to Kendra made Tom keep up the pretense of joking around. "The real reason I will show Kendra is because you suck at teaching. You'll just get mad when she doesn't catch on fast enough and yell at her. Then you guys will fight and she'll give up because she can't stand you. That will not help her. You know I'm right."

Marcus scowled in irritation, but he conceded Tom's point. "Yeah, I know. I try, but—"

"You suck at it."

They turned to see Tom's other best friend, Lexie Walker, standing near them. Marcus's expression darkened again, but Tom was thrilled to see her.

Lexie had been in the same auto mechanics class as Tom and they'd become firm friends. She was a stunning beauty, but for some reason their friendship had always remained platonic. Tom had taken Lexie into his formula one team on the European circuit. They'd had so much fun on the circuit until she fell for one of the rival team's drivers—Jason Colter.

"Lex!" He embraced her. "What the hell are you doing here? You didn't tell me you were coming into town."

Lexie hugged him back, but Tom felt how tense her shoulders were and grew concerned.

"It was a surprise," she said.

Pulling back, Tom met her dark eyes, but her gaze slid away slightly. "Everything okay?"

"Not really. Can we talk?"

Tom was further surprised when he saw her blink tears away. "Yeah, sure. Come on to my office."

She and Marcus traded scathing glances while Tom motioned for her to go ahead of him and he almost sighed. The two of them would never get along. Marcus hated Jason. And unfortunately, Lexie was part of Jason's life, her husband, when the accident on the race track happened. Jason's recklessness caused the crash and Marcus just couldn't get passed his career ending like it did. He'd been on target to win the driver's championship for the second time.

There it was. Now his two best friends were at odds and it made things awkward for Tom whenever they were together. He'd tried to get Marcus to see that Lexie wasn't to blame, but Marcus's memory was long—and twisted with bitterness.

Once they settled in his office, Tom behind his desk and Lexie in a stylish black leather chair, he asked, "What gives?"

Lexie looked at the ceiling a moment and then back at Tom. She was trying to hang on to her composure. "Jason and I are done. For good this time. I caught him with another track whore. I can't take it anymore."

Once again today, anger surged through Tom. "Son of a bitch. I'm sorry, Lexie." He wasn't overly surprised though.

She slapped her hands lightly down on her thighs. "Don't be. You tried to warn me, but I wouldn't listen. Well, that's the last time he makes an ass out of me. I filed for divorce last week, licked my wounds, and now here I am, ready to get on with life."

One side of Tom's mouth lifted. "It takes a little longer than that to recover from that kind of thing, Lex."

The pain in her eyes made Tom's fists tighten with the need to bash Jason's skull in with a tire iron. If he ran into the scumbag, Marcus would have to get in line.

"I don't have time to sit around gnashing my teeth and wailing. I'm flat broke, Tommy. Jason took off with all my cash, any that was left that is. He sniffed most of our money up his nose."

Tom leaned forward in shock. "He's using again?"

Lexie gave a sarcastic laugh as she pushed her dark hair back from her face. "Yeah. I don't think he stopped, but he hid it well until a couple of weeks ago. I came home from being out with some friends and caught him doing a line off the kitchen counter. We got in it, and that's when he told me we were poor. He's not worked since he got kicked off the racing team. We're so poor he's sold the car to pay off his drug dealers."

Tom rubbed his jaw. "Christ. Listen, I'll give you as much money as you need, honey. You just—"

"No. I don't need money from you," she said.

"Okay, then what? Just name it."

Lexie blew out a nervous breath. "I need to work. I need money to live on, but I need to work just as much as I need the money. I need a job. Hire me."

Tom relaxed back in his chair as dismay set in. "Lex, I'd love to, but we just don't have a spot right now. And even if we did, you and Marcus would eat each other alive. I can't have that kind of drama around here."

Lexie's expression filled with something Tom had never seen on her beautiful face. *Desperation.* She was desperate.

"Don't make me beg, Tommy. Find something for me to do. Sweep the floor, wash windows—anything just so I can be around the cars," Lexie said.

"Lex—"

"I'll be good as gold around Mucous, I mean Marcus."

Tom laughed at her derogatory name for his business partner. "Look, I might be able to throw some part-time work your way and recommend you for some side jobs. Or you could go work at another garage. I have contacts."

His suggestion made Lexie look like she'd just swallowed gasoline. "What other garage? You mean like a garage-garage? Oh, hell no! C'mon, Tommy."

Tom cast a glance at the office door. "It's not up to just me."

Lexie let out a disgusted sound and flopped back in her chair. Then she shot to her feet and stalked out of the office. Tom scrambled after her. He knew that crazy gleam in her eyes, and he needed to make sure that all hell didn't suddenly break loose in the garage.

"Marcus!" she shouted.

Tom caught her arm. "No, no. Don't you dare."

Marcus came walking over to them from somewhere towards the back. "Yeah? What do you want?"

"To say goodbye," Tom said. "Lex was just leaving."

Lexie yanked her arm away. "Like hell I was. Why would I leave my new place of employment?"

"Lexie," Tom warned.

Marcus looked back and forth at them. "What's she talking about? Did you hire her? We don't need another mechanic! All of our bays are full, Tom."

Tom hated being caught in the middle of the two of them, which happened a lot. Just like now. They glared at him as though willing him to pick a side. "She's kicked Jason to the sidewalk, and he's left her broke. Have a heart."

"Hey! Did you just hire her?" Sully shouted.

"Yes!" Lexie hollered at the same time Tom said, "Sort of," and Marcus yelled, "Wait a minute… "

Sully frowned. "Well, which is it?"

Marcus said, "No, we didn't hire her. We really don't need another mechanic."

Sully sauntered over and gave Lexie a slow once-over. "Haven't seen you in a while, Lex. Looking good."

Lexie returned the favor. "Not looking so bad yourself, silver fox."

Sully laughed and motioned for her to follow him. "C'mon. I got some places that need fixing that only small hands can get to. As I recall, you have great hands."

"You might be gray on top, Sully, but there's nothing wrong with your memory," Lexie said.

Sully grinned and then said, "Zip! Get Lexie a pair of your coveralls! You're the closest to her size."

Zip popped out from under the hood of a sleek, silver Maserati. "Sure!"

He trotted off like an obedient puppy to do Sully's bidding while Lexie followed Sully, leaving Tom and Marcus fuming as they faced off.

"What the fuck just happened?" Marcus asked.

"Sully happened," Tom commented.

Marcus snorted and started for the office. "Who the hell are the bosses around here? I need a drink. Want one while I rip your face off for being a dumbass?"

"I can't," Tom said. "You know that."

Marcus stopped. "Sorry. I might be pissed at you, but I'm not trying to be an asshole by tempting you back to drinking. Sometimes I forget."

Marcus had been a great help when he'd first decided not to drink. He was the buffer between the rest of the gang who always tried to get him to drink. Fast cars and alcohol were like models and bikini's—they just went together.

"Look we could do with an extra mechanic. We've got a waiting list already. Can't you see that she's nothing like Jason."

Marcus sighed and handed him a coke. "I'll try but—it's just when I see her, I see Jason and the bad memories rush back. I can feel the car flipping and the pain…"

"Yeah, I know," Tom said. "but that was Jason not Lexie."

"I'll adjust. I always do." Tom stood up. "Where are you off too," Marcus asked.

"I have to go get Kendra's van and bring it back here. She has a new keyboard in it and I don't want it to melt. She was coming back from picking it up today when the van died. I don't know why you're letting her drive that heap of crap."

Marcus said, "I don't want her driving it, either. I dropped a nice Jeep off to her one day, but she refused to drive it. It sat over there outside that place she calls a home for two weeks, but she never got in it. I had to take it back before someone stole it."

Despite being irritated, Tom had to admire Kendra's tenacity. "Okay, well, I better get going."

"Fine, but when you get back, we will discuss this Lexie thing. I have a few rules," Marcus said.

Tom met his gaze. "It won't do any good to talk to me about it. Talk to the boss."

Marcus groaned. "When the hell did we lose control?"

"The day we hired Sully," they said in unison.

Tom snagged the keys for the tow truck off one hook that lined the wall outside of the office, then gave Marcus a last look. "Lexie needs a job, Marcus. That shit of a husb-ex-husband left her high and dry. If you recall, in this industry we help our friends. And Lexie is my friend."

He noted Marcus's slight nod. Tom had been by Marcus's side every minute after his crash. Tom had been there when they'd told him he'd never walk again. He'd also been with him for most of his physical therapy, and he'd definitely been there when he had proven the doctors wrong and walked again.

You did not leave your friends in time of trouble. That is what loyalty was and unlike his traitorous mother and his drunken father, loyalty meant something to Tom.

Chapter Ten

Kendra jerked awake when someone knocked on her door. She forgot where she was and almost rolled off the couch when she turned over. However, she caught herself on the coffee table and avoided winding up on the floor. Looking at the wall clock, she saw that it was shortly after seven.

"Oh, God." She got to her feet and finger-combed her hair while the knocking came again.

It was most likely Tom, but she never took chances.

"Who is it?" she called through the door.

"It's me."

Opening the door, she found Tom standing on the landing holding a huge bunch of roses—her favorite flowers. That's what she missed about having a garden—she couldn't grow her own flowers or vegetables. The muscles in his arms bulged under the weight of the huge bouquet, and she noted he obviously still worked out.

She took the flowers, not sure what on earth she would do with them. She didn't have a vase big enough, and certainly not a cupboard full of vases to use. "Thank you, these are gorgeous."

He brushed a curl off her cheek. "Not as gorgeous as you."

She looked down at her clothes. "I fell asleep on the couch. I look—"

"Like a busy mother who needs a bit of spoiling." He closed the door behind him and followed her into the kitchen.

"Could you reach the vase on the top shelf for me, please?"

His movements pulled the t-shirt up and Kendra's cheeks heated. She'd never been so jealous of a piece of clothing in all her life. The glimpse of the eagle tattoo she remembered so well teased her senses.

"Would you like some iced tea?" she asked, heading for the kitchen.

Tom followed her. "Love some. Where's Connor?"

"In bed. He was worn out from today so I put him down early." Kendra took a pitcher out of the fridge and got a glass from the cupboard next to it.

"I thought he was going to Stella's so we could talk."

She shrugged. "He's so tired he'll sleep. We can still talk. I'm hoping we won't be yelling at each other. But we might have to order in. I haven't prepared anything. Connor practically fell asleep in a bowl of cereal, and then I never bothered to figure out what to have for dinner."

"No problem. How about I pop out and pick up some Chinese while you look through these listings I've bookmarked on my phone?" He handed her his phone as if he had nothing to hide on it. Didn't he know what woman did when they got their hands on a man's phone? "The code's 8639."

She handed him a drink, which he promptly put on the counter. "I'll be right back with dinner and your keyboard, it's in my car."

"You left my keyboard in your fancy car in this neighborhood."

He smiled like a sly fox. "You just made my point about living here. Check the listings." He pressed a soft kiss to her lips.

Kendra shrugged. "Clever, aren't you?"

Tom grunted and then headed for the door. Kendra followed

him just so she could admire his muscular shoulders and back. If her little apartment got any hotter, she'd combust.

Tom nodded. "Right. Well, start looking. There are several places I thought might suit you and Connor, but it's up to you. Be right back."

As soon as the door closed, Kendra was going through his phone. And she wasn't looking at the listings. She'd gone straight to his text's. She knew it was wrong, but he would be an important person in both Connor's and her life, and she wanted to see if she could trust him with this sudden desire to be a one-woman man.

To her surprise, there was nothing of note to read. There were a few text's from a woman called Lexie but they seemed to be about work. Ashamed of herself, she swiped sideways and looked at the listings he'd selected. Surprise, surprise they were mostly in his neighborhood which she knew meant they were expensive.

She hated how already she suspected Tom's motives. She didn't want to be that clingy, needy woman, chasing after her man every minute of the day. How was she ever going to believe he was here for her, not just his son?

She found a couple of places she would love to look at even if they were in his neighborhood and was just about to put the phone down when Tom arrived back with her keyboard and she rushed to grab the Chinese takeaway from his over loaded arms and watched each muscle flow as he found a space for the keyboard on the table along the wall.

She moved to the kitchen, fighting the heat growing deep inside at his proximity. As she dished out the food, she called over her shoulder, "I looked at some listings. You have good taste and knowledge of what would work for me and Connor."

He spoke from just behind her and she longed to turn into his arms. "I thought about my childhood and what I would have wanted and never had."

She turned then and laid her hand over his and squeezed. He

may not be honest about his feelings for her, but it was clear he wanted nothing but the best for their son.

Over delicious Chinese they made a list of what she was looking for in an apartment, as they looked at the rest of the listings.

"I would really love three bedrooms so I can have one as a music room, big enough to fit my piano. Fully air-conditioned would be luxury and some outside space for Connor."

He remembered she had a wonderful voice. "What's happening with your music?"

Her face flushed before answering his question. "It's moving slowly but I've sold a few songs, mainly for commercials and I top up my money through doing piano lessons." She hesitated but added, "I have told no one else yet, but a producer downtown is interested in some of my work and asked me to write a song for a well-known singer. If she likes it, then… I won't be worrying about money for a while. It could be my big break."

"Wow, that's fantastic. It's an indescribable feeling to achieve something you have always dreamed about and worked hard for."

Her smiled disappeared. "Do you miss the racing circuit? You didn't have to give it up just because Marcus could no longer drive."

"It wasn't the same without Marcus."

"But I heard you had a huge offer from another racing team. Marcus thought you were nuts not to take it."

That's what everyone had told him, but he'd reached his dream because of Marcus, and his friend needed him. For a man of action, being told he might not walk again… Tom knew he had to give Marcus the will to fight.

He'd achieved all his dreams, the ultimate being helping Marcus win a Formula One World Drivers Championship. It wasn't the same after he saw Marcus's crash. He had seen the footage, and it wasn't because of anything wrong with the car, but still he could not help feeling responsible. He realized perhaps after eight years on the circuit, his luck had run out and, like Marcus, it was time to come home.

He decided it was time to change the subject. "What about a pool?"

She pursed her lips making him want to taste them. "Perhaps. Although it needs to be properly fenced for Connor."

Tom smiled to himself. Kendra was really enjoying this. Wait until she got to look at them in person. This might actually work. He knew for a fact the house across the road from his was up for rent. It had a wonderful backyard with a fully fenced off pool. He could imagine teaching Connor to swim. But he was jumping ahead of himself.

He couldn't believe how relaxed she was in his company. She sat cross-legged on the couch, her laptop on her knee, going through rental listings. She looked adorable in her denim cutoffs and spaghetti strap top. A bead of sweat trickled down between her breasts and his eyes traced it, wishing he could lick it up with his tongue. The open window did little but let the warm air in. He really needed to move them to a better house and fast.

Glancing at Kendra, he caught her staring at him. She jerked her gaze away, but not before he saw the desire in her eyes. *She still likes me.* Pretending not to notice her preoccupation with him, Tom gathered up the remains of their take out.

"So, do we have some places you want to view?" he asked.

"How many can I see?" Kendra responded.

"As many as you like. You don't have to settle. We'll find someplace you really like, take your time."

"Thank you." She chewed her bottom lip and his groin tightened. "These look expensive."

Facing her, Tom said, "You're welcome. And remember, I have three years of financial support to make up for."

Her expression tightened, and wariness entered her eyes. "Yeah. I guess so."

He didn't want her to withdraw because he'd raised the topic of money, so he sat down right next to her. Heat came off her, and the scent of fresh lilies wreaked havoc with his senses.

The proximity to her sinfully delectable body made him ache. Shoving that away as best he could, he asked, "Don't let money come between us. We have more to worry about and if money raises its head, we might not stand a chance."

Kendra smiled wryly. "I guess this *is* more than about money. It's about all of our futures, including Connor. But our relationship can't just be about Connor. Why now? Why this desire to have a relationship with me? You must see how it looks."

He felt the guilt flicker across his face and Tom turned away. "I suppose it is time for some truths to come out. I promised Marcus I'd stay away from you when we first met, and he was right to warn me off. We were both young, and you'd just beaten cancer… but the fact is, I liked you as soon as we met."

Her eyes widened. "You did? You never said anything, and I chased after you like a bull after a red flag."

Tom laughed and leaned back against the couch. "Marcus caught me eyeing you up and made me swear to stay away from you, so I couldn't tell you."

"He had no right to do that. I was old enough to make my own decisions."

"You were sixteen. Try to understand where he was coming from. I'm the first one to admit that I was not in your league, and he wanted better than that for you," he said. "Turns out he was right. I never should've slept with you, especially when I knew nothing could come of it, I was heading back to Europe the next day but damn it—I wanted you."

Kendra shifted away from him. "Well, I'm not sorry that I slept with you because I have Connor. He's the best thing I've ever done and I wouldn't change it for anything."

Her wounded expression made Tom feel like an ass for hurting her feelings. "Kendra, it's complicated. Look, I'm not good at this relationship stuff, but I want to try. My parents weren't great role models for relationships. That night with you was incredible. I don't regret sleeping with you; I regret the timing. I regret putting friendship before what we could have had. I didn't think it would work between us."

Kendra nodded. "My parents aren't fabulous role models either, but not because they broke up, because they stayed together. Mum puts up with so much shit and I swear I'll not do that."

"I'd never want you to. And I'd never treat you like your father treats your mother. That's why I hate this secrecy. Hiding this from Marcus…" He knew Kendra wasn't just thinking about herself in trying to hide this from Marcus, but it still hurt. "I can do that, but it puts me in a terrible position. Until yesterday, I didn't have to lie about Connor. If he asks me outright I can't or won't lie to my best friend."

Kendra lifted an eyebrow. "And I'm not marrying you just to make a family."

Tom had thought about that all day, and he'd decided that he'd gone about it all wrong. He gave a self-deprecating laugh. "Sorry for trying to order you into it. That was stupid. But I want to make a home for Connor and be his dad." He pointed at some listings they had printed out. "Moving closer to me will help."

Kendra shook her head. "I can't figure you out. I never thought of you as the marrying type. You always hopped from bed to bed."

Tom shrugged, "I never had a kid before. It makes a big difference. I had a shitty childhood and I don't want that for Connor. I want him to know that he has a father he can count on."

"Want to share? I'll tell you my terrible childhood stories if you tell me yours."

He wanted the ground to open up. Her cancer topped his physical beatings for sure. "I don't talk about it much. No sense to it as I can't change what happened to me. That was in the past, so I try to leave it there. My old man was too busy cheating on my mother to pay much attention to me." He shrugged. "Mom finally tired of it and took off when I was thirteen. That's when Dad's drinking escalated. I always swore to be a better man than that." Tom let out a sarcastic laugh. "Talk about an epic fail. Fast cars, fast women, and all the booze I could handle. For quite some time I was just like him or turning into him."

Kendra cocked her head. "Was?"

"On a trip state side, Marcus and I had gone to Daytona to see the 500 when Sam called me to tell me that Dad had cirrhosis of the liver from all his drinking. There I stood in the stands right before the race with a beer in my hand while he's telling me that Dad had pickled his liver."

"He told me that Dad would die unless he got a liver transplant, and it felt like I was holding a cobra in my hand instead of a beer. And I knew that if I kept drinking, I really would end up like Dad. I didn't drink that beer. I gave it to Marcus and I haven't drunk since."

* * *

Kendra couldn't believe it. "But you go out all the time."

Tom's smile looked a little sheepish. "Yeah, but I'm the designated driver a lot."

Astonished, Kendra could only stare at him for a few moments. Why hadn't Marcus ever told her that? Then it came to her. After she'd thought Tom had abandoned her and Connor, she'd expressed no interest in Tom. In fact, she'd purposely acted disinterested in anything Marcus had to say about Tom, and her brother had started only mentioning him in passing.

"I go out to have a good time with the gang—"

"And to pick up women."

Tom frowned at the censure in her voice. "Don't be like that. All holier than thou. It's not like you were a virgin before we slept together, and I'm sure you're not hurting for dates."

"You're right. I have no right to judge," she said.

He sighed and stretched. "Yes, you do. But I can't change my past. I'm not sure how we'll work this out, Kendra. We both want different things that we think are the best for Connor. I want to make a stable, happy home for him."

Kendra said, "I want the same thing, but getting married for his sake is the worst idea in the universe. Look at our parents. Isn't it better to remain friends and leave sex out of it?"

Tom twisted so he faced her. "Did you ever wonder what would've happened if I hadn't gone back to the circuit?" His chest muscles flexed as he rested his arm on the back of the couch behind her. "Did you ever think about what it would've been like to see where things might have gone between us?"

Kendra couldn't speak. *I must be dreaming. This can't be real. It's like he's plucked my thoughts right out of my brain.* "I did for a little while, but after two months of not hearing from you I stopped having stupid fantasies. I had a baby on the way and he was my focus."

She could see the remorse in his eyes. "I get it. I do. I don't blame you for hating me, but no more than I hate myself for not reading your emails or listening to your voicemails." He lifted a hand and laid it against her cheek. "I'm sorry that I wasn't here then, but I'm here now. Please give us a chance."

Danger signs flashed in Kendra's mind, but she smashed them with an imaginary hammer. His rough palm on her skin ignited a hunger that had lain dormant for so long. Tom was right. There had been a couple of guys since Connor had been born, but they'd been just brief, meaningless flings. When it came to sex, they'd paled in comparison to the way Tom had made her feel.

"I'm here and I'm not going anywhere," he practically whispered.

Kendra tried so hard to keep her eyes on his, but she couldn't help glancing at his sensual male mouth. Her breathing quickened as he leaned closer and cupped the back of her head. She should turn away, shove him away, and run away, but she was trapped by desire.

The first contact with his lips as he brushed them over hers, sent need coursing through her and any objection she might have made fizzled and died. It was a good thing she was sitting down when he kissed her in earnest because her knees would've turned to jelly. *Oh, to hell with it!*

Kendra gave up fighting against what her body wanted and wrapped her arms around Tom's neck. Parting her lips, she invited him to invade her mouth, reveling in the warm, soft collision of their tongues. She'd lied to him about not fantasizing about him like this.

She liked the feel of his short hair against her palm as she ran her hand over the back of his head. He hauled her over onto his lap, making her gasp into his mouth. Tom angled his mouth a little more and Kendra kissed him back like a starving woman.

Nothing could cool the fire Tom had lit inside her. No man had ever kissed her with this kind of intensity. It had been the same way on the night they'd slept together. He was everything she'd wanted, needed… and he had given her a night she could never forget.

Iced tea had never tasted as good as it did on his lips, and she drank deeply while her temperature continued to climb. He slid a hand down her back to her hip and kept it there even though she wanted him to strip her naked and kiss every inch of her heated skin.

A cute little voice said, "Mama kish Tom," followed by an adorable giggle.

Tom jerked so hard in surprise that he almost bucked Kendra off the couch. "Hi!" he said to Connor, who stood smiling at them. "Mommy had something in her eye and I was helping her."

Kendra clung to Tom's shoulders until she regained her balance and then stood. His ridiculous excuse and the stark fear in Tom's expression struck her as hilarious, and she promptly burst into laughter even though desire still hummed through her body.

Connor laughed and jumped up and down in delight as Kendra braced herself on the couch.

She could tell Tom didn't find the situation amusing in the least. It was obviously his first time being interrupted during a passionate moment by a kid, and his son at that, and he wasn't sure what to do.

"Tom kish Mama!" Connor shouted, still jumping up and down.

Tom ran a hand over his face. "Shit. I hope he doesn't say that around Marcus."

Kendra's mirth faded at that thought. "Oh, God. You're right." Then she waved away their concern. "I'll just say that I kissed your cheek to thank you for your work on my van."

Tom stared at her. "Have you always been this good at lying?"

"Pfft! Please. I had to be, or else I wouldn't have ever gotten to do anything," Kendra said. "Even after I was given the all-clear, everyone treated me like I was still sick and I wasn't hardly allowed to leave the house."

"Shit!" Connor said and laughed.

"Sorry about that."

"Don't worry about it. Stella accidentally taught him that one. Kids can sneak up on you, as you just found out. They overhear things that they shouldn't."

Tom leaned back against the couch, and she shivered in his heat. She wanted him so much but Connor came first. He sighed and chuckled. "Okay. I'm glad I didn't teach him that word."

Connor ran over to the couch and used Tom's leg to help him clamber onto it. "What's dat?" He pointed at the forgotten laptop on the floor.

Kendra said, "It's mummies laptop. You've seen this before. We play Mr. Caterpillar on it."

"Me see!" Connor slid back off the couch and ran over to where it lay discarded in their passionate moment.

Tom grinned when Connor couched down and touched the keyboard. "Can you see Mr. Cattapillar?"

"No." He looked at Tom.

"I bet he's gone to bed as it's late," Tom said to him.

Connor thought about that and nodded. He stood. "Mama, me thirsty," the little boy said.

Kendra chuckled. "Okay, but only a little water."

"'Kay."

"I better go." Tom rose and prepared to leave. He snagged the printouts of the rentals they would inspect, and Kendra had to stop herself from saying, 'don't go'.

She was still so into him.

Perhaps she could give this relationship idea a chance. She would try to protect Connor from it, but ultimately, she would begin a relationship with someone. Why not the man who owned her heart? She couldn't protect Connor from her own needs.

Connor went to run by Tom and he grabbed him, turning him upside down. Connor squealed with laughter and Tom laughed with him. Seeing her son's eyes shine with happiness made Kendra warm inside.

Tom hugged Connor close. "I'm going bye-byes, buddy."

Connor frowned and took Tom's face in his little hands. "No. Stay."

Kendra's heart squeezed and damned if she didn't feel like crying. She wanted him to stay too.

"I can't right now, but I'll see you soon. Okay?"

Connor's gaze never wavered. "Promise me?"

"I promise."

"You see me morrow?" Connor wanted to know.

"Yeah. I'll see you tomorrow," Tom replied.

Connor's frown gave way to a smile. "'Kay." He hugged Tom's neck and patted his shoulder.

Tom rubbed his back and turned towards the kitchen.

Kendra blinked away tears at the sweet picture that big,

strong Tom and their cute son made as they hugged. How many times had she dreamed of the three of them being a family? Too many to count. That was all it was, though—a dream. Did dreams ever come true?

Despite his insistence on getting married, Kendra would never do it because he didn't love her. Eventually, his excitement over being a father would fade and he'd hate being trapped in a marriage that he didn't truly want. Then they'd have horrible fights and end up divorcing. She refused to put Connor through that, no matter how much she loved Tom.

"Heading out?" She walked over to them.

Tom smiled. "Yeah. That way someone will go back to sleep."

Kendra appreciated his consideration. "Okay. Thanks again for everything."

Reluctantly, Tom gave Connor to Kendra. "No sweat. If you're free on Thursday and can get a sitter, I'll organize times for us to view some of these," he waved the pages in his hand.

"That'll be great. I'll ask Stella," Kendra said, shifting Connor to her other hip.

"Okay. I'll see you tomorrow when I bring your van back."

"Thank you. That went better than I thought. Night."

He looked at her and Connor. The want in his gaze unmissable. "Way better."

Kendra locked the door behind Tom and looked at Connor. "Okay. Time for a little drink and then off to dreamland. Got it?"

Connor gave her a nod. "Got it."

As she settled Connor back in bed, Kendra couldn't prevent her mind from reliving the fantasy again. Perhaps she should seriously consider dating Tom. The idea, like the man, was very attractive.

She slipped into bed and decided.

Tomorrow she'd face Marcus. Trying to build a relationship while keeping secrets was a recipe for failure.

Chapter Eleven

The longer Tom worked on Kendra's van the next day, the angrier he became at Marcus. One of the rear struts needed replacing, two of the tires were worn down, and there were spots of rust on both rocker panels. The battery terminals were slightly corroded, and the vehicle had a small oil leak.

His first instinct was the same as Marcus'; just buy Kendra a brand-new car and be done with it. That wasn't an option because Kendra would never accept it and everyone would find it odd. The one complicated thing about Bad Boy Autos was that they were all up in everyone else's business most of the time.

So, the next best thing was upgrading the van as much as possible for the time being. That meant all new tires, fixing all the engine issues, and a decent paint job. He couldn't do the paint job right away, but he could take care of all the other stuff.

After double-checking the tire size, Tom grabbed his keys from a hook. He turned around and startled when Lexie stood there.

"Jeez, Lex. Trying to give me a heart attack?"

She grinned. "Nope. Just wondering what's up with you."

"Well, I'm going to Kix's place to get new tires for Kendra's van and a few other things. We don't have those kinds of tires, so…"

Lexie shook her head. "That's not what I mean. You're acting weird."

"I am? How?"

"Well, you're not a chatterbox, but you're really quiet today. And you blew me off last night. We were supposed to meet, remember? You never usually put 'getting some' ahead of me. What gives? Who is she?"

Tom swore inwardly over Lexie's perceptiveness. "Uh, shit. Sorry about last night. I've just got a lot on my mind with Dad and all."

"Oh. How's he doing?"

Tom shrugged. "Okay, I guess. Sam said that he'll be in the hospital for a couple more weeks unless he's doing okay, then they'll let him go home."

Lexie's expression turned sympathetic. "Sam wants you to go see him, doesn't he?"

A long sigh escaped Tom. "Yeah. He keeps trying to force me to make amends with Dad and I just don't have it in me."

Lexie put a hand on his arm. "I know he put you through hell, but maybe you should consider it."

Her statement incensed Tom because it seemed like she was siding with Sam. But then he'd told no one how bad things had gotten with his father. The beatings, the neglect—sometimes having to steal because there was no food in the house… "I gotta get going. I told Kendra I'd have her van back by noon."

Lexie gave him a resigned look and dropped her hand. "Okay. Go. But we will talk—and soon. If you like, I'll come with you when you visit with your father."

Tom left the shop, his mind churning with mixed emotions. He hated lying, or misleading his friends—both Lexie and Marcus.

* * *

Kendra paced across her living room as the time neared for

Tom to collect her so they could visit the rentals she'd selected. She'd tried to contact Marcus, but he'd gone out of town. Telling him would have to wait.

She'd only seen Tom briefly when he'd dropped her van off that afternoon and she'd wanted to confess her desire to give their relationship a go, but he'd acted distracted and distant and it made her wonder if he regretted kissing her last night. Although she knew that it wasn't a good idea to show Tom how much he still affected her, she hadn't been able to control her yearning for him.

She remembered the night of her prom. It was about twelve months after she'd gone into remission. She had hardly been at school over her senior years, and the word cancer seemed to put all the boys off. No one want to touch her, or kiss her, as if she carried germs they'd catch.

Her parents wanted Marcus to take her, but she refused to go to prom with her brother as an escort. She would not go at all until Tom reminded her it was her life and why should she care what anyone thought.

She told her parents she'd prefer to go solo with Stella.

When they arrived at the entrance to the prom, Tom stepped out of the shadows with the boy Stella was dating, and he escorted her to her prom. Stella and Tom had set it all up.

She'd been the envy of the senior girls. Tom in a tux was something to behold. Sexy, strong, older—suddenly it seemed as if dreams came true. He'd given her a night she would never, ever forget.

And when they danced… being held in his arms as if she was the most important person in the world, his gaze never leaving her face…, she fell completely in love. What young girl wouldn't?

And the kiss he'd placed on her lips when he'd put her in the limousine to go home sealed her heart as his.

She shook away the memory. She'd never met a man who stirred her heart like Tom had—and still did.

The kiss last night proved to her she was still susceptible to his male charisma. But one-sided love did not make for a good marriage.

She heard movement on the landing outside her door, and a moment later, someone knocked.

"Who is it?"

"It's me."

Opening the door, Kendra's breathing stopped at the sight of Tom. The black jeans he wore hinted at his strong thighs. He wore a solid red button-down shirt with the sleeves rolled up to his elbows. It emphasized his broad shoulders and brought out the color of his eyes.

Tom was dressed to impress and he surely did. He usually always wore old jeans and T-shirts or tank tops. He looked incredible and her desire to kiss him almost overwhelmed her.

He gave her a quizzical look. "Can I come in?"

"Oh! Of course." She waved him inside. "Sorry. You look nice."

As he walked past her, the faint scent of an expensive fragrance reached her nostrils. It only increased her hunger for him. How was she supposed to concentrate on rentals when he looked and smelled so good?

Tom smiled as he turned to her. "I clean up pretty good— when I feel like it, which isn't too often. You look nice, too."

Kendra looked down at her blue skirt and white spaghetti strap top. "You're just being kind," she said. "These are just old clothes. Gone are the days where I could afford designer anything."

His gaze raked over her. "You could wear a burlap bag and still be sexy as hell, Kendra."

Why was it so hot in here? Kendra suddenly couldn't breathe as desire gleamed in his eyes. "Don't look at me like that."

"Like what? Like I want you? Like you drive me crazy? Because you do. You always have. I just couldn't let you know it."

Kendra couldn't lie to herself or him. "I wish you would've."

His lips curved in a wry smile. "I should've, but I was scared."

"Scared of what?"

He lifted a hand and cupped her cheek. "Screwing up with you just like my parents. All those fights… And then losing my best friend over nothing."

His touch made her pulse speed up. The remorse in his eyes filled her with sympathy. "It wasn't all your fault, Tom. I wanted you so much that I jumped at the chance to be with you when you'd made it very clear it was a onetime thing. I'm ashamed, but I was young and had stars in my eyes. I was so stupid and reckless once I found out I'd had a second chance at life."

He stared into her eyes. "If you'd asked, I might have postponed going."

"No you wouldn't. I have thought about that a lot." Kendra put her hand over his. "Besides, I couldn't ask you to put your career on hold. I didn't want to hold you guys back. I'm not sure my brother would have won without you."

"You could've come with me."

Kendra's eyes widened. "What and sit at the hotel? Like a track bunny? Not me, sorry."

He sighed. "You're right. I wasn't good enough for you after everything you'd been through. You deserved more than to tag along behind me. You had a life to live, and I had to make my way in mine. Maybe that's how it was meant to be? Because we both had time to grow and mature to the point we know what we want."

"Maybe…" Kendra thought maybe there were second chances. She broke away from Tom so he could not see how much she would have wanted to be with him. "And you were being loyal to Marcus too, right? I know the bro code." She crossed the room to the windows.

"We were all too young but we aren't now."

Soon he was next to her and turned her around. "I'm done

worrying about what Marcus thinks. He's an adult and needs to get over it. I was just trying to be respectful to him and you. I didn't want to ruin my friendship with Marcus if there was nothing serious between us and back then I wasn't ready for anything serious. But I am now. Now we have Connor to think about too."

"I'm not sure you really are. It simply suits you to say so because of Connor, but you haven't been interested in me since you've been back."

Tom's gaze wavered. "I know but—"

Kendra poked a finger at Tom's chest. "Don't lie to me now. You've always told me like it is... And I can't start a relationship based on lies." She poked him again. "That's partly what hurts so much. I thought you were different, but if you're going to try to twist our situation to suit you, you're not."

He took a gentle hold on her wrists. "I'm sorry, Kendra. I'm sorry that I let you down and hurt you like that. Let me make it up to you."

Kendra didn't hide the tears that welled in her eyes. "I don't know if I can. How can I trust you? How can I believe that you really want me and not just Connor? Us marrying won't help Connor if we later divorce. Connor comes first."

"That was the past. This is a different time and place in our lives. I didn't know what I wanted before, but now I do."

His unwavering gaze held Kendra prisoner and she couldn't look away. Could she, should she, take the risk when there was so much more at stake than her own heart? What if Connor became attached to Tom and everything fell apart? It would devastate her little boy, and she didn't want him to go through that. But Connor was so young he'd bounce back, wouldn't he? And he could still see Tom. Tom had never lied to her before. Could she depend on him to show her that same honesty now?

"What makes you think you're ready for a commitment now? What's changed?"

"I'm getting older. I've had time to look back over my life

and see a few home truths. I know what it takes to be a good father. I'm not saying I'm not scared. I'm petrified, given my parent's example. But we aren't our parents. I know that I want to try. Will you at least give a relationship with me a chance?"

She wished he didn't push so hard. She turned and grabbed her handbag. "Come on. We have a busy day of house hunting to get through."

Tom grinned. "I guess that's a start. It's not a no and I'll take it."

* * *

Kendra admitted to herself she was enjoying the day. The apartments and houses they had selected to view were such a step up from her current living conditions that she could have said yes to any of them. In fact, deciding on which one would be hard.

And the added bonus of spending the day with Tom made her heart scream to say yes to dating him. When they'd stopped for lunch, the waitress flirted with him outrageously and her temper had soared. But in fairness he hadn't flirted back, in fact he'd never taken his gaze off her.

Who was she kidding? She would give him a chance to prove he wanted her just as much as he wanted their son. Not want— love. She wanted his heart more than his money or body—okay, she *really* wanted his body too.

"This is the last one." Tom pulled into the drive of a beautiful California bungalow. "This is the one with the pool."

Kendra looked at google maps and knew the area would be perfect. There was a kindergarten around the corner and a school a few blocks away that was supposed to be fabulous. Then it hit her. She'd seen this house before. She looked around and then looked at Tom with disbelief. "That's your house," and she pointed across the road.

"Yip. Is that a problem?"

She sat speechless. Was it? "What are you up to?"

"You selected this property to look at if you recall. I didn't push you into anything."

That was true. "Well, let's go look then." Kendra loved how Tom's face lit up with such a sexy smile. Her heart flipped in her chest. "Look being the key word."

Tom leaned over and pressed a quick kiss to her lips. "Thank you. I bet you love it."

"Have you seen it already?"

He hopped out of the car and walked round to open her door for her. He hesitated before saying, "Only from afar and online, I swear."

The realtor came out to greet them and gave them the details and low down on the house. The minute Kendra stepped into the hall and saw the polished wooden floors and period details, she fell in love just as he guessed. As they walked through the fully furnished property, which even had one bedroom decorated for a little boy, it almost seemed too good to be true.

She moved through the spacious bungalow and fell in love. She could make a fabulous home for Connor here, and there was even a music room with a grand piano in it. She suspected she'd find more clients in this area, too. Many of those who knew her reputation hated coming to her current neighborhood, and she suspected that was part of the reason she was finding it difficult to grow her business.

She swung to face Tom. "This must cost a fortune to rent."

"I owe you a lot in back maintenance so let me do this for you."

She wanted to dispute his words, but she swallowed her negative response. This was what was best for Connor, not how it made her feel about being able to provide for her son. Tom was his father, after all. And once she got on her feet, she'd be able to contribute substantially more. If she sold a few songs to this big star…

"Come on, we've not seen it all yet," and Tom took her hand and led her into the lovely open plan kitchen dinner with bi-fold doors out into the garden. *A garden.* Connor could play outside! On real grass. It even had an outdoor room with shade louvers to keep them cool. Then she spied the pool area. Fully fenced in, it had a toddler's pool leading into an adult's pool. The temperature was as hot as Hades today, and she knew the pool would be bliss, along with the fact the house was centrally air-conditioned.

She turned and noted Tom was staring at her. "It's perfect, isn't it? Perfect for our son."

Tom's face lit up at her words, 'our son'. "It would certainly be handy for me too. I promise not to pop over unannounced though. This would be your house."

"What about the upkeep—the grounds, the pool... "

Tom pointed to the realtor sitting in the kitchen. "All of that is covered in the rent, apparently."

She wanted to jump at this amazing offer. "I going to have to explain it to Marcus."

Tom's lips thinned before he uttered what she knew was the truth. "Aren't you sick of worrying over what Marcus thinks? If we are to give our relationship a real chance, then we can't hide our situation from those closest to us. I for one can't wait to tell the world I'm Connor's father."

"I know. Last night I decided to tell him." She had to laugh. "Marcus will kick your ass."

"I probably deserve it. I've made so many mistakes—"

"No more regrets from either of us. Besides," she spread her arms and twirled around her new garden. "You're making up for it now."

"So, you'll take it?"

She stopped twirling and looked across the grass to where Tom leaned against the pillar. He looked so sexy, so masculine, and so like a man who could steal her heart, if he didn't already own it. She ambled across the grass until she stood right in front of him. She rose on tiptoes and threw her arms around his neck.

"You know me too well. You knew I would say yes before

you brought me here," and then she kissed him, softly, urgently, and thoroughly.

He pulled her tight against him, and she could feel his erection pressing into her belly.

She broke the kiss. "Right now I'm feeling pretty pleased that you live across the road," she purred seductively.

Tom immediately turned and took her hand, all but dragging her back through the house. He stopped when he reached the realtor. "She'll take it. Can you draw up the papers and send them to this address to sign? She'll move in this weekend." He passed the realtor his card, and then they were gone. He even left his car parked in Kendra's new driveway and pulled her across the street with him.

Chapter Twelve

Tom's hands were shaking and he could barely get his keys out of his pocket to unlock the front door. His raging hard on didn't help either. He almost yelled with relief when the door finally opened, and he could pull Kendra inside. He immediately turned her and pressed her against the door.

He groaned inwardly when she caught her bottom lip in her teeth. What was it about her that made him so hot for her? Just the way they stood so close had him nearing the edge of his control, and he hadn't even kissed her. *That was about to change.*

Taking her face in his hands, Tom brought his mouth down on hers in a hungry kiss. Her lips were as soft as he remembered, and his need for her intensified when she responded to him. She wound her arms around his neck and pressed against him, meeting his questing tongue with her own.

Her breasts flattened against his chest, and Tom's groin burned with need for her. He nipped at her lips, tasting and teasing. Caressing her back, he worked his way down to her hips and then cupped her firm ass, pulling her hard against him. He molded her curves to his body, letting her feel his arousal.

He wanted her with a ferocity that he'd only felt for her. No other woman had ever made him so wild with need. He wanted to take her right here against the door.

With a shove against his chest, she broke the kiss. Then grabbed his hand and tugged on it, only he didn't move and she stumbled backwards a little.

"Where are you going?" he asked in a husky voice.

Giving him an inviting smile, she replied, "You're taking too long. Which way to your bedroom? Would you like to come with me?"

Her double entendre wasn't lost on Tom. He wanted to bring her that kind of pleasure more than he'd ever wanted anything. "You sure?"

"Oh, yes. I'm positive."

Tom turned the tables on Kendra and practically dragged her past his kitchen and down the hallway into his bedroom. "I'll have to set up a direct debit into Stella's bank account for babysitting duty."

"Just as well you're rich." He loved that she'd finally accepted he could help her. He tugged her towards him, but Kendra surprised him by pulling her hand free and turning him around.

She worked on his shirt buttons, quickly unfastening them and spreading the garment open.

His breathing quickened when she ran her hands over his chest and kissed his skin. She flicked her tongue over his tight nipple and he growled as hot sensation shot straight to his groin.

He started shrugging out of his shirt, and Kendra went to work on his jeans. His arms got caught in the sleeves just as she freed his hard shaft from the confines of the denim, and he sighed in relief.

Kendra saw that he was trapped and at her mercy. His chest and abs rippled as he tried to free himself, and he loved how she admired his body as she started stroking his penis.

"Damn it." Tom continued to struggle. "I can't get the hell out of these sleeves. That feels so good. Help me get loose."

Giving him a wicked smile, Kendra said, "Not just yet," and went down on her knees.

Tom groaned and closed his eyes as she ran the tip of her tongue along the underside of his shaft. He reopened his eyes when she grabbed his jeans and pulled them down to pool around his ankles, before running her hands up his strong thighs and taking him in hand again.

When she closed her mouth around his cock, Tom sucked in a sharp breath. She was pretty talented and she hit the most sensitive places, making his body tighten. His chest rose and fell faster as her tongue fluttered and swirled around him.

"Kendra, for God's sake, stop before I come," he practically begged.

Instead of complying, Kendra took him deeper and he had to brace his hand on the headboard behind him. He could tell she loved being in control, and he was more than happy to let her. The sensations coursing through him were intense. He closed his eyes, willing himself to hold off. Finally, he wound his hand in her hair and tugged.

Releasing him, she rose licked her lips which almost had him beg her to finish him off but he wanted to be inside her so badly.

She helped him out of his shirt. No sooner was he free than Tom picked her up and tossed her on the bed.

Kendra giggled as he grabbed the waistband of her shorts and yanked them down.

"I hope you're ready because this will be quick and hard. It's your fault because you got me so hot," Tom said, stepping out of his jeans.

Kendra lifted her hips when he reached for her white, satiny panties. He made short work of them and then spread her knees wide.

"Goddamn is that pretty," he said. "Stay just like that. Don't you move." Bending over, he fished his wallet out of his pants and took a condom from it.

Kendra smiled as she glanced at it. "I'm on birth control, too."

"Good to know." A tiny stab of regret pierced him at her words. The idea of getting her pregnant again was surprisingly erotic. This time he would be here to experience the event with her. He shoved that thought away as he tore the packet open and rolled the condom down over his throbbing erection.

When Tom climbed onto the bed and kneeled between her legs, Kendra lifted her hips and reached for him. He had other ideas, though. His powerful muscles made it easy to slide her up in the bed until she could rest her head on the pillows. Pressing her legs apart, he bent and kissed her stomach before his tongue slipped lower.

Kendra gasped as blissful sensations coursed through her when his warm tongue found her center. Pure raw hunger gripped her and she opened even wider to him. The night they'd slept together she'd been ready so fast and her need for him was even more urgent now.

She trembled as he stroked her with the flat of his tongue. "Please, Tom, please."

He growled but he kept to the slow, leisurely pace, torturing her. Kendra rested her head back and closed her eyes as he continued his ministrations. He was thorough in his pleasuring of her, missing nothing. She cried out when he came back up to concentrate on the swollen nub between her folds.

His fingers dug into her flesh a little as she started moving her hips in response to his attentions. She edged closer to a climax and grabbed the comforter on either side of her. Her eyes flew open when Tom halted.

"No, no! Don't stop." She wanted to hit him with a pillow when he gave her a cocky grin.

"Payback's a bitch, sweetheart." He moved up between her legs, hooked a hand around the back of her neck, and pulled her into a sitting position. "I want to see the rest of that hot body and be inside you when you come."

Kendra practically ripped off her shirt and bra, flinging them away. She ravenously kissed Tom, melding their mouths together roughly, while she pulled him down on top of her.

She loved how Tom's eyes filled with a fiery need. She pushed out her chest. What was a girl to do when he wanted to take things a little slower? Rolling, he positioned Kendra on top and guided himself to her center. Their gazes locked as she slid down his length and leaned back.

Sitting up, Tom wrapped his arms around her, gave her a languid kiss, and trailed his tongue down her neck. He kissed the little hollow at the base before moving lower.

When Tom's mouth closed over her nipple, Kendra whimpered and moved her hips in response to the heavenly feelings he evoked in her. He laid back down and pressed his pelvis upwards, completely filling her.

"Oh, God, yes," she said.

"What gear, Tiger?"

She smiled. "What?"

"What gear? First?" He demonstrated with a slow pace. While it felt good, it wasn't going to be enough. "Second?"

She caught on. Bracing her hands on his shoulders, she said, "Let those ponies run."

His sexy grin excited her even more. "And you said you didn't know car stuff!"

Kendra's laugh was cut short when Tom kicked into high gear, thrusting fast and hard. In the waning light of day coming through the French doors of his bedroom, Kendra' eyes closed in ecstatic joy. He planned to put that look on her gorgeous face as often as possible.

Sweat broke out all over his body as he concentrated on bringing her to the peak. Her nails dug into his shoulders as at the same time she tightened around his rigid shaft, and he watched in wonder as she climaxed.

Tom's piston-like rhythm sent Kendra flying into a shuddering release. It was so intense that she couldn't breathe for several moments as undulating waves of sensation crashed through her. There was no holding back her cries as she rode the tide.

Tom wanted to bring her to a second pinnacle, but he was too turned on and she felt too good to hold back. Grasping her hips tighter as he came, Tom pumped his pelvis and ground to a stop as ecstasy flooded his body. Kendra flopped down on top of him just as his climax began ebbing and he wrapped his arms around her.

Their pants filled the room as they relaxed together.

Kendra listened to Tom's heartbeat thunder under her ear as she rested her head on his chest. His hands slid down over her back, along her thighs, and back up again. She liked the way his rough palms felt against her skin.

"Mmm. That feels nice," she murmured.

"Yeah," he agreed. "That was amazing." It had been beyond amazing, but Tom didn't know how to accurately describe the experience.

Kendra lifted her head and looked at him shyly. "Any regrets?"

A lazy smile spread across his face. "Just one. I should've gone slower."

Laughter shook Kendra, and Tom chuckled.

Sitting up, Kendra caressed his chest. "You don't hear me complaining, do you?"

"No, but still… We'll take our time next time." At her surprised look, he said, "What? You don't think this will be the last time we do this, do you?"

She merely gave him a small smile.

Tom sat up and held her by the shoulders. "I want to be with you and get to know Connor. Will you let me? Will you give us a chance?"

Fear gnawed at Kendra. "Are you sure? The repercussions with Marcus…"

"I can handle Marcus. I should have done so long ago, but

I'm man enough to admit that I used him as an excuse, because you were getting too close. My parent's marriage made relationships something I avoided like the clap." Tom said, "But now… I haven't thought about anything else since you told me about Connor."

"That's what I mean. You wouldn't have approached me if I hadn't confronted you," Kendra said.

"I know, but you know why now, and it was a mistake. My mother walking out on my father screwed me up." Tom replied. "Let's not go over the what ifs. Why make this more complicated than it has to be?"

"Because I have Connor to think about." She rested her hands on his shoulders. "His welfare comes before anything else."

Tom clenched his jaw. "You're worried that I'll let him down, let you both down, aren't you?"

"Yes. Your track record with relationships is—well—you don't do relationships. You chase women just as much as Marcus. If we get together, how can I be sure I'll be enough for you?" She laid her hand along his jaw. "It would kill me if I got more involved and you cheated on me." She couldn't bear that kind of hurt.

It astounded Tom how much he wanted a relationship with Kendra. "Ever since the night you came to the shop, you're the only woman I've thought about, the only one I want. I want you again. Right now. I've never wanted a woman the way I do you. That's no bullshit, Kendra."

Kendra's breath hitched in her throat when he cupped her breasts and toyed with her nipples. Hot need pooled between her legs, and she moaned. "I want you again, too, but hot sex doesn't make a relationship. I want a man who is there for the good times and the bad. I want that special person who will stand with me when things go pear-shaped. We have both seen what happens when one person bails when the going gets tough. Your mother left, and my mother shut down and became a doormat. It's important that the sex is wonderful, but it's not enough."

He looked at her and remained silent. She saw it in his eyes. He knew she spoke the truth.

"Then let's just be boyfriend and girlfriend and see where this takes us. I have earned the right to try, because he's my son too."

She nodded and pressed a kiss to his lips. "That's a good place to start. And me moving in across the road should make it easy for us to see each other, and for you to get to know your son. I know that's important for both of you."

"Connor's so easy to love. You did good, my girl."

She loved the praise because she had done good. It had been tough, but so worth it. Connor was a good kid. "He is, but don't you go spoiling him."

He rolled her under him and tickled her. "Just a little, maybe."

She laughed. "I suspect what you consider a little is not what I'd consider a little."

His smile faded. "I just want to love him and hope that he grows to love me."

She cupped his cheek. "Of course he will. There is a lot to love. I should know."

His slow, deep kiss set her body on fire once again. "When did you say you'd pick Connor up?"

She looked at the clock. "We have another hour."

He started kissing down her body. "Plenty of time for first gear, maybe even second gear loving!

Chapter Thirteen

"Y ou slept with him, didn't you?"

At Stella's question, Kendra almost dropped the bottle of wine she was pouring from. "What?"

Stella came over to lean a hip against the counter. Her eyes zeroed in on Kendra's face. "You slept with him. Did the nasty. Knocked boots." She pointed at her. "Don't you try to deny it."

Kendra laughed as she handed a glass to Stella. "You have such a way with words. So romantic."

"You have that after sex glow."

Kendra left the kitchen and settled on the couch. They'd spent all afternoon packing her belongings, ready for the move on Saturday. Kendra was so excited. Tom had arranged it all, and because the house was furnished, she simply needed her personal possessions.

"The look suits you." Stella followed her, sat down on the opposite end, and tucked her feet under her. "Spill it."

Knowing that Stella had investigative skills that would impress the FBI, Kendra figured that it was useless to lie to her best friend. "Yes, I slept with him."

Stella squealed in delight.

"Shh! You'll wake Connor up," Kendra admonished her.

"Sorry." Stella lowered her voice. "I'm just excited for you. The fact he's managed to get you to move some place more appropriate, makes him a hero in my book. And the fact he gave you an orgasm as well... I'm warming to him."

Kendra's mouth dropped open, but Stella just gave her a sardonic look. Her shoulders drooped. "You're changing your spots."

"Mmm hmm. You haven't been with anyone since Tom got back to town because *he's* the only one you're interested in," Stella said.

"Shut up," Kendra grumbled, but couldn't refute her statement.

"So, now what?" Stella asked.

"He's my boyfriend." Kendra sat her glass on the coffee table. "He wants to give things between us a shot and it's all I've dreamed about since I first met him, but..."

Stella nudged her knee with a foot. "But?"

"If it doesn't work, I will have my heart broken again. He might be with me just because of Connor." Kendra got up and paced across the room. "I mean, what if we wind up hating each other? I don't want Connor subjected to that kind of fighting. And what if we have more kids and he walks out on us...? Do you see why I'm so twisted up about this? Love. He has to love me and this is all so sudden."

Stella's eyes filled with sympathy. "I do, but you're driving yourself crazy for nothing."

Kendra threw her hands up. "Nothing? How can you say that?"

"Chill, okay? You will never know unless you try. Are you going to throw away this chance because you're afraid to fail? You faced a greater fear. Don't lose something good because of fear. Maybe hold off on the sex—" Stella sputtered into laughter.

Kendra glared at her.

Stella gave an apologetic little wave. "I'm sorry, but I couldn't say that with a straight face. I know you love Tom, but don't you dare let him know that. You want him to declare his love for you. You both need to get to know each other again. Both of you have changed so much in the past four years. In the meantime, enjoy yourself." She pointed at Kendra. "And don't let Marcus interfere. He has no right to. I know he means well, but he has to let go of the... he doesn't have apron strings, so what's an appropriate analogy? Steering wheel! He has to let go of the steering wheel and let you drive your own car of destiny. Damn, that was good. I should write that down."

They broke into laughter and Kendra sat back down. "I think you're right. I'll just try to take things a little slower."

Stella patted her knee. "Good. Well, I have to get going, but I'll come around and help christen the new house with a bottle of the best champagne."

"Okay."

Kendra followed her to the door, and they hugged goodbye. While she locked up for the night, she gave the situation a lot of thought and followed Stella's suggestion to ease into a relationship with Tom. *Easy does it,* she warned herself, and hoped that she could heed that mantra.

* * *

The move went well, and Connor, goodness, he was in heaven. He loved the backyard and the grass. Tom had given him a soccer ball and Connor spent most of the day outside kicking it around.

Tom had also introduced Connor to the paddling pool, and her little boy had never been so happy. She'd been selfish not letting anyone help her. She now saw all that Connor had been missing out on before, but could have had if not for her pride.

So, she let Tom help her again.

They had hired a nanny, Jackie, who came in from 10am to 6pm Monday to Friday, so Kendra could work without scrambling for babysitters. It also meant she could suddenly drop everything and head to her music room when the lyrics of a song hit, without having to watch Connor. She'd also already picked up three more clients for music lessons. Word of mouth was amazing once she'd told her current customers where she'd moved back to Beverly Hills. It proved that the area she'd lived in had been holding her back.

Best of all, for the first week at least, Tom had kept his word. He never came over without checking with her first. He'd even stayed a few nights but left before Connor woke. She didn't want her son seeing him living there until they knew where this new relationship was going.

Today she'd finally agreed to let Tom teach her a few things about car maintenance, so here she was at Bad Boy Autos. Although it probably was about time she bought herself a new car. She had the most important meeting of her career coming up with one of pop industries biggest female singers, a young girl who was riding a wave of success from a single #1 bestseller. If the pop princess liked her song and bought it, with the payment and royalties, she'd have more than enough for a new car. She still didn't have the lyrics down, but she couldn't push her muse. It would happen. She still had a month.

While she was proud of two advert jingles, she'd written the chance to write songs for a big recording artist…

"Hey, are you listening?" she heard Tom ask.

She stopped day dreaming and focused on the task at hand.

"Why won't this damn thing move?" Kendra said through gritted teeth as she tried loosening a lug nut on the rear driver's side wheel of her van.

Tom crouched down a short distance away. "Does the expression 'righty tighty, lefty loosey' ring a bell?"

Kendra let the tire iron fall to the concrete floor and stood straight while she panted. "No. Should it?"

Tom tilted his head as he looked up at her. "Have you ever used a screwdriver or a wrench at all? To put together furniture or *anything*?"

Kendra felt like a dumbass. "No. Marcus did all of that and

anytime I need something fixed, him or Melvin from downstairs helped me."

Tom groaned and let his head drop forward. "Okay. No problem." He raised his eyes to hers again. "The rule of thumb when you're dealing with lug nuts, screws, or just about any fastener like that, is this; turn it to the right to tighten it and turn it to the left to loosen it. Righty tighty, lefty loosey. Get it?"

It dawned on Kendra as she looked at him. "I was turning it the wrong way!" She picked up the tire iron. "Okay. I can do this. Lefty loosey."

She fitted the socket of the tire iron over the lug nut until it was snug. Then she gave a mighty shove in the correct direction and screamed when the lug nut gave so easily that her momentum pitched her forward.

Tom grabbed her by the shoulders and pulled her against him so she didn't fall on her face. "Whoa! You okay?"

Kendra held onto his strong arms while her heart knocked against her ribs. The fast rhythm had more to do with being in close contact with Tom than any fear of falling.

"Yeah, sure." She glanced at his mouth and whispered, "If I get any booboos, will you kiss them and make them better?"

One side of Tom's mouth lifted at the corner. "Honey, I'll kiss every inch of that luscious body if it'll make you feel better." He cast a wary glance around. "But for now, let's get back to our lesson before I get wound up, okay?"

Kendra let go of him and nodded.

"Take the other four off, now," Tom instructed.

As she bent to the task, she hoped Tom thought she looked adorable in the black overalls and steel-toed work boots that she'd borrowed from Lexie. She'd put her sleek, black hair in a ponytail, hoping for once she would not be the only one hot and bothered.

Kendra loosened the last lug nut and laid it on the floor beside the others. "I did it! Now what?"

Tom smiled at her enthusiasm. "Now we jack it up and take the tire off."

"But I don't have a jack."

Tom pointed at the back of the van. "Yeah, you do. Look under the donut. I found the right model at a junkyard the other day and tested it."

She tossed him a grateful smile. "You think of everything."

"I don't know about everything, but I do okay."

Kendra lifted the hatch and opened the compartment that housed the donut. She loosened the wingnut that held it in place and put it to the side. The heavy weight of the donut surprised her as she struggled with it. She almost had it out of the well when someone nudged her aside, and it fell back down.

"Hey!" she protested.

Marcus said, "I'll get that for you since he won't. You don't need to strain something."

Tom took Marcus by the shoulder. "Let her do it. There will be no one out on the road to help her. She has to learn to do this for herself."

Marcus shrugged him off. "I can teach her, then."

"You haven't before? I'm happy to do it." Tom shook his head. "She needs to learn the whole process from start to finish."

Kendra grabbed hold of the donut and tried to wrestle it away from Marcus. "I want to do it. Truly. Tom is right. I can't always rely on anyone being available to help me, and you know me. I hate being helpless."

Marcus was immovable thanks to his brawny, superior strength. "You're making me feel like shit. You're right, I should have taught you this stuff. So let me."

"You and I would fight. I'll stick with Tom." Kendra refused to give in and gave it a hard tug. Her hands slipped off the donut and she fell hard on her ass. Pain shot up her back and she let out a loud cry.

Tom jumped around Marcus and kneeled by her. "Don't move. Where are you hurt?"

Marcus appeared next to Tom in Kendra's line of vision. Both men's eyes filled with concern.

She gritted her teeth for a moment and then let her breath out. Sometimes she wanted to knock these guy's heads together. Over protective or what? "I'm fine." She sat up, and Tom supported her shoulders.

"Did you hit your head?" he asked.

"No. I'm fine. I just want to get up and finish the job," she replied.

Marcus shook his head as Tom helped her up. "I think you've had enough for the day."

Kendra tried to rein in her temper, but Marcus was pushing all her buttons. This is what he always did. He tried to protect her from things she did not need protection from. She wasn't sick anymore. She thought of Tom and all the wasted years. Marcus was ruining what had been a lovely morning with Tom. "I'll tell you what I've had enough of; you, bossing me around." She poked Marcus' broad chest. "Stop interfering. Tom was doing just fine instructing me until you showed up. I can do this!"

"Why Tom? Why not Sully?" Marcus said, eyeing Tom with suspicion.

She flashed a gaze at Tom and took a deep breath. Like a band aid, she ripped it off. "I can make my own decisions, like whether I want to learn how to fix a car, or who I want to date!"

Marcus' eyebrows shot up. "Who you want to date? What are you talking about? Are you dating someone?"

Tom nodded at the question in her eyes. She put her hand on Marcus's arm and quietly said, "Yes. I'm dating Tom!"

Stepping closer to her, Tom put an arm around Kendra's shoulders. "That's right."

Marcus looked between them and then his gaze bored into Tom's. "You lied to me the other day, you son of a bitch. You told me you were kidding about Kendra. You know how I feel about this, but you went behind my back anyway."

That did it. Marcus needed to hear the truth. "Who do you think you are? I love you dearly big brother but it's my life. I fought really hard for the curtesy to live it. What gives you the right to warn someone away from me? Who I date, who I sleep with, or who I don't, isn't any of your business!"

Marcus pointed at Tom. "He's not the right guy for you. He's my best friend, and a good guy, but he's not the settling down type, and you're not the type of woman who just screws a guy and moves on to the next one. Look how the last guy treated you. He took off and left you pregnant and all on your own."

Tom's jaw tightened; Marcus' disapproval obviously bothered him. "Thanks, Marcus. Nice to know that you don't think I'm good enough for Kendra. Good to know what you really think of me." Tom didn't blame Marcus. He was probably right. Tom had never had a long-term relationship. He'd let no woman close. What was the point, marriage wasn't a priority to a man like him—but suddenly none of that rang true to him because it was important to him now?

Marcus said, "Tom, you know that I think of you as a brother, but I gotta be honest. You've chased skirts all over the world, just like me. You're not cut out for a serious relationship. I'm not saying that in a shitty way. I'm not cut out for that either. Neither of us will ever settle down. We both know it. I don't want Kendra to get hurt."

"Like she said; Kendra is a big girl and can handle herself. We are dating, it's not a crime. It's a shame you don't give her— and me—more credit. Do you think I'd do anything to hurt her?"

Marcus didn't give any ground. "I don't think you'd mean to, but it's just who we are. We are not one-woman men. I love Kendra, but I think her judgment is a little off sometimes. Like when she let some guy get her pregnant and refused to tell me who it was. Now she's a single mom trying to make ends meet." He threw a hard look at Kendra. "Which is why she's always borrowing money from me." His gaze returned to Tom's. "I don't want something like that happening again."

"It won't. My song writing is beginning to pay. I've even moved into a new rental on Tom's street. He told me about it and I grabbed it." She wasn't really lying, just not revealing the whole truth.

"On Tom's street. How convenient," Marcus hissed.

Tom looked pissed at Marcus. "You're a real asshole to talk about your sister like that. Throwing Connor in her face. Nice way to show her you love her."

Tears streamed from Kendra's eyes, and she couldn't breathe. This is what she'd been dreading—friend hurting friend. She needed space to think about what to do to calm her brother down. She ran to the door leading outside, flung it open, and rushed out into the sunshine.

   * * *

"Way to go," Tom said to Marcus. "I can't believe you."

Marcus pointed at his chest. "Me? You're the one who started all this. You promised me you'd leave Kendra alone."

Tom nodded. "Yeah, eight years ago when we were kids. You can't seriously hold me to that now. Unlike you, I've grown up. I've always liked Kendra. I should've never listened to you back then."

Marcus' eyes turned a deeper shade of green and his face flushed with anger. He grabbed Tom's overalls by the collar. "I don't want you seeing Kendra!"

"You better get used to it. Nothing will stop me, not even you," Tom countered.

"Oh, yeah? We'll see about that."

Marcus cocked his right fist back, but a strong hand grabbed it and jerked Marcus away from Tom, who was coming right for Marcus. Lexie inserted herself between the two furious men and Sully hauled Marcus backwards.

"Knock it off, boys," Sully said. "You're acting like a couple of jackasses."

"Men!" Lexie kept ahold of Tom, who was trying to get around her. "Stop it, Tom! You should go after Kendra."

Marcus tried to get away from Sully. "I'll go."

Sully shoved him towards the office. "No, you won't. You're the problem. Let's go in the office. We'll have a beer and you can cool off."

Marcus pointed at Sully. "Who the hell do you think you are? I think you're forgetting who the boss is here."

Sully gave him a stern look. "No, I didn't forget. You're the boss, but I'm your friend and real friends tell their friends when they're acting like a damn idiot. Marcus, you're acting like a huge ass. So, before you say something you can't take back, it's best that you go in the office until you get yourself under control."

Marcus glared at Tom and Sully and then stomped into the office. He slammed the door, and they heard the lock slide shut.

Tom took a huge, calming breath and then went looking for Kendra.

Chapter Fourteen

Kendra sat on a chair on the porch of the big storage building that flanked the main shop. It held their client's expensive cars overnight for the longer jobs. During lunch or after work, the gang sat there in the shade to drink a beer and unwind. She'd helped herself to one from the fridge inside the staff workroom kitchen.

She set her bottle on the small metal lawn table next to her and unbuttoned her overalls with trembling hands. Standing up, she took the garment and her boots off, glad that she was only wearing a pair of gray workout shorts and a matching sports bra. Feeling cooler, she draped the overalls over another chair and sat back down.

Her stomach ached from stress. Or she hoped it was stress. She'd been feeling so tired the last few days. Perhaps the move had taken more out of her than she'd thought.

How had things gone so bad so quick? She should have kept her mouth shut. One minute she'd been having fun with Tom, and then she opened her big mouth. A fist formed tight in her stomach. She'd pushed because she'd wanted to test Tom. To see how committed Tom really was. Would he risk his friendship, his business for her…?

How selfish could she have been? She should have told her brother differently.

Now everything was ugly.

Kendra sat straighter as she realized something. Tom had corroborated her story, had stuck up for her. Tom and Marcus were at each other, but she couldn't help the feeling of her heart singing in her chest. He'd stuck up for her—for them. It was enough for her to let down her defenses.

She made a decision.

She would throw herself into this relationship and give Tom her heart if he wanted it. But if he broke it again—fool me once, all on me. Fool me twice—never again. There would not be another chance.

He thinks he wants it all, wants a family, well let's find out.

On that thought, the workshop door opened, and Tom stepped through it. He was so gorgeous she almost forgot to breathe. Just watching the man walk filled her with hunger. His muscular arms swung a little as he came towards her, his strides loose and sure. What a prize winning this man's heart would be…

Although his gait was relaxed, his shoulders and expression were tense as he came up on the porch. "You okay?" He sat down by her and put a hand on her knee.

Kendra ignored the way her heartbeat sped up at his touch. "Yeah, I guess. Sorry to dump you in it. I am just so sick of being scared to show what I really want in this life. I've always held back because of all the sacrifices everyone made for me when I was ill; I'm apprehensive to say—do—what I want. I shouldn't have to care what my brother thinks. He should love me unconditionally as I love him. But my parents didn't and if I lost Marcus too…"

She put her hand over his and traced one vein on the back of it. "Any regrets about my announcement?" The memory of how good his caresses had felt the other night came back to her.

Feeling daring, she took his wrist and pulled his hand up higher on her thigh.

He linked his fingers with hers. "Not a damn one. Marcus will calm down and if he doesn't," Tom shrugged. "Him and I will sort it out. This won't destroy us. We've known each other too long for that. Besides, he loves you. He's only likely to kill me if I hurt you, and I will make sure I don't."

She looked at him. "Is it true you've never had a long-term relationship? I mean, I figured as much with all the women you dated, but can you tell me why? I doubt it's because you want sex with hundreds of women. It has to be something more."

He let go of her hand and hung his head.

She pressed him for more. "You say you want a relationship with me—to marry me. If that is true then why is it so hard to talk to me. To share your past?"

He stood and put his hands in his pockets, his back to her. All that did was pull his jeans tight showcasing a superb backside.

"My mother walked out when I was twelve. Sam was seventeen. I can't blame her for leaving my father, he was an unfaithful, drunk bastard—"

Kendra sucked in a breath. "But she left you too." Tears welled. "I have Connor and I cannot understand any mother leaving their children behind—for any reason."

He turned to face her. "I thought it was because of something I'd done. Sam tried to tell me it was because of Dad, and after a while I worked out that that was true. But to this day, I do not understand why she didn't take me with her. I thought I was bad, or unlovable…"

"I can't imagine what that must have felt like at such a young age." A mother's rejection—she of all people understood the pain. Her mother had said nothing when her father virtually threw her out when she wouldn't reveal the identity of Connor's father, but she was older, almost twenty-one. And she'd had Marcus to help her out. Tom was just a little boy.

"I know her leaving affected me. But it's only now, now that

I've reviewed my past, I've understood why I let no one close. I feared losing someone again. That pain of being left behind, of being rejected, is indescribable. I was protecting myself from that pain. I thought I didn't need anyone."

She nodded. "But now, because of Connor, it's worth risking that pain?"

He moved to stand before her, reaching out to cup her face. "And because of you. For some reason I believe my heart will be safe with you."

She slowly rose to her feet and slipped her arms around his neck. "It is. And always will be."

They stood together holding each other. He slid his hands up and down her sides.

"That feels nice," she murmured, meeting his gaze. "But it's not what I need."

His eyes darkened as he kneaded her buttock. "What *do* you need?"

"You." The sudden fire in his eyes and his tightened grip intensified her craving. Kendra gave him a sultry look. "Come on."

Tom got up, followed her into the workroom kitchen, and locked the door. As they went to pass the fridge, he spun her around and shoved her up against it. Hooking a hand around the back of her head, he captured her lips in a demanding kiss that she matched. They practically devoured each other as they urgently started undressing one another.

Tom ripped his wallet out of his work pants, took out a condom, and tossed the wallet over his shoulder. Kendra had his pants unzipped by that time, and she shoved his boxer-briefs down. His rapidly hardening member stood up between them.

Kendra snatched the condom from his teeth and did the honors. Tom sucked in a breath at her touch.

"Slow down, this is for you," he said with a smile as he kneeled.

Kendra giggled as he freed her right leg from her shorts and panties and lifted her leg over his shoulder. She shivered as his warm breath tickled her sex and gasped the next moment when he grazed her nub with the tip of his tongue.

"Don't you dare stop this time or it'll be the last time you touch me," she growled.

Tom's chuckle rumbled low in his chest and he set swiftly to work. Pressing closer, he thoroughly tasted her until she could hardly bear it. Her fingers curled, pulling his short hair, and he growled at the pleasure-pain. Her pleasure spiraled as he flicked and swirled his tongue.

"Don't stop, don't stop," Kendra whispered as she started shuddering.

The cool metal of the refrigerator pressed against Kendra's back as she rested her head on it. Having sex with Tom in the storage building, only yards from the shop made Kendra feel wicked. It was wild and reckless, but that was what she craved right then. She didn't want to think. She just wanted to feel the pleasure that only Tom could bring her.

With every stroke of his tongue, Tom took her higher, and she was helpless to do anything but enjoy the ride. She couldn't hold still and trembled as she got closer to the brink. Her orgasm took her by surprise, the sharp bliss making her shout Tom's name. She barely heard Tom's groan of approval as the tempest of sensation held her prisoner. It hadn't faded when Tom hoisted her up, giving her no choice but to grab onto his shoulders.

Tom wrapped her legs around his waist and slowly entered her tight heat. "Oh, shit. You feel so good, baby."

"So do you."

Their gazes locked as he started thrusting with masterful strokes. The bottles and cans inside the fridge clanked together as he pounded away. Kendra had never felt anything so intense as being with Tom. Every time he filled her, she inched towards another climax. The laser beam focus of his gaze and the way his shoulders bunched under her hands enthralled her.

The first pulse of another climax hit her. "Yes, yes, yes."

"Tell me, Kendra. Tell me," he demanded harshly, thrusting even harder.

"I'm coming, I'm coming." Her words ended on a high-pitched note that turned into a scream.

Tom muffled it with his mouth, but the sound was music to his ears. Knowing that he made her feel like this gave him immense satisfaction. He dragged his lips from hers as a powerful release rocked him. He dropped his head to bite her shoulder as he let out a hoarse groan.

As the ripples of ecstasy died away, Kendra sagged a little. She took Tom's face in her hands and smiled. "That was just what I needed, and it was incredible. You're incredible. I'm thrilled that I'm giving us a chance."

Tom was in no hurry to relinquish his hold on her and gladly kept supporting her. "You're pretty incredible yourself, Tiger. Damn. I've never had a woman get me hard so fast before. I always knew you were special."

"You don't have to say that."

Tom frowned. "I know that. You know that I say nothing I don't mean. I'm being straight with you."

She wiggled and smiled in his arms and his heart pounded with joy. "Okay. I'm glad I do that to you."

His naughty grin made her smile. "Me, too."

He released his hold on her slowly, loving the feel of her body sliding down his. His groin tightened, and he wondered if he would ever get enough of Kendra. He wanted to haul her back up and do it all over again, but he had to get back and sort this out with Marcus, and she had to pick up Connor from Stella's.

"Do you think Jackie will be okay with sitting with Connor later this week so we can go out?" Tom asked.

"I'm sure I can organize something. Where are you taking me?"

He pressed a kiss to her forehead. "I want to show you off. I think a nice restaurant for a change. Let's dress up and go fancy."

She laughed. "I haven't dressed up fancy since before Connor was born. I'd love to be wined and dined in style."

Happiness flooded Kendra and he planted a hot, hard kiss on her delicious lips. Abruptly releasing her, he said, "Wednesday night. Eight o'clock. Be ready and wear something nice."

He moved towards the door, but Kendra stopped him. "Wait!" She motioned at his lower half.

Looking down, Tom saw that he still had his pants round his ankles. They laughed together as they finished dressing. Then they left the building and started for the shop. Halfway there, Tom reached over and took Kendra's hand. He didn't give a damn who saw them holding hands.

Exchanging a smile with her, Kendra wondered when was the last time he'd walked along holding a woman's hand. Maybe never? But Tom held her hand!

Tom opened the shop door for her and motioned her inside. Her shoulders relaxed when she noted Marcus was not in sight. She'd have to talk with him, but she preferred to do it without Tom around. To their surprise, Kendra's van was back together, and she suspected that Lexie had done it.

Kendra got in the driver's seat and Tom stood between the van and the open door. "Don't think for a minute you're getting out of learning how to change a tire and stuff."

Meaning it, Kendra said, "I don't want to get out of it. I need to know how. It's time I became much more self-sufficient."

"Glad to hear it." He leaned inside the van. "Do I get a kiss goodbye?"

She grabbed his overalls, pulled him closer, and pressed her lips to his in a kiss that heated his blood again.

When it ended, Kendra said, "Wednesday night. Eight o'clock. Don't be late and wear something nice."

Tom grinned at her, repeating his earlier request back to him. "Yes, ma'am."

He shut the van door and opened the bay door. He guided

Kendra as she backed out of the bay, waved her away and stood watching as she drove off.

Lexie appeared at his side. "Something you'd like to tell me?"

Tom gave a curt nod. "Yeah. I'm going to marry that woman."

Lexie's jaw dropped open. "What? You! The man who swore marriage was for suckers, if I remember correctly. You thought I was nuts marrying Jason."

"You heard me and that's all I'm saying about it." He smiled at Lexie's shocked expression. "And you were nuts. It wasn't the marriage part I really objected to, just the groom."

She narrowed her eyes at him. "Okay, for now, but you will spill the beans soon. Oh, and by the way Marcus has left."

"Shit." He ran a hand over his head. "Do you know if he's coming back?"

She scoffed, "Me? I'd be the last person Marcus would confide in."

Lexie grumbled to herself as Tom went to bring in the Jaguar he was pimping for a boy band singer who had more money than brains. While he worked, Tom planned how he would win Kendra's heart. He almost snorted out loud at that thought.

Him, one badass who'd founded Bad Boy Autos, was plotting how to make a woman fall in love with him. Him, a man who could drive a test car around a track at 200mph but who was scared shitless by four little letters—L-O-V-E. Still, his body wanted to reject his thoughts of a relationship with Kendra, but his heart... It pumped strong and true in his chest. It wanted the chance to have a family, to wake up each day with the same woman by his side, a woman who loved him unconditionally. A woman he could trust completely. For the first time in a long while, he felt as if he deserved this chance. He almost laughed aloud at the absurdity of it, and then he turned his attention to the Jaguar.

Chapter Fifteen

Looking in the mirror on Wednesday, Tom swore as he fumbled with his tie. Why'd he say they'd dress up? Because he knew Kendra would love the chance. He couldn't remember the last time he'd worn a suit and he'd never been good with ties. Sighing, he unknotted it and started over. A knock sounded on the front door and he growled in frustration at the interruption.

He strode through his house, frowning at how ugly it was. It was time to do something about that. The house would likely take eighteen months or two years to renovate from scratch by the time architects and permits had been granted. However, it would be the perfect home for Kendra, Connor, and God willing, any other kids they had. Making a mental note to look for contractors, he pulled open the door to discover Sam standing on the porch.

He held in a curse, trying to be happy at seeing his brother standing there. "Hey, bro. Come on in."

Although they had the same brown eyes, Sam's hair was a dark brown instead of blond. Both men were about the same height, but Sam was a little thinner than Tom.

"Thanks." Sam walked past him and looked around the

living room. "Why the hell do you live here?"

Tom laughed. "The land. I already told you that. Lots like this are hard to find, and the neighborhood is good. Good schools—"

—"Schools? Not something I thought was high on your list."

He didn't answer. Kendra had told no one yet, and he'd promised her…

Sam being the good elder brother didn't push. He took in the dark blue suit Tom wore. "Wow. Don't you look snazzy. What's the occasion?"

Tom suddenly felt bashful and got pissed with himself. "I have a date."

Sam's expression filled with surprise. "*You* have a date? I didn't think you did dates, just women."

Tom smirked at him. "Hilarious, jackass." He held out his tie to Sam. "Tie this for me?"

Sam took the tie and went to work. "So, this lady must be pretty special, huh?"

Hating the blush that crept up his neck, Tom replied, "Yeah. Hey, where did you get Tonya's engagement ring?"

Sam froze, his eyes going wide. "You're going to propose? I think I'm missing something here. Care to fill me in?"

Tom hadn't meant to ask him that question, but he wanted to be prepared when the time came to show Kendra how serious he was. And right now he needed a sounding board, and he knew that Sam would keep his secret. "Yeah, not enough time to explain. I don't want to be late picking Kendra up."

Sam resumed tying the tie. "Kendra. As in Marcus's sister Kendra Black?"

Tom couldn't stop the silly grin that lit his face at the mention of her. "Yeah." *He knew he shouldn't but he was just bursting with pride and Sam was his brother.* "If I tell you something you have to promise to keep it a secret until I say you can share." Sam nodded. "You know her little boy? Connor?"

Sam nodded. "Yeah. I've seen him a time or two."

"He's my son. He's mine." A rush of love and pride hit Tom and he smiled. "I'm his father."

Sam stopped tying. "I'm sorry, but did you just say that Connor is your son?"

"I did, but you can't tell anyone," Tom said. "No one else knows. I didn't know that I was his father until last week."

Sam finished with the tie and blew out a breath. "Holy shit. Why didn't you know? Didn't she tell you?" His face took on that brother protecting frown.

The now familiar guilt gnawed at Tom. "It's a long story, but I don't have time right now to spill. When it's all out in the open, I'll explain everything." Sam looked as if he was about to protest, but Tom folded his arms over his chest and Sam closed his mouth. Staring at his brother, he asked, "So why are you here? I mean, why didn't you just call me?"

Sam sobered and the hair on the back of Tom's neck rose. "It's Dad. His body is rejecting the liver transplant from Aunt Sonya. They're going to look for another donor, but there's no guarantee they'll find a match. They've already tested me, but you know I'm not a match."

The blood drained from Tom's face as a myriad of emotions flooded his mind. "He's going to die, then."

Tears shimmered in Sam's eyes. "Yeah. Unless…"

A wave of sadness hit Tom with surprising intensity. "Unless what?" But he knew what was coming and his hands clenched in fists.

Sam cleared his throat. "There's you."

"You want me to get tested?" Tom's heart throbbed inside his chest. "Shit."

Sam put a hand on Tom's shoulder. "Will you let them test you to see if you're a match? And if you are, would you be willing to donate a piece of your liver to Dad?"

A lump formed in Tom's throat and he couldn't answer.

"I know this is a lot to dump on you, little brother, but I wouldn't ask if it wasn't so important." Sam squeezed his shoulder. "I know that things aren't good between you and Dad, so if you don't want to do this for him, do it for me and for my kids. They love Dad and he's a good grandfather."

Tom couldn't deny that. Vincent had been a crap father, but with his grandkids… Vincent seemed to try to make up for being a shitty father by showering his grandkids with love. But Tom hated his father, didn't he? He expected to feel a sense of satisfaction that his father was getting what Tom thought he deserved, but sorrow crowded his heart instead.

You don't feel sad over people you hate; he reasoned. "When do these tests have to be done?"

"Tomorrow morning," Sam answered. "The sooner the better. His time is running out. Will you do it?"

Tom thought of his son. Connor would love to have a grandad. His other grandad had washed his hands of him. Was Tom going to hold on to anger for something that couldn't be changed and deny his son? Vincent was all the grandparent Connor might have. "Yeah, I'll do it. What time?"

"Eight. I'll meet you at the hospital," Sam said with a brotherly smile.

"Okay."

Pulling Tom in for a hug, Sam whispered, "Thank you."

"Don't thank me." Tom returned the manly embrace. "I've done nothing yet."

Sam drew back. "Just you agreeing to be tested means a lot, Tommy. It will mean everything to Dad. You can visit him tomorrow." He smoothed down Tom's tie. "There. You're all set. Have fun tonight. Oh, no eating after midnight. You have to fast for the tests. You can drink water, but that's it."

Tom masked his fear with a smile. "I will. Now get out of here so I can get going, too."

"Right. See you tomorrow," Sam replied, going out the door. He stopped on the threshold. "Congratulations. I think you'll make an excellent father, little brother. I can't wait to meet Connor and introduce him to our family."

Tom closed the door with his heart thudding in his chest. He stood in the foyer trying to absorb all the changes that were suddenly in his life. His earlier good mood vanished, and the worry meant the last thing he felt like doing was going out to a fancy restaurant. However, he didn't want to disappoint Kendra.

With a groan of dismay, Tom pulled off his tie. Kendra was a perceptive woman and she'd see through any facade he'd put up. He flopped down on the couch, pulled his cellphone out of his pocket, and hit Kendra's number.

"Hello, Mr. Lorde."

He grinned at the smile in her voice. "Hello, Miss. Black."

"Did you call to tell me you're running late? I warned you not to be," Kendra said with mock-severity.

Tom sighed and leaned his head back against the couch. "No, I will not be late, but do you mind if we order in, or if I pick up something?"

"Oh. Yeah, sure." Her voice went flat. "That's fine."

"I was ready, except for my tie when Sam showed up," Tom said. "I—It's Dad. His new liver isn't working."

"What new liver?" Kendra asked.

"Marcus didn't tell you?"

"Um, Marcus doesn't mention you much around me."

Pain slashed at Tom. "Wow. I didn't realize just how much he disliked us together." He stomped the hurt down. "Dad had a liver transplant, but his body is rejecting it."

"Oh, Tom, I'm so sorry."

He gave a short, mirthless laugh. "Yeah, me too, which surprises me. Anyhow, I have to go to the hospital tomorrow to see if I'm a match. I'm so sorry, honey. I was really excited about showing you off. But I feel like shit being happy when Dad's facing death."

"I completely understand about this kind of stuff, Tom, and I think it's generous of you to do this for your dad. You've said before that you two didn't see eye-to-eye most of the time," Kendra said.

"That's an understatement." Tom leaned forward and rubbed his forehead. "God, I want to get drunk."

"Don't you dare, Thomas Lorde!"

Kendra's shout startled Tom so much that he almost dropped his phone. "Okay, okay! I won't, I was just saying—"

"I'll go grab some food and come over. Pointless wasting a babysitter—unless you'd rather be alone."

"I'd love some company—" The line went dead and Tom looked at the phone.

Then he laughed at Kendra's text, "See you soon," and got off the couch to go change.

Chapter Sixteen

K endra used her foot to knock on Tom's door, as her hands were full of food.

She heard Tom approaching and when he opened the door, she sucked in a breath. His jeans rode low on his hips and he was shirtless. "Damn, Kendra. You look amazing. Gorgeous," he said.

She smiled. "Thank you." She winked, "I like this look on you but I'm not sure a fancy restaurant would allow shirtless men in—you might cause a riot."

Tom smiled. "I was just getting changed out of my fancy gear but I can get dressed again?"

"I'm very happy with the look you're wearing right now."

"As am I. I wish I hadn't canceled going out so I could show you off." Tom noticed that she carried a large reusable grocery bag. "You grabbed some dinner but I'm not sure I'm that hungry?"

"I might have something in here that will tempt you."

"You tempt me." Their eyes clashed and sparks flew. "Come on in." Tom stood back to let her pass.

Kendra kept walking until she found the kitchen and deposited her bag on the table. Turning around, she watched him walk into the kitchen wearing those low riding jeans sitting tantalizingly on his hips. Had they made love only two days ago? His scrumptious body made her hands itch to touch him, but that would have to wait.

"There's a box in my van," she said, noting the answering longing in his eyes. "Please, will you get it?"

"Sure. No problem." He gave her a curious look, but didn't comment any further before leaving the kitchen again.

Kendra looked around. Although the kitchen was plain and desperately in need of remodeling, it was clean. The black and while linoleum floor was worn in places and the white counter-tops needed to be replaced. A small, round wooden table and four chairs stood in the center of the room.

Sitting her bag on the counter, Kendra took out a nice white tablecloth, crystal candle holders, and tall red candles. She put the cloth on the table and centered the candle holders on it.

Tom entered the kitchen with the box and sat it on the counter. He looked at the table and smiled. "What are you doing?"

Kendra said, "I'm bringing dinner to you since we're not going out."

He rubbed the back of his neck and grimaced. "I'm really sorry about that."

Going to him, Kendra wrapped her arms around his waist and looked into his eyes. "It's okay. I completely understand. If you don't feel like dinner, we can simply talk."

Tom laid a hand alongside her face and ran his thumb over her cheek. "No. It will be nice to watch you cook. Take my mind off things."

"Well, I can't say I cooked it." She rose on tiptoe and gave him a brief kiss. "Okay. Time to eat."

Tom let her go and watched as she started taking cartons out of the box. The scents of garlic and tomato sauce filled the kitchen and his stomach growled. "What is that? It smells good. Sounds like I'm hungry after all."

"Me, too." She opened an aluminum container and he moved closer. "I hope you like chicken parmesan. And we have salads, garlic bread, and cherry cheesecake for dessert."

"Wow. You thought of everything." He nudged her aside. "Let me do that before you get something on that pretty dress. You'll never get the sauce out of it."

Kendra appreciated his thoughtfulness. "Okay. I'll fix our salads."

"Well, you can fix a salad for you, but I'm not into rabbit food," Tom said, getting plates and dessert dishes out of a cupboard.

Kendra teased thoughtfully. "You should learn from your son."

Smiling, Tom answered. "I'm glad he likes healthy stuff but it's just not my thing." He scooped the dinners onto their plates. "Plus, with going to the gym, I need to carb load."

Kendra playfully reached over and squeezed his bicep. "I'd say that you're a very healthy specimen."

"Thanks," Tom grinned smugly. He placed the plates on the table and then got a pack of matches out of a drawer. Lighting the candles, he stood back a little. "Looks really pretty."

"Yes, it does," Kendra sighed softly.

Tom's gaze swung from the table to Kendra, and then down at himself. "I'll be right back."

Kendra looked up from fixing her salad. "Okay."

* * *

Tom went to his room and took the suit he'd been wearing earlier out of his closet. He changed as fast as possible. It was only right that he make the extra effort since Kendra had gone to so much trouble.

Picking up the dreaded tie, he attempted to tie it, but got too frustrated. Checking his appearance in his bureau mirror, he thought the suit looked fine without the tie and tossed it on his bed. He put on a pair of gold cufflinks that Sam had given him a few years ago and straightened the shirt cuffs.

He smoothed a hand down his front and walked back out to the kitchen. Kendra's double take and sensual smile made his effort worth it.

"Oh, my God. I almost didn't recognize you for a minute," she said as he strolled toward her. "I take back my earlier comment. You look amazing in these clothes. You clean up pretty good for a grease monkey."

"Thanks. I just couldn't sit here in jeans while you looked so damn beautiful." He wanted to kiss her so badly, but he knew if he started he wouldn't be able to stop at just a kiss.

"Well, I appreciate that very much. You look so handsome." She played with his collar a little. "I've never seen you in a suit before."

"I only wear one to weddings or funerals," he said with a wry twist of his lips.

She laughed and stepped away. "I can believe that. Come on. Let's eat before it gets cold."

Tom held out a chair for Kendra, seated her, and then sat in the chair beside her. He caught her looking at him with an odd little smile on her lips. "What?"

"This is a different side to you. I like it."

Tom lifted an eyebrow. "Maybe I'll show my gentlemanly side a little more often." And he slowly cupped her nape, his fingers gently stroking her soft skin.

The flirty look she sent him made his temperature rise. "I wouldn't have a problem with that."

She started cutting up her food, so sighing Tom did the same. However, he cast quick glances her way, surprised that he found watching her do such a mundane thing such a turn on. He returned his attention to his own meal and took a large bite.

"Mmm. This is great," he mumbled through his overfull mouth. "Where did you get it?"

"Flora's Kitchen."

Tom frowned. "Never heard of it."

Kendra said, "I'm not surprised. It's a little Italian restaurant in my old neighborhood. Great food at reasonable prices."

"You drove all the way over there?"

"I wanted food that might tempt you into eating," Kendra spoke shyly.

"Well, I'm duly tempted. Flora makes some fine chicken parmesan," Tom gratefully replied.

Kendra took a drink of her water before asking softly, "What happened between you and your dad?"

Her question caught Tom completely off guard. His hand tightened around his fork; with a refusal to answer driving through his mind. But he forced him-self to relax. Kendra had a right to know about his past, especially since he planned to persuade her to marry him one day.

"When I was seventeen, I got mixed up with the wrong crowd. I'm sure that doesn't surprise you. Marcus probably told you," he said.

With feigned shock, Kendra smirked, "No! He's mentioned a bit about your past. But I could never imagine the surly young boy I met years ago got in trouble…"

Tom chuckled. "Smart ass. Anyhow, to cut a long story short; I got accused of mugging an elderly woman because I was in the vicinity. I didn't do it. But the lady ID'd me since I looked a lot like the guy who snatched her purse. I ended up spending six months in juvey for something I didn't do.

"Dad left me in there because he didn't believe I was innocent. He'd gotten me out of vandalism charges and stuff like that, but that was the last straw for him." Tom shook his head. "In all fairness it was almost nicer in juvey than living at home with dear old dad. He was always drunk and when he got mad, I became his punching bag."

Kendra's eyes welled with tears. "I'm so sorry, Tom. No kid deserves that. I don't really know what to say. My parent's kicking me out at twenty-one seems lame in comparison. Dad thought he owned me, especially as he thought I'd beaten cancer because of him. I should spend the rest of my life thanking him. I was grateful to him for the best hospital care, but who won't help their child just because I wouldn't reveal the father of my baby? Dad knew Marcus would look after me, but he also thought I'd come crawling back." She grimaced. "That didn't work out as he planned, so now I think he doesn't know how to fix it."

"Kicking out a pregnant daughter with no money or support —I'd like to have a talk with your father one day," said Tom shaking his head angrily.

She shrugged. "At least we know how *not* to treat our son. We have to listen, support and guide him. But we also have to make sure we don't hurt him. Promise me that whatever happens in our relationship, we won't let it affect how we both parent Connor?"

He watched her face but she betrayed nothing of what she was feeling. Did she think this relationship would fail? He put his fork down and reached across the table for her hand. "I would never let Connor suffer the way we suffered. That, I swear. But I'm not starting this relationship thinking it will fail. I'm hoping you're not either."

He felt her reassuring squeeze before she withdrew her hand. "Good point. How did you get to be a mechanic? Someone must have helped you because I doubt your father did."

Tom half-smiled at her quick return to their original discussion. "You're right. Living with dear old Dad was no picnic, but there was one bright spot from being in juvey. There was this balsy lady named Clem who taught auto mechanics. She took a shine to me and started teaching me about fixing cars. And that was that. I knew right then tinkering with cars was what I wanted to do."

"I started studying books, watching videos, and working on any car I could get my hands on to gain experience. Once I got out, Sam had me take my GED and sent me to auto mechanic school. That's where I started working on racing cars and streetcars. My teachers rode my ass hard, but only because they saw that I had real talent."

Kendra said proudly, "And that's why Marcus hired you. He's always said you were the best in the business."

"I used to hang at the local amateur racing track to help with the cars. That's where I met Marcus. We became best friends right away. We just 'clicked', you know? He's right; we're like brothers, which is why the way he acted today really upset me."

"Me, too." Kendra sighed. "This is why I never revealed who Connor's father was. I knew the pregnancy would tear you two apart. Gosh, just the idea of us dating has him all riled up. I'm dreading what might happen when he learns about Connor."

"You of all people should know Marcus's all full of piss and wind. He'll come around once he sees how committed I am to you and Connor."

Kendra shrugged her shoulders. "Let's not talk about him, okay? Let's enjoy our night. Tell me about your Dad's condition."

Tom looked down absently at the table. "Okay. He's pretty ill. His body is rejecting the liver transplant. So Sam wants me tested to see if I'm a match. If I am a match, I'm supposed to give a piece of my liver to the man who made my life hell." Lifting his head to look in her eyes, Tom whispered, "Sam's right, though. At least he stuck around. Mom left when I was twelve."

Kendra's heart hurt for him as she replied quietly, "I still can't believe that she left you both behind. Have you never wanted to find her and ask why?"

He swallowed against his gut burning desire to confess to her he was too scared to. What if she said it was because that she left, did he really want to know that? "I thought if she wanted me, she'd find me. I'm not chasing after a ghost."

Even he could hear his pain in those words.

"I can relate. Parents aren't supposed to cut their children out of their lives. I know how much that hurts," exclaimed Kendra, nodding sternly.

"I know you do," Tom said. "I still can't believe you wouldn't tell anyone that I was Connor's dad. That was brave and also stupid."

Kendra twirled some spaghetti around her fork. "There were several reasons I stayed silent. As I said before, I was afraid that if Marcus knew about us, it would mess up his racing career and then also your business. But most of all, I was afraid it would mean I'd never see you again."

"What?" Tom uttered, his heart beating like a drum in shock.

Kendra couldn't look at him, as she twined her sweat-dampened hands together in her lap. "Since you never answered my emails, I assumed you wanted nothing to do with me and Connor. If you and Marcus had stopped being friends, I'd never have had the chance to confront you. You might've skipped town and never looked back." She shrugged hesitantly. "It happens." She raised her eyes to his. "And I wanted you to be the first to know that Connor was yours. Okay, well, Stella knew, but only because I needed someone to talk to about it all."

Tom released his breath harshly after hearing the pain in Kendra's voice, and though he had no right to be mad that Stella knew about Connor before him, he couldn't help feeling angry, anyway. He'd missed out on so much of Connor's life already. He gave a wobbly smile and said, "I'm glad she was there to help you. You needed someone." He pounded a fist on the table. "Damn it! I should've read—"

"Tom, stop!" Kendra interjected sharply. "We can't go back and undo it all. We just have to move forward. Both of us need to stop feeling guilty about it. It's not doing us any good and it won't do Connor any good, either."

Tom acknowledged the wisdom in her words, quietly saying, "You're right. I am trying. I just feel robbed because I've missed so much."

Kendra smiled with her eyes bright and whispered, "But now you can make up for lost time."

Tom smiled lovingly back. "Damn straight. By the way, I told

Sam about Connor when he was here earlier tonight. Don't worry, he won't tell anyone."

Fear gripped Kendra. "Are you sure? If Marcus finds out from someone other than me and you... it won't be pretty."

"I know and I won't tell anyone else, but Sam's my brother and I trust him," Tom responded calmly. "Besides, you have one person you can talk to about it, so I should get one person to confide in, too."

"You're right. It's only fair," Kendra said.

Tom laid his silverware down and wiped his mouth. "Kendra, there's only one reason I don't tell people I'm Connor's dad."

"What's that?"

"I need to prove to myself that I'm worthy to be his father before other people know. I need to know that I can be the dad he deserves," Tom replied solemnly.

"What you really mean is that you need to prove to yourself that you're not like *your* father," Kendra snapped straight back at him.

How was she always able to see past his words and know what was truly in his mind? Kendra seemed to understand Tom so clearly it was scary. "Exactly. I was beginning to resemble him," he said. "But when Dad got sick, it really made me think about things. About the things I wanted from my life. I always thought a family was not my scene. But when you told me I was a father... it was as if my world lit up. I just knew I would be a good father and that I wanted to have children."

Kendra nodded and said, "I know what you mean. Mortality seems to make you test what is important to you. When I was at my sickest and thought I would die, I swore to myself that if I made it, I would make my dreams come true. And I would do it on my own terms."

The thought of her dying distressed Tom, and he had to swallow hard to keep tears at bay. He cleared his throat, but his voice still came out slightly thick. "I know you can do anything you set your mind too. You were so brave and gusty during your illness. I admired you then and I admire you now. You kept going even though the odds were against you. I don't think you realize how incredible you are."

His compliments made her blush. "Stop it. I'm not incredible. I'm just determined."

Tom continued softly, "Strong, talented, and sexy as hell."

"Stop it," she replied, giggling like a teenager. "You're embarrassing me."

He grinned, got up from the table and held out his hand to her. "Dance with me?" he asked suggestively.

"There isn't any music," Kendra answered with quiet longing.

"There will be."

Curious about what he was up to, Kendra slipped her hand into his and allowed him to lead her to the living room. A Bose sound system was on a stand next to a big flat screen TV by the bay window.

Suddenly Tom said, "Wait here and close your eyes."

"I feel silly standing here with my eyes closed. What are you up to?"

"Just do it, okay?"

Kendra played along and closed her eyes.

Hurrying out to the kitchen, Tom retrieved the candles from the table and took them into the living room. He sat them on the fireplace mantle and ran back out to the kitchen where he hastily rummaged around in the cupboards.

"Yes!" he cried upon finding what he was after. He dashed back to the living room, grinning like an idiot. This was the first time he'd ever done something romantic for a woman, and he wanted it to be special. Lighting the tiny tea lights, he carefully placed the glowing candles all over the room. Left by their last owners; he silently thanked them for their gift.

Grabbing his cellphone from the coffee table, Tom brought up Pandora on the screen. Searching his playlists, he chose one with romantic songs, one playlist he rarely used. Scrolling through it, he stopped at the song his mother had played when she'd taught him to dance. It was one of the few happy memories from his childhood he had of her.

Quickly sitting his phone on the dock of the Bose system, Tom hit the play button, and adjusted the volume slightly as *Unforgettable* by Nat King Cole floated in the air. Turning to Kendra, he murmured, "You can open your eyes now."

Chapter Seventeen

Kendra had been listening avidly to Tom's movements, but upon opening her eyes she gasped. All she saw were tiny dancing lights that cast the room in shimmering shadows, creating a cozy, intimate space.

"You're just full of surprises," she mused as he enclosed her in his arms. "I can't believe you know songs like this."

Tom smiled. "My mom taught me how to dance and we danced to all kinds of love songs. I was twelve and wanted to impress my date for the Junior Ball that year."

His movements as he danced were smooth and graceful. "Well, if you danced then, as well as you are right now, I don't know how she couldn't have been impressed."

Tom smiled, drew back from her, and propelled her into a slow spin. Then he drew her back, fitting her intimately against his body. "Mom taught me how to slow dance and she even taught me how to waltz."

Kendra smiled shyly at him. "I know. You waltzed with me at my prom. I never forgot that."

The song changed to Elvis' *Can't Help Falling in Love*, and Tom twirled her around in a slow, sexy waltz.

Am I dreaming? Am I really here, waltzing with Tom again? Kendra wondered as she looked in his eyes. She was enchanted by this other side of him, and it almost seemed like he was a different man. He was so handsome in his suit and he'd styled his hair differently, too. This suave, debonair man was a far cry from the tough guy mechanic she knew. She adored this softer side of him.

Between the warm, lovely light from the flickering candle flames, the romantic music, and the hunger in Tom's eyes, Kendra felt like a princess in a fairy tale. Closing her eyes, the magic of the moment swept her away.

Putting a hand around the back of his neck, she coaxed him to lower his head so she could press her lips to his. Their kiss was slow and sweet. When it ended, Tom pulled her close and she laid her head on his chest. She sighed when he rested his cheek on the top of her head. Snuggling closer, Kendra closed her eyes, swaying with him to the rhythm of the music.

The romance of the moment was so moving, her heart so overflowing with emotion that she couldn't contain it. She needed to tell Tom how she felt about him, but in a special way. Suddenly a grin curved her mouth because it came to her while she danced.

As the current song ended, she drew away from him. "Stay right here," She ordered.

Tom gave her a quizzical look when she left the living room. She returned, replaced his phone with hers and connected it to the Bose dock. Let him wonder what she was up to.

Quickly, she brought up the karaoke version of Christina Perri's *A Thousand Years*. She rejoined Tom, moving smoothly back into his arms while the intro played.

At the proper cue, she sang, *"Heart beats fast, colors and promises, how to be brave. How can I love when I'm afraid to fall, but watching you standalone, all of my doubt suddenly goes away somehow…"*

By the time she'd sung the first chorus, she saw a light of

understanding blazing in Tom's eyes. She was trying to show him. This wasn't just a song. This was her admission of love.

"I have died every day waiting for you, darling don't be afraid, I have loved for a thousand years, I'll love you for a thousand more."

Close to end of the song, tears welled in Kendra's eyes and she couldn't stop the way her chin trembled as fear, love, and longing coalesced inside. Would he crush her heart or push her away now that he knew how she felt about him? Gathering her courage, she readied herself to face his reaction.

Kendra cupped his face as she sang the last line while tears streamed down her face. As the song faded, she started, "I fell in love with you the first time I saw you and I've loved you ever since. When you left, you took my heart with you. Now you're back in my life asking me to risk my heart again, to commit to this relationship. So here I am." Her voice trembled, "I couldn't wait any longer to tell you. I love you, Tom."

* * *

She had sung those lines with such conviction that Tom couldn't miss the meaning behind them. *She's loved me all this time?* There was no mistaking the message she was sending him and he felt humbled, happy, but also unworthy because he'd broken her heart almost four years ago. He'd deserted her and hadn't been there for her when she'd needed him the most.

How had he missed it back then, before he'd left? He thought her infatuated with her big brother's best friend. Why would a young woman with her social standing be interested in some schmuck mechanic?

He stared into her eyes, and his heart thumped in his chest. He cursed himself for being so blind. For being a coward. *I'm such an idiot.* It hadn't been the broken condom that had scared him away four years ago. It had been his own feelings for Kendra. She was unlike any women he'd ever known and he'd believed he didn't deserve someone as good and wonderful as Kendra.

The feelings he'd locked securely away behind the walls of

his heart broke free of their chains and he could no longer deny them. When they were younger, terror stopped him telling her what was in his heart, afraid she'd reject him because he'd been such a hellion from the wrong side of the tracks. Would she have believed him? Would she believe him now?

Once again, her bravery touched him because he understood the thoughts that haunted her. Kendra's declaration gave him courage. Lowering his head, he kissed her forehead and the tip of her nose. She closed her eyes and he kissed them while he brushed away her tears with his thumbs.

Resting his forehead against hers and breathing deeply, Tom said the words he'd never said to another woman. "I'm so thankful to hear you say that because I love you, too."

Kendra shook her head a little as she opened her eyes. "No, Tom—"

Tom shook his head and settled a finger over her lips. "You know that I don't lie, Kendra, not even to spare your feelings. I was a coward. A guy like me couldn't have a woman like you, or so I thought. Someone so smart, talented, and good. So, like a dumbass, I ran. That's why I didn't read the emails. I was too scared that you'd discover the real me and dump my sorry ass. I knew you deserved better than me."

He saw the anger and pain on her face as she fisted her hands in his suit lapels, latching on with a little shake. "That wasn't your decision to make! I wanted you so much. You're a better man than you think. I could see that even when you didn't!" She pounded a fist against his chest. "Why couldn't you tell me this back then?"

Tom caught her hand and kissed it. "Because I was young and stupid and I'm not as brave as you. I'm sorry that I didn't tell you then but I can tell you now because both you and Connor are worth fighting for." He flattened her hand over his heart. "I love you, Kendra. And I love our son."

The blazing light in his eyes as he stared into hers convinced

Kendra that he meant it. Overwhelmed by emotion, Kendra rested her head against Tom's chest and shook with sobs.

Tom gathered her close and held her as she cried. He shut his eyes against the tears that filled them. A few escaped and trickled down to fall into her hair. Then he scooped her into his arms and carried her down the hall to his bedroom.

Setting her on her feet, he turned on a small lamp on his dresser, casting a soft glow around the room. Tom cradled her face in his palms, his gaze steady as he met her gaze for a few moments. Dipping his head, he brushed his mouth tenderly against hers. When she wound her arms around his waist, he settled his lips firmly over hers.

He plundered her mouth and she responded in kind. Taking all the pins out of her hair, Tom laid them on the nightstand and embraced her again. Her body heated as he caressed her back and shoulders.

She offered no objection when he unzipped her dress and dipped his hands underneath it to cup her bottom. Kendra needed to be as close to him as possible. She held him tighter and kissed him harder.

His hands traveled up to the clasp behind her neck that released the top of her dress. Tom undid it and slowly pulled it down, exposing her breasts. Her nipples tightened and she gasped as he brushed the backs of his fingers over them.

He drew the dress slowly down her body and helped her step out of it. Crouching, he kissed her stomach, trailed his lips downward, and pressed them against her mound through her panties. Hooking his thumbs under the sides, he removed the lacy garment and her high heels.

Kendra shivered with need as he kissed his way up to her breasts. A moan escaped her as he kneaded them and teased her nipples with his fingers. Hunger filled her and she needed to feel his skin against her own.

She pushed his suit jacket off his shoulders and pulling it off his arms. As she unbuttoned his shirt, she kissed every inch of the muscled chest that she exposed. With shaking hands she took off his cufflinks and laid them on the nightstand before tugging the shirt the rest of the way off. When Tom stood naked before her, she thought no man could ever be as sexy as him. He was sculptured perfection.

Although he burned for Kendra, Tom was determined to show her how much he loved her. Picking her up, he laid her in the center of his bed and stretched out beside her. Meeting her eyes, he ran his fingertips over the silky skin of her thighs.

He took his time, caressing and kissing her everywhere—worshipping this amazing woman who had given him her heart. With his hands, mouth, and tongue, he tried to show her how much he cherished her. Her back arched when he took a turgid nipple in his mouth and lazily circled it with his tongue. Cupping her mound, he coaxed her legs apart and found the sensitive nub within her folds.

He wanted the fire he felt to consume her, too. He sighed when she lifted his head, kissing him and shifting her body in clear invitation.

Unable to resist any longer, Tom gently broke the kiss and covered her body with his. Savoring the moment, he gradually pressed forward until he filled her. He spread her dark hair over the pillow, admiring the glossy locks.

Raising up on his hands, he pulled out partially and pushed steadily back in. The sensations were more intense than normal. *Blast, no condoms.* Remembering that Kendra was on birth control, he shoved away his concern and began moving again.

Moaning, Kendra wrapped herself around Tom, running her hands down his muscular back to his buttocks. Gripping them, she urged him into a faster rhythm. As they rocked together, she felt his love in every kiss and touch. The dam inside Kendra burst. She cried out in bliss and shuddered against his hard body.

Determined to take her with him to another sensual pinnacle,

Tom didn't give her time to recover. Instead, he rose on his hands and pumped his hips faster, driving them both onward. A desire to completely fill her heart, to brand himself on her soul burned in his veins. To make her his forever.

Moving with him, Kendra clutched at his back as she strained towards their mutual goal. Her whimpers of need turned to moans before a powerful orgasm made her call his name so loudly that it echoed off the walls.

Hearing the sounds of pleasure he gave Kendra sent Tom over the edge. His release tore through him with the intensity of a cyclone, and he wrapped his arms around her as ecstasy crashed over him. A long, low groan left him as his thrusts slowed and then stopped.

Completely spent, he relaxed down on top of Kendra. Lifting his head, he met her emerald gaze and smiled down at her. She returned his smile and he couldn't resist kissing her. Their tongues twined as their hearts calmed.

Ending the kiss, Tom cupped her face and made her look at him. "I love you, Kendra. I've never loved any other woman. Just you. Got it?"

She nodded. "I hear you and I believe you." She covered his hands with hers. "I love only you. Got it?"

He grinned. "Got it."

Kendra let out a cry of surprise when he flipped them over in a lightning fast move. She giggled when he laughed. Squeezing his shoulders, she said, "I love these muscles of yours too."

He gave the same treatment to her rear end. "And I love these and a lot of other things about you."

With a chuckle, Kendra laid her head on his chest. They lay together like that for several minutes, just enjoying their closeness.

Kendra lifted her head when Tom sighed. "What's wrong?

"I'm so glad that you don't have to go home tonight, because I want you again. And again and again."

She giggled. "I'm all yours to have again and again and again."

His kiss was fierce and excited Kendra with surprising swiftness. Soon they were lost on another ride into passion and stayed in each other's arms until almost dawn when sleep finally claimed them.

Chapter Eighteen

Someone shook Tom and he opened his eyes to see Sam smiling at him. For one moment he forgot where he was —at the hospital. Kendra had left early wanting to be home when Connor woke. Living across the road from her was working out mighty fine. Tom'd had to get to the hospital anyway for the tests, so although he didn't want her to leave, he had his own commitment to his family to consider.

Now, he'd had his tests, and he was resting from last night's marathon love session with Kendra, in a really uncomfortable hospital chair, waiting for the results.

"Long night?"

Images of his and Kendra's special night played in his mind. "Yeah, but the best kind of long night."

Sam grinned. "I've had a lot of those myself."

Tom looked around the hospital waiting room, which was just outside the laboratory where he'd been poked and prodded. Surprisingly, there were only two other people in it and they were across the room.

He leaned closer to Sam. "No, it wasn't just sex. Until last night, I didn't understand what lovemaking meant or why it's called something besides sex. I mean, it's sex, but more, you know?"

To his credit, Sam tried to contain his mirth, but he lost the battle. "God, you're adorable. My baby brother is growing up."

"Shut the fuck up," Tom said under his breath. "Forget it."

Sam chuckled. "I'm sorry, Tommy. I know exactly what you mean. I had plenty of sex in college, but when I met Tonya senior year, that was it. Love at first sight. We didn't sleep together until we'd been going out for four months and I never once cheated on her."

Tom raised his eyebrows. "Four months? Wow." Then he frowned. "Wait a minute. You guys started dating in February that year and you got married in June right after graduation." Tom gasped. "You waited for your wedding night?"

Sam pounded on Tom's thigh. "Why don't you just tell the whole hospital? Lower your voice."

Tom resisted rubbing his leg, even though it hurt like hell. "Sorry. I'm just surprised, that's all."

Sam smiled. "So was I. Tonya was saving herself for marriage and I knew as soon as we met that I wanted to be with her forever. I took a lot of cold showers and did some other things to blow off steam, but she was worth waiting for."

"And that night, I discovered that being with someone you love has so much more meaning. Sure, sex is fun and feels good, but lovemaking?" Sam shook his head. "Infinitely better."

Tom was about to respond when his number was called, but in his mind, he agreed wholeheartedly with his brother. Being with Kendra last night had been unlike anything he'd ever experienced, and he wanted to always share that with her.

"What gets me, little brother, is why did you never read any of Kendra's emails?"

His stomach clenched as he looked at the floor. "I was scared about what she would say. I never imagined it would be to tell me that she'd got pregnant. The condom broke, but the hospital had indicated she might not be able to have children from the chemo. She even froze some of her eggs in case. So, we didn't think much about it. Not reading those emails was more about my feelings for her and not being brave enough to face them. Let's face it, good old mum and dad didn't set a very good example of happily ever after."

"You were young. You just needed time to work out what is important in life. It's not cars, wine, and women. It's love and family."

"You and I have plans tomorrow, Sam," Tom said, standing.

"Oh, yeah? Doing what?"

Rising, Tom let out a happy sigh. "Ring shopping."

He turned away, leaving Sam laughing behind him.

A nurse appeared from the laboratory and suggested, "Why don't you go visit your father while you wait. I'll come find you if we have any news."

The bother's nodded in agreement and went to find their dad.

Tom stood looking down at his sleeping father, who lay in a hospital bed. Tubes and wires connected Vincent to IV bags and a heart monitor, among other machines that Tom wasn't familiar with.

Although he'd been at the hospital with Sam for his father's surgery, Tom hadn't visited Vincent. His father's eyes had sunken and his pallor was tinged with yellow from his failing liver transplant. He was much thinner than when Tom had last seen him. His throat closed as he took in his father's declining condition.

"Remember what we agreed," Sam whispered.

Tom nodded. They'd decided not to tell Vincent that Tom was being tested as a possible donor in case he didn't qualify. They didn't want to get Vincent's hopes up.

"Okay. I have to get to that meeting," Sam said.

Tom's head whipped around. "What? You're leaving?"

Sam explained, "Yeah. I can't be late. Besides, you need some time with him, just in case."

Tom glowered at Sam and walked out of the room. Sam followed, grabbed his shoulder and turned Tom around.

"I'm not doing this," Tom said. "I'm not forgiving him for making my life hell so he can die with a clear conscience. That's what you want me to do, isn't it?"

Compassion filled Sam's eyes. "Maybe a little for him, but mostly for you."

"What do you mean?" Tom snorted.

Sam hesitated, "I know that Dad isn't perfect. A couple of months ago, he told me about everything he put you through. I feel so bad that you were dealing with it all while I was away at school. You should've told me."

Tom jammed his hands in his jeans pockets and looked at the floor. "I didn't want to ruin college for you." He shrugged. "Besides, there wasn't anything you could do about it."

"Yes, there was. I could've talked to Dad, but I also could've been there for you. I'm your big brother and it's my job to look out for you."

"Anyway, hanging onto all this bitterness isn't doing you any good. You need to find common ground with him before it's too late or you'll regret it, Tom. Now, I have to go. I'll call you later."

Tom waved him off, "Fine."

Sam pursed his lips and walked away.

Leaning against the corridor wall, Tom calmly considered Sam's advice and thought perhaps he might be right. Squaring his shoulders, Tom stepped back into his father's room and sat on the chair close to the bed.

It wasn't long until Vincent stirred and opened his eyes. They widened when he spotted Tom. "Tommy? Are you really here or did I die?"

He might be sick, but his dad hadn't lost his dry wit. "You didn't die. I'm really here."

Vincent pressed the button on the bed that raised the head. "You look good. Still got all those tattoos?"

Tom laughed. "Yeah, I still have them. I keep telling you I'm not getting rid of them."

Vincent grinned, his brown eyes shining despite being sick. "I think I'll get one."

Tom snorted. "A little late in the game, isn't it?"

"Exactly. At this point, it's like, what the hell? Why not? I'm already dying. What's a little ink poisoning?" Vincent responded with a tiny shrug.

"Knock it off, Dad. That's not funny."

"Tom, I've made my peace with it and the truth is, it'll be a relief to be out of pain," Vincent said.

Tom's jaw worked as he fought to retain his composure. "If you're going to talk like that, I'm leaving."

Vincent closed his eyes and sighed. "Okay, okay." Opening them, he looked at Tom again. "So, did you come here to yell at me and tell me what a horrible father I was? How much I hurt you? Or maybe that you hate me?"

Damn it. How was he supposed to look a dying man in the face and stay angry at him? "I've tried to hate you, Dad, but I couldn't quite do it," Tom admitted.

"I'm glad to hear that," Vincent whispered. "No matter what you think, you're my boy and I've always loved you."

Tom crossed his arms. "You have a rotten way of showing it."

"I know. I screwed up big time with you, but I've been trying to make up for it. Even before I got sick, but you wouldn't listen to me," Vincent trailed off.

"You would've just told me the same bullshit that you always did."

Vincent pleaded, "No, I wouldn't have. I would've told you exactly what I'm going to tell you now. I should've believed you when you told me you were innocent." Tears gathered in his eyes. "I hate myself for not being a better father to you. I don't expect you to forgive me, but I just wanted you to know how sorry I am that I hurt you so much."

Tom didn't know how to respond, so he just nodded and acknowledged, "Okay."

To his surprise, Vincent started chuckling, which led to a full belly laugh.

Even though he didn't know what had amused his father, Tom grinned. "What's so funny?"

Vincent got himself under control. "*You* are. You always were closed-mouthed and you haven't changed. I just bared my soul to you and all you can say is 'okay'?"

"What the fuck do you want me to say, Dad?"

"Good! That's right. Get mad."

Tom's fists clenched. "*Get* mad? I've been pissed at you for so long that it's hard to remember when I wasn't. Women and booze were more important than me! I started running around with Doug's gang to get your attention." He rubbed his forehead. "What a pathetic cliché I am."

Vincent replied, "If you're a cliché, then so am I. I was always so drunk I couldn't figure out where I went wrong with you. Not until it was too late and you'd washed your hands of me. *I* was the problem, not you."

Tom wondered if Vincent was just blowing smoke up his ass or if he was being genuine. "Part of it is my fault. I shouldn't have been stupid enough to do that stuff with Doug, but I was young and hurting. I'd lost my mother and I may as well have lost you too. I can understand why you would've thought I was guilty at first, but why didn't you check into it more?"

Vincent groaned, "My brain was too flooded with alcohol to think properly. I admit that I was a complete ass. People tried to get me to go AA. I didn't think I had a problem and told them to go hell. And now I'm paying for it. I put myself in this situation."

Tom couldn't argue with that.

"I'm really glad that you came to see me, Tommy," Vincent said, laying his head on his pillow. "I needed to apologize to you, not for my sake, but for yours. Maybe you won't think so badly of your old man once I'm gone."

Tom hung onto his composure by a thread as he stood up and approached Vincent's bed. Looking in his father's remorse-filled eyes, the tentacles of anger and pain wrapped around Tom's heart began loosening their hold. Bending down, he carefully embraced his frail father.

Tears filled his eyes as he remembered how big and strong the man used to be. "I love you, Dad."

Despite his weakened condition, Vincent hugged Tom tightly. "I love you, too, buddy. I always have and I'm so proud of you for making such a success of your life despite having me as a father."

"Thanks. That means a lot." Tom decided as he drew away. "Dad, I have a son. He's almost three and his name is Connor."

Vincent's eyes grew huge. "What? Why didn't you tell me before this? Sam never said anything, either."

Tom explained the situation to Vincent. "I loved him the minute I saw him, Dad."

Vincent grinned. "I felt the same way when you boys were born." He grabbed Tom's hand. "Bring him to me, Tommy. I want to meet my grandson. Please?"

Tom couldn't refuse. "I will."

Vincent squeezed Tom's hand. "Promise me you'll bring him."

"I promise."

"Thank you." Vincent's eyes drifted close.

"Get some rest, Dad. I'll bring Connor tomorrow, okay?"

Vincent let go of Tom's hand. "Okay. I'll see you then."

Tom watched his father fall asleep and quietly left the room. Finding the nurse, she advised the labs were running slow and that they'd ring him when they had the results back.

With relief, he rushed from the hospital and headed for his car. Once Tom was in the driver's seat, he slammed the door and leaning over the steering wheel, let the tears come. Hoarse sobs wracked his body as his pain poured out.

It hurt, but it was also cathartic. After several minutes, Tom reined in his turbulent emotions, wiped his face with his hand and relaxed for a few moments before leaving the parking lot. As he made his way to Kendra's he hoped that she'd understand why he'd told Vincent about Connor.

Chapter Nineteen

Taking advantage of having a morning with no piano lessons, Kendra worked on the song she had to deliver for one of the pop princesses of the day. She was excited at the prospect that this could be her big break. Kendra had a good voice but knew her real talent lay in song writing. Besides, she much preferred to be behind the spotlight than in front of it. She saw what that kind of life could do to people, and their privacy.

She was struggling to find the right lyric, and she was listening to Connor laughing in the yard, when a knock sounded on her door. As soon as she opened it, Tom swept her into his arms and held her close. Kendra returned his embrace, stroking his hair and kissing his cheek.

Since she didn't know what was wrong, Kendra just hugged him, trying to soothe him with her closeness. When he drew back and kissed her, it was a different kind of kiss, one that sought comfort instead of passion.

Kendra gladly lent her support to him and kissed him back tenderly. By the time the kiss ended, her heart throbbed in her chest, but concern overrode all her desires. The pain in his eyes made her scalp tingle with fear.

"What is it, Tom? What happened?"

"Where's Connor?" he asked.

"In the kitchen."

Tom released her and headed for the other room. Kendra knew something had happened with his Dad. Entering the kitchen, he saw Connor scooting a train engine across the floor and the smile that lit his face brought tears to her eyes. He loved his son, and he knew right then that Kendra had no right to stop him from announcing his paternity to the world.

Catching sight of Tom, Connor threw up his hand. "Hi, Tom!"

Tom grinned and scooped Connor into his arms. "Hi, buddy." He kissed Connor's soft cheek and hugged him. "I love you and I will be the father you deserve. I promise. I know you don't understand what I'm saying, but one day you will. You'll never have to wonder if I love you."

Connor wiggled in his arms. "Are you my Daddy?" He'd understood one word. His little serious face broke Kendra's heart.

"I am your Daddy. Is that all right with you?"

Connor threw his small arms around Tom's neck and giggled. Her son saw her over Tom's shoulder. "Mama, I have a Daddy now. Tom will be my Daddy."

Kendra kneeled down next to her two favorite men. "He's always been your Daddy, but he's come home now." And the three of them collapsed on the floor of her kitchen, hugging and smiling and crying.

Finally, Connor got bored with sitting still. "Mama, can I go for a swim?"

"I'll take you in a minute," Tom said. "Find Jackie and she can put your swimsuit on." Connor was running from the room before he'd finished speaking.

"How did it go at the hospital?" she asked as they both rose to their feet.

He tried to smile, but couldn't quite manage it. Taking a huge breath, he said, "I went to see Dad after getting my bloodwork done. God, he looks like… crap. He's so thin and he's hooked up to all these monitors and stuff." He shook his head. "Seeing him like that… was so hard. We had a good talk and got a lot things out in the open. I wasn't expecting that. I was so mad at Sam for making me do it, but I'm glad he did."

Kendra rubbed his back. "That's great that you reconciled with him, Tom. I'm sure that it's a big relief. I often wonder if I should reach out to my parents, or my mother maybe."

Tom let out a shaky sigh. "I can't advise you on that. You'll know when it's time."

"Probably. I hope so."

"I told Dad about Connor because I want them to meet. If I'm not a match as a donor, he will die, Kendra. I want Dad to see his grandson before he goes. I hope you can understand that," Tom shared. "It'll still be a secret for now because it's not like Marcus or anyone else will see Dad."

Tears of sympathy filled Kendra's eyes. It was only right that Tom's father met Connor. Tom had missed so much of his son's life, he should be able to share the news with whoever he wanted. "It's okay. I think you should be able to tell whoever you want. I shouldn't have asked you not to acknowledge Connor. I think I'll have a housewarming party for our friends this weekend, and we will tell them then—together. If that's what you want?"

He pulled her close and kissed her. "I think that's a wonderful idea. Should we tell Marcus separately?"

"He's gone out of town for a few days to the parts expo. But he'll be back this weekend. I think we tell him at the same time. If there are people around who might rejoice at our news, he's less likely to try to kill you. I kind of like having you around."

Tom smirked. "Do you now. That's fine with me. The being around a bit I mean." He kissed her long and hard.

When the kiss ended, she stepped back and stated quietly, "I'd like to go with you to the hospital."

Tom's face registered surprise. "Really?"

"Really. I want to meet him," Kendra responded.

"I'd like that," Tom agreed. "I have to get to work after I take Connor for a quick swim. Shall we go tomorrow morning?"

"Sounds like a plan."

He ran a hand over his head. She felt exhausted, so she knew this must have been more draining on Tom. His father was dying. He looked so tired. The stress of his father, Connor, and their late night of love-making were tiring both of them.

"How about I bring pizza tonight and we watch some movies?"

Kendra smiled up at him. "I'd really like that. We can have an early night."

"I can stay here?"

His whole face lit up and Kendra felt tears well in her eyes. "I guess I'm committing to this relationship. Connor needs to know his father."

Tom's excitement filled the room. "I'll try to be here by six so I can visit with Connor before he goes to bed."

Kendra wrapped her arms around his waist and squeezed tight. "That would be awesome."

Tom planted a firm kiss on her mouth. So lost in each other, they didn't hear Connor approach.

"Daddy kish Mama," Connor said with a giggle.

Tom laughed and swung Connor into his arms. "That's right." He blew a raspberry on Connor's cheek and the little boy squealed with laughter. "Daddy kiss Connor, too."

Connor took Tom's face in his chubby little hands and tried to blow a raspberry on his cheek. Tom and Kendra laughed at his antics.

Reluctantly, Tom set Connor down on the floor. "I'll see you tonight, Kendra, okay?"

Kendra laughed as Tom pulled her against him and rubbed his hips against hers.

"Maybe tonight Tom kiss Mama."

Hunger rose inside Kendra and she wished they could play house right now. "I'm counting on it."

Tom groaned. "I wish I didn't have to go to work." He gave her another kiss and let her go. "Let's have that quick swim, Tiger."

Kendra couldn't stop smiling even after they left. She watched them through the window as Tom and Connor played in the toddlers pool. Humming a song, she went back to her music room, happier than she'd ever been. Suddenly the lyrics bloomed in her head and as she heard Connor and Tom splashing in the pool, the song flowed.

* * *

Tom arrived home at five, not six. He was the boss, after all. Lexi needed the overtime, so he'd left her to finish the car he was working on.

Connor squealed when he saw Tom and raced into his arms. His son put a little finger to his mouth and went, "Sssh, mama is sleep."

Tom looked at Jackie. "Kendra wasn't feeling well, so she went to lie down about two hours ago."

He lowered Connor to the floor. "I'll just check on her." He handed Jackie some money. "I ordered the Pizzas as I was leaving work. They should be here soon. Then you could take the night off."

He made his way to Kendra's bedroom and quietly opened the door. The curtains were pulled but light poured in from the open door behind him. Kendra was curled on her side, sound asleep with a throw over her. He tip-toed over to the bed and stood looking down at her. She looked so beautiful. His heart was so full of love for her. He couldn't wait to marry this woman and start a new life with her. He hoped they had more children. He would be by her side this time; nothing would keep them apart.

How silly of him to have been afraid of love. Scared of not knowing how to be a good husband and father. All he'd needed was to give his heart to the right woman, and it had taken him this long to understand what he'd felt four years ago. Kendra was that woman. The only woman for him.

She looked tired. He decided not to wake her. It would give him and Connor an evening to get to know each other. He tiptoed out of the room and went in search of his son and family pizza.

T wo hours later, Connor was lying on the couch pressed snug against Tom, with his favorite cuddly toy, just freshly bathed and full of food. Tom was reading him a story before he tucked him in to bed, when Kendra wandered sleepily into the den.

She looked all soft and warm from her sleep, and his body reacted to her immediately. He wanted to take her right back to bed and—

"Mama, Daddy is reading to me."

Kendra squeezed onto the couch on the other side of Connor. "I hope you've been a good boy?" she asked with a yawn.

"I have, Mama. I had pizza too."

"Well, it's past your bedtime, so as soon as Tom—Daddy—finishes this story it's off to bed with you."

"Can't I stay up with you? Please—Daddy?" Connor begged wistfully. His big round eyes opened wide.

Tom wanted to laugh. His son was clever. Already he was trying to pit mom and dad against each other. "Hey bud, I think you have to do as your mom says."

Connor's face crumpled, and she could see it was Tom's first experience of parenting. You're not there to be your child's best friend, but to help him settle, to understand boundaries and expectations. But Kendra knew how hard it was to ignore the wishes of their wonderful son.

But Tom gave Connor a kiss as he snuggled quietly into her arms, and Tom finished the story. His little eyelids were struggling to stay open as Tom stopped reading. Kendra made to stand and carry him to bed when Tom laid a hand on her arm. "May I? I've never put my son to bed before," he implored her gently.

Without a word, she handed her precious bundle to Tom, and he softly crooned to Connor as he carried him from the room. Kendra was beyond happy; life right at this moment was wonderful. She'd never expected to be this happy—Tom was in her house and it just felt right.

Suddenly feeling hungry, she went in hunt of leftover pizza to zap in the microwave.

She'd just taken a huge mouthful when Tom's arms slid round her waist. "Are you feeling better?" he enquired as she turned in his arms.

"I was just tired. But now I'm really hungry."

He laughed as he noticed the slice of pizza missing from the box. "So I see."

"No." She pressed closer and rubbed against him, loving how his body roared to life. Kendra whispered, "I'm hungry for you."

He swung her into his arms, but she grabbed one more slice of pizza before he carried her to her bedroom. "For sustenance," she chuckled.

He placed her gently on the bed and stepped back. He undressed as she lay watching, finishing her pizza with her eyes glued to his body. Soon he was standing naked in front of her and her mouth watered for something other than pizza.

She rose to her knees and crawled to the end of the bed with a huge grin on her face. Tom stood there in all his naked glory, well aware of what the sight of his magnificent body did to her. The soft lighting of her bedroom cast shadows, making his pecs and his abdominals look like they'd been deep-carved by Michelangelo himself. The prominent wings of his hip bones were a protective funnel for his towering erection.

She could barely raise her eyes back to his face, but when she did, the love she saw was brighter than the world's largest fireworks display.

Still on her knees, she leaned forward and pulled Tom's hand until his thighs were flush against the bed, and then she kissed the flat, ripped muscles of his stomach. She loved how he shuddered under her touch. His smooth, satin skin beneath her lips was pure heaven.

As her lips trailed lower, a soft growl rumbled deep in Tom's chest. Her tongue meandered across his lower belly, and she loved how his erection jerked. Her fingertips skipped up his strong thighs, and as she stared up at him, she saw his eyelids flicker closed as she finally took his shaft in her palm.

Tom's ragged inhale stoked her arousal as she stroked him. Parting her lips, she extended her tongue and licked her way from his heavy sac all the way up the underside of his erection.

"Holy, shit," he cried, before she saw his jaw clench and his eyes flare. He obviously liked it, so she did it again.

She teased him—slowly. Her tongue ran up his cock and then her lips hovered over the tip. Would she, wouldn't she take him in her mouth? She almost laughed out loud when he hissed, "Pleaseeee," from between clenched teeth. Taking pity on him, she smiled slyly and finally took him deep into her mouth.

Tom closed his eyes on a groan. She loved to tease and she withdrew right to his tip, her pink tongue swirling in the slit, making his toes curl and his sac tighten. Then she sucked him down again, her whole throat somehow enveloping his entire length. His hands rose to tangle in her hair, pulling the dark silk aside touching her face. She looked up to see how much he was enjoying her pleasuring him.

The rhythm started slowly, but soon he helped, moving his hips. When her palm slid round his cock, he let out a loud moan. She could do this all night just to hear him, watch him take his pleasure.

"I want to be inside you," he panted as his cock popped from her lush mouth.

He pushed her slowly onto her back as he crawled up her body, helping her shed her sundress as he went. He used his teeth to remove her thong, and her body hummed with arousal. By the time he reached her beautiful breasts, she was braless. "Why the hurry? We have all night."

She lay back and sighed, but lifted her hips in impatient offering. "I just want you so much." With her words ringing in his ears he slid into her heat and began to love the woman who owned his heart.

L ater as they lay cuddled together under the blanket, Tom brushed the hair from her face so he could kiss her. But as his hand found her skin all he felt was clammy heat. "You're hot."

She cuddled closer. "Thanks. But I think you're the hottest."

"No. I mean you're hot. Are you feeling all right?"

She stretched beside him. "I feel fabulous, but I will admit I'm a bit tired."

He stared at her and she looked a bit flushed, but after their lovemaking that was expected. "Shall I turn the air up?"

"No. Then I'll just get cold during the night. I just need some sleep."

Accepting her words, he kissed her forehead. "I'll just go check on Connor."

"Okay," came a muffled response.

He grabbed his jeans and dragged them on, not bothering to do them up and made his way quietly to Connor's room. His son's night light was on, but Connor was fast asleep. He'd kicked his blanket off, so Tom covered him again and pressed a kiss to his cheek. His heart overflowed with love, and he couldn't believe how lucky he was to have Kendra and Connor in his life.

He couldn't wait to bring Connor to meet his Grandad tomorrow. He hoped these new relationships were not too overwhelming for the little boy. So much had changed in Connor's life over the past weeks.

Finally, he pulled himself away from watching his son sleep. Tiredness pulled at him. He needed sleep before facing the hospital and all that might entail tomorrow.

He quietly got into bed, noting Kendra had fallen asleep. Tom reached across and switched off the bedside lights, plunging the room in to darkness. He curled his body behind her and it took him barely moments to slip into a deep, contented sleep.

T om didn't know what had woken him, but he bolted upright. Kendra wasn't in bed and his heart raced—Connor. But then he noted the light in the bathroom was on and he walked over to see if she was all right.

He pushed the door wider only to see Kendra lying face down on the floor, the hand-wash container broken on the floor beside her. He raced to her side, his heart pounding. He felt her forehead with the back of his hand. She was burning up. With growing alarm he gently shook her, but she didn't wake up. Scooping her into his arms, he placed her on the bed, panic setting in.

He raced down the hall to Jackie's room and knocked. He thanked God that Jackie's apartment was being repainted, so she'd moved in for a week or two.

She finally poked her head out and gasped in shock. Tom was naked. "Something's wrong with Kendra, she's fainted and burning up," he stated fiercely, not concerned at all by his state of undress.

Jackie hurriedly followed him back to the bedroom. She went straight to Kendra and tried to revive her, but Kendra wouldn't stir.

"Should I call an ambulance?" Tom's heart was thundering in his chest.

But Jackie had already picked up his phone and was dialing 911. Tom paced across the bedroom floor.

"Please put some clothes on," said Jackie grimly. "You must let paramedics in and accompany her to the hospital. I'll stay here with Connor."

Tom nodded and dressed.

It seemed like hours but was merely 15 minutes before the responders arrived. They asked him questions, but he barely remembered answering them before they loaded her in the ambulance and he clambered inside with Kendra.

They were halfway to the hospital when he suddenly knew he had to make a call. He pressed Marcus's number. "Pick up. Pick up for once in your sorry life—"

"It's five in the fuckin' morning, this better be good," came a muffled curse over the phone.

"I know you're out of town but something's wrong with Kendra. We're on the way to UCLA Medical Center."

"I didn't go—last-minute thing. I'm on my way!" and the phone went dead.

Tom sat there, not knowing what to do. Helplessness swamped him. He remembered the last time he'd felt like this. It was when they pulled Marcus's lifeless body from his mangled car.

And that incident had turned out fine in the end. He remembered to breathe.

Tom watched Kendra's face for signs of her waking, but all he heard was the monitor and the noise of beeping.

At least that meant she was alive.

Chapter Twenty

Tom hated the smell of hospitals. The antiseptic scent filled his nostrils, and he choked on the sterile odor. Or was it his own fear he was choking on?

He paced impatiently up and down the waiting room. It had been almost two hours and if someone didn't tell him something soon, he would lose his shit.... He blew out another long breath. No one would tell him anything. Not since Marcus had arrived. Tom wasn't a relative or Kendra's husband, so they excluded him, even though he loved Kendra more than life itself.

How ironic that his father was in this very hospital. He was supposed to meet with the transplant team today to go over his results. He hadn't noticed the smell nearly as much when he'd visited his father. But then he didn't have so much at stake.

Suddenly the doors to the ward opened and Marcus appeared. He looked like he'd been hit by a car.

"How is she?"

Marcus scrubbed a hand over his face. "They've rehydrated her and she's awake, but they're keeping her in for tests. Her temperature is still up."

"Do they have any idea what's wrong with her?"

Marcus shook his head, "It could simply be a virus, or flu.

They don't know, but because of her medical history they are doing tests to be sure."

"Can I see her?" asked Tom as he made to walk round him, but Marcus grabbed his arm.

"She doesn't want to see you."

Tom shook off Marcus's hand. "You're just saying that to keep us apart, but I'm not leaving her. I love her. Get out of my way." He didn't even notice he was yelling.

Marcus's eyes filled with tears. "I know you do. I know about Connor. She just told me you're his father. I'd like to beat the shit out of you but now is not the time."

"So let me pass."

"She doesn't want to see you. I'm so sorry, but once she gets something in her head… you know how stubborn she is."

"What are you trying to say?"

Marcus sighed, looking over Tom's shoulder. "Go home. Be with Connor. He will wonder where his mother is and he could get scared. He needs his father."

Tom couldn't believe this. Fear weaved through his cells. Marcus wasn't even mad about Connor. What was really wrong with Kendra? "Why? Why is she pushing me away?"

He watched Marcus swallow hard. "She's got this fool idea in her head that her cancer is back and she doesn't want to drag you through that—"

"Bullshit. That's not her decision to make. What? Does she think I'll leave her if the going gets rough? If her cancer is back, we'll fight it together. I want to be there fighting for her all the way."

Marcus glared and drew Tom away towards the exit. "It's not you she's protecting. It's herself. Can't you see? When she battled before, she didn't have you or Connor to lose. Both of you are her world. She's scared she'll lose this next battle, if there is one, and it will be worse with you there because she knows what she's leaving behind. If she pushes you both away, she thinks it will be easier for her to face her own mortality."

"What about Connor? He'll need to see her. We both need her."

"She doesn't want him here either. She doesn't want her son to remember her sick. She wants you to take care of him." Tom's mouth dropped open. She didn't want her son… "Go home, Tom. Go be with your son. He needs you now."

Tom brushed the tears off his face. "I'll be back. I'll keep coming back until she sees me. Until she realizes I'm not leaving her alone. And I'll have Connor with me."

Marcus nodded. "Good. You fight for her. She needs you to make her fight too, if it is cancer. It may not be, but of course she's thinking the worst. Especially as a friend's cancer returned recently and it's now terminal."

At the word terminal, Tom's blood turned icy in his veins. He smelled his own fear, but nothing would scare him away from her this time. It wasn't like his mother. His mum chose to leave him. With cancer, no one had a choice. A cold malady seeped through him, and he suddenly wanted to be home holding Connor tight. He couldn't lose Kendra, not now. "All those bloody wasted years," he said. "I should have opened her emails."

Marcus hugged him before stepping back. "I can't believe I got it so wrong. All this time I worried you'd break her heart. I never for one minute imagined she'd break yours." With that, he turned and walked back through the doors towards his sister and left Tom standing there like a helpless dick.

Yes, getting home to Connor was what he needed. But he'd be back. There was no way Tom would allow her to push him away. He looked at his watch. He had just enough time to get home, see Connor and shower, check on Jackie, before he had to be back here for his test results.

   * * *

"Thought I'd find you here."

Tom closed his eyes in dismay. "Fuck."

"Well, I was about to when Marcus called me."

With a groan, Tom lifted his head from where it lay on the bar top and watched Sully light up a cigarette. "Marcus?"

Sully took a long drag and turned away to exhale. "Yeah. He called me and told me about Kendra. Gosh, who'd have thought she'd get sick just to escape your sorry ass."

Normally, a crack like that would've made Tom laugh, but not tonight. He'd tried to see Kendra when he came out of his meeting with the transplant team, but she still refused to see him. Stella was there, of course, and she told him that Kendra's fever was still up and more tests were being run. The doctors just wanted to be thorough. Stella agreed she'd try to get Kendra to see him tonight.

"She will be fine. I know it."

Sully nodded. "Of course she is, so what's got you sitting at this bar?"

"I was a match for Dad."

Sully frowned and looked around the little hole-in-the-wall dive known as Pitstop. "Isn't that a good thing?"

"It would be, but the doctor said that Dad won't survive the surgery. I'm too late, Sully. Why didn't I listen to Sam?"

Sully sighed. "Because you're pigheaded, just like most men. Me included. Listen, you can't beat yourself up about this. No one told your old man to drink himself to death. The same goes for me. I lost my family to the bottle because I thought I was handling my drinking just fine. Same as your dad, and same as you."

Sully paused before saying, "The difference is that you were smart enough to quit earlier than a lot of alcoholics." He eyed the money Tom had out, sitting on the bar. "What's picking up that bottle again, going to solve Tommy? Huh? Is it going to change your dad's condition?"

Tom rubbed his eyes. "No."

"Will it help Kendra or make this easier to get through?"

"No."

"Right. Will it screw things up with Kendra and your boy?"

"Yes." Tom sat straighter and stared wide-eyed at Sully. "Did Marcus tell you about Connor?"

Sully exhaled and laughed. "I can't believe how stupid everyone else around the shop is. I mean that in a nice way, of course. How did Marcus not see it every time he looked at Connor? The boy is you out-and-out. He has Kendra's hair color and nose, but that's about it. How come you've told no one?"

"We were going to this weekend when we had you all over, but then Kendra got sick."

"How is she?"

"I only know what Stella told me today. She still has a temp and they don't know what it is. Kendra thinks her cancer is back." Tom looked at the bottles that lined the wall behind the bar and fought back the thirst that had never been quenchable. Hard liquor had always been his weakness. "What if it is? And to top it all off, she's pushing me away. I don't deserve that."

Sully snorted. "She's scared. I've never seen her so happy, so I bet this is hard for her to face. To have such happiness and then maybe she's going to lose it…"

"But I'm right here now," Tom said. "I love her and I want to be with her. What if her cancer is back and she only has a short time left? I want to spend every moment with her even if I lose her."

Sully smiled. "Have you told her that?"

"She won't let me."

"Let me give you some advice."

Tom was curious about Sully's conspiratorial attitude and leaned closer.

Sully asked, "You know what?"

"What?"

Sully motioned him even closer and Tom complied.

"*DON'T FUCKIN TAKE NO FOR AN ANSWER! BARGE IN THERE.*"

Tom recoiled and almost fell off his barstool. His ears rang as he stared at Sully.

Sully pointed at him. "If you love her fight for her. No one said love was easy. If it was, we'd all be loved up. All I know is that when you find that special someone you let nothing push or pull you apart. She loves you so much. She's hurting and she's scared. So go to her. Find a way. Make her listen and understand you'll be there when things get scary. She doesn't have to do everything on her own anymore."

Tom slid back on the stool but didn't get too close to Sully in case he started yelling again. He was right. Since her scare with cancer, Kendra always believed she had to do everything on her own. She'd protected him and Marcus by not revealing Connor's father, and she'd refused to bow to her parent's pressure. She'd done it all on her own.

Well, she wasn't on her own now.

"Now, about your dad. That's a bitch and a half, but it ain't your fault, son."

Tom shook his head. "I should've listened to Sam and reconciled with Dad as soon as I found out he was sick. Dad tried, but I wouldn't listen and meet him half way."

Sully grunted. "Hindsight is a bitch. Can't blame yourself, just like I don't blame my kids for not believing me. Josh and Lindsey are starting to trust me more, but not Will. He's old enough to remember the worst of it. Just like you. It was easier for Sam to forgive your dad because he didn't go through the stuff you did. You had every reason to not believe that Vincent had changed. He told you he would, but never did."

Tom shrugged. "Then how come I feel so guilty? I could've saved him, Sully."

"Coulda, woulda, shoulda. You'll drive yourself crazy with that. Maybe your dad didn't want to ask you to be tested because *he* felt too guilty. None of that matters now, Tom. What matters is how you spend the time you have left with Vincent? Are you going to sit around whining or are you going to make the most of it?"

Tom said nothing as he looked at all the booze just mere feet from him. Thinking about Kendra and Connor, Tom knew that if he was to have any chance at lasting happiness, he had to resist temptation. One drink would lead to two, and two would lead to five, and so on. Their faces rose in Tom's mind and he couldn't, wouldn't put them through the same hell he'd endured as a kid. Kendra would then have the excuse she needed to push him away. He wouldn't make that easy for her.

Grim determination took hold of him, and he looked at his friend. "Sully, I've made up my mind."

Sully arched an eyebrow. "Oh? What are you going to do?"

Tom got off the stool and stood tall. "I will go see my woman and look out anyone who stands in my way."

"Attaboy!" Sully clapped his shoulder. "Let's get out of here."

Chapter Twenty-One

Tom marched into the hospital ward with a look that dared anyone to stop him. He rode the elevator to Kendra's ward and stepped out onto the main floor, ready for a fight. But no one was around. He looked down the corridor towards Kendra's room, but there was no Stella or Marcus standing guard. Perhaps they were in her room? As he walked forward, his mouth dried. But he was not leaving here until he told her how much he loved her. He looked through the little glass window in her door and all he saw was Kendra in bed, so he took a deep breath and entered.

She swung towards him, and for a split second he saw the flare of want and need in her eyes before she tried to hide it. "I told Marcus I didn't want to see you."

"Hello to you too, my darling." And he walked to the bed, took her face in his hands and gently kissed her. She tried to pull back, but it was a very halfhearted effort. "How are you feeling?" He looked her over and she definitely had more color in her cheeks. He felt her forehead and it was cool. "Because if you say you're feeling better, I just might put you over my knee and spank you for trying to push me away."

"I'm doing what I think is best—for all of us." But her voice trembled.

He sighed and stepped away from the bed. "No, you're not. Your running scared. Believe me. I know because I ran from you four years ago. Too scared to let anyone close in case they left me again. I couldn't believe a woman like you could really want a man like me."

She lay back and closed her eyes. "I don't... I don't want you. I don't want you here either, and I don't want you in my life. This was all a big mistake. I have already instructed my lawyers to set up a visitation and maintenance schedule. Now please leave me alone."

He stood looking down at her, but she refused to open those lovely eyes and look at him. "So that's it? At the first hurdle you give up on us? You might have given up but I haven't."

Her eyes flashed open and speared him with anger. "You have no right to preach to me. You who ignored me for four years and only decided I was worth consideration when you learned about Connor. Well, you can have access to your son, but I've decided you and I are wrong for each other. So understand that."

"Oh, I understand all right. I'm not going to sugarcoat it. I'm pissed as hell at you. I had to prove to you I committed to this relationship, I'm here and I am, but at the first chicane you blew out. Abandoned the race. Let us run out of fuel—"

"Enough with the racing metaphors. This is real life." She thumped her chest. "I can't count on anyone but me. This is—"

"Scary? Terrible? Frightening beyond measure?" Her beautiful eyes filled with tears, but he pushed on. He had to. He had to make her understand. He took her hand and drew it to his lips. He pressed a kiss to her palm. "But it's not so frightening when I'm holding your hand in mine."

A tear tracked down her cheek. "It is for me because... because if I'm really sick again... I don't want you to see me that way. Besides, with you by my side I'll fight, and I'll fight hard, but this time if I lose... I lose too much. Better to fight on my own. When death comes calling, you're on your own. No one else can help you. Besides, you've lost so much already, you'd end up hating me. Find someone else to love."

"It's a little too late because I love you, so there goes that argument. And I'd never hate you. I might be pissed at you, at God, at life, but I'd love you for the rest of my life. If, heaven forbid, you lost the battle, I would know that it wasn't your choice. I'd never blame you for that. What I blame you for is pushing me away without a fight. You aren't fighting for us —for me."

She said nothing.

Tom wasn't letting her off easy. "Right from the start, you worried I wouldn't stay the course. You wanted me to prove that I was in this relationship for real. That you meant as much to me as Connor. Well, this is real and I'm here. It's you who's bailed."

Like a knife being shoved in his chest, she leaned over and pressed the buzzer for the nurse. "Just go. I'm so tired. It's over."

"You don't mean it. You love me as much as I love you."

She turned to him and almost snarled. "I don't have the energy to love you. Right now you're just an added complication that I don't need."

Tom's sympathy was diminishing like an ice cube melting away. "So that's it? You've given up on us? I thought you were a fighter."

Before he could make her answer, the door opened. A nurse entered, "Everything all right in here?"

"Mr. Lorde was just leaving."

Tom gripped the railing of Kendra's bed so tight he thought his knuckles would crack. He stood staring at the woman who held his heart in her hands and fear seeped in. She wouldn't look at him. He tried to imagine what thoughts must run through her head. The thought of her cancer being back was Kendra's kryptonite. She would immediately worry about Connor and what this would do to him. Kendra not wanting to see her son—that scared him the most. It was as if she'd given up.

Obviously, she was in self-preservation mode. To finally be this happy and then have it ripped away would be unthinkable to him—losing Kendra was unthinkable to him—he could understand why she was reacting this way. Fear made people into strangers. But he couldn't live his life scared that bad things would happen. He couldn't go through the pain of being rejected again and again.

"I'll leave. For now. But unlike you, I'm not giving up." He brushed a tear from her cheek with his thumb. "This might not be cancer so don't ruin something wonderful for nothing. If you can't let me be a part of everything in your life, the good, the bad, the heartbreaking, then I can't be part of only the good times, because I'll be sitting waiting, every day, for you to decide to push me away again. My heart can't take that."

That made her look at him. But instead of saying 'yes, I'm being silly. I need you…' she merely nodded.

He tried to leave, but he couldn't pry his fingers off the bed rail. He wanted to get down on his knees and beg her to fight for them, but he knew it wouldn't do any good. She had to come to that conclusion herself.

He would wait. He would pray her cancer wasn't back and he would pray she was strong enough to let him into her life—all of it.

He finally backed away from the bed as the nurse cleared her throat. He had to tell her. "In case you're interested, I am a match for my father, but he's not strong enough to have the operation. I don't know how long he has, so I'm taking Connor to see him."

This time her head snapped up and her eyes welled and he thought he saw her hand move toward him. "I'm so sorry, Tom."

He nodded. "So am I." Then he turned and left before he started yelling and screaming at her to think about what she was doing. He bumped into Stella as he stepped into the corridor.

Her face broke into a huge grin. "She let you visit with her.

That's…" Her words petered out as he shook his head. "Shit. I'm sorry. Just give her time. She's so scared."

"And I'm not? I love her. I've finally found her and Connor."

Stella placed her hand on his arm. "Imagine what it's like for her then. She's the one that could die. She is brave enough to face this if she only has herself to worry about. But she knows what it will do to you and Connor to have to watch. And she's decided she'd rather lose you now than later. Stupid, I know, but I can kind of understand. She finally thought she had it all, and now it's being taken from her."

"Can't you talk to her. Make her see I want to be with her."

Stella simply shook her head. "One thing our Kendra is, is stubborn. Once she's made up her mind—how do you think she beat cancer last time? She stubbornly refused to die." She looked at Tom and added, "If her cancer is back, and pushing you away is what Kendra needs to do to beat it again, I'll support her decision. I may not like it, but it's not about you and I right now. It's about supporting what Kendra needs."

Tom's anger drained away. Stella was right. This was about Kendra and what she needed. But deep inside a wall was building. It was obvious Kendra didn't need him like he needed her. How could he marry her when she wasn't in this relationship 100%? Would she bail again when things got tough?

"I'll be back tomorrow morning. I'm bringing Connor to see my father. I'll try and see if she'll see Connor and me then."

Stella hugged him tightly. "You know you're not such a bad guy. Just give her some space and time."

Tom nodded and as he walked away all he could think about was what would happen if Kendra continually wanted space and time. And time ran out…

* * *

Kendra ignored the tears that rolled down her face as Tom left without looking back. She was doing the right thing. All he really wanted was Connor, anyway. He'd not once thought about her until he learned he was Connor's father. She just couldn't let herself believe that there was more to his wanting to be in her life, because he'd not been in touch for over four years. He'd not even read her emails.

She didn't want him around should this turn out to be her cancer returning. She didn't want him staying around out of some kind of guilt or duty just because they were Connor's parents. Besides, she couldn't bear to have him see her sick. He was the only person who'd never treated her like brittle glass. He was the only one who had told her to chase her dreams and not let anyone tell her she couldn't do it. But that was because he was one of the few people in her life who had not seen her when she'd been fighting cancer. He did not understand what was to come.

He'd not seen her when she couldn't keep any food down. Or when she lost all her hair. Or when her mouth and hands had blistered so badly, she couldn't use her hands.

The thought of him seeing her go through that when he might not really love her… He would see her differently, treat her differently, maybe want to leave her—what they shared would be different. If Tom started treating her like Marcus did— well, she couldn't bear it.

"Wipe those tears, super K, because they are self-inflicted."

She automatically did as Stella said. Super K had been her nickname when Stella had held her hand the last time she'd faced cancer.

"Why are you pushing the man you love with all your heart, away?" She said nothing, so Stella added, "I know why. You're scared. You're scared the cancer is back and you are protecting everyone, including yourself."

"He doesn't know what it will be like, but I do. What if it's too much for him? What if he doesn't love me enough?" There, it was out. She didn't trust him to hang around, and if he left when she needed him most—it would kill her. He'd left before and never looked back. Only learning about Connor saw him come knocking on her door.

Stella sat on the end of the bed and sighed. "He loves you."

She shook her head and wiped away the tears. "Does he? I know he desires me, has fun with me, but Connor is the real reason he's with me. I'm not sure that's enough."

"Don't be ridiculous. It's not the fifties where men step up and do the right thing. He doesn't have to be with you to be in Connor's life."

"He told me right at the beginning we should marry to make a family for Connor. That had nothing to do with how he felt for me."

"Keep telling yourself that lie. The man's in love with you, and you know it. I suspect he always has been, but friendship, Marcus, the racing circuit, and plain fear kept you apart. He only needed Connor to remind him of who and what was important. He didn't need to marry you, to make a family. Both of you are lying to yourselves if you believe that. He wanted to marry you. I suspect you've always been 'the one'."

Pain lanced her chest. Stella knew her too well.

"So, come on special K. Don't shove those who really love you away."

She burst out crying. "I'm so consumed with the fear of losing him and Connor this time round, that I can't focus on the fight."

Stella pulled her into her arms and they sat on the bed rocking each other and crying. Finally, Stella pushed Kendra back. "Look at us two. Crying and we don't even know if it's cancer yet."

Kendra blew her nose on a tissue and suddenly the weight on her shoulder's seemed less heavy. "You don't think if I have to fight cancer again that it will chase Tom away then? Do you think he'll look at me differently?"

"Probably. I did." Stella rushed on at Kendra's frown. "You were different after the cancer. You were stronger, more confident, and you grabbed at life. Maybe it was you simply getting older, but I think everything we face in life changes us in some way. Look at Tom coming into your life. I've never seen you happier, yet you've let Tom guide you and help you. Miss. independent is changing, and that fills me with hope and joy. Life is lonely without the odd helping hand."

"Kettle—pot—black. When did you ever need a man for anything but pleasure?"

Kendra watched her friend's face and her smile faded away. "Like I said. It's lonely sometimes. I envy you Tom."

They sat in silence until the nurse arrived to check her vitals once again. Once the nurse left, Stella said, "Tom's bringing Connor this evening to see his father. Please think about seeing them both. Connor won't notice a thing, you look fine."

Just then the door opened and the doctors and residents walked in. Dr. Spencer was smiling, so Kendra took that as a good sign.

"Miss. Black, can we chat if you have a moment?"

Kendra looked at Stella who promptly reached for her hand and said, "I'm staying."

Dr. Spencer merely nodded. "We have run an exhausted set of tests and it's relatively good news. You have infectious mononucleosis commonly known as mono, 'the kissing disease'."

Kendra swallowed hard and squeezed Stella's hand. "So, no cancer?"

"No. You made the right decision to come in for tests given your history, and the symptoms are similar. Fatigue, fever, nausea. But we cannot find any signs of cancer at all. You just need to go home and get plenty of rest and drink lots of fluids. Your spleen is slightly enlarged so no physical activity, and we'll check you again in a few weeks."

She wanted to burst into hysterical laughter or song. The relief dancing through her body could have powered a city. She wasn't terminal. She didn't have cancer.

She wanted Tom.

Even though she was bursting with joy, she calmly said to the team of doctors standing in her room, "Thank you. You say it's infectious. I have a three-year-old boy."

"What I suggest is you keep your distance, no hugging or kissing. Keep a separate set of cooking and eating utensils and a separate bathroom if that is possible." She nodded that it was. "You'll be infectious for about another two weeks but you may feel fatigue for a few months so you must have no stress and rest."

She'd kissed Tom a few hours ago. Shit. And Tom was with Connor. She better ring him. Taking the coward's way out she asked Stella, "Can you ring Tom and let him know. I kissed him this morning or he kissed me. Either way, we both have to be careful around Connor."

"You ring him," and Stella promptly broke down in tears. "I am just so happy. I was so scared."

Kendra laughed. "You hid it well."

"One of us had to stay strong and you were falling apart." Stella pulled out her phone. "Call Tom. I'll call Marcus and let him know." She slipped off the bed. "I'll call from the corridor and give you some privacy. I suspect you'll need to do some heavy duty groveling. Do you want me to call your parents?"

"I don't think they know I'm sick."

"Marcus rang them."

"And they didn't visit me?" Hurt replaced her joy for one brief moment. "It's their loss. Let Marcus tell them. I don't care." But she did. Why couldn't her parents love her the way she was —faults and all? They really didn't care about her or Connor. She had a long memory and her parents were slipping out of her life for good.

As the door clicked shut behind Stella, Kendra stared at the phone in hand and didn't know how she would tell Tom. How did she make a man who feared nothing understand how afraid she'd been? Would he be angry at her? She hadn't trusted him. He'd been right, she had overreacted, pushing him away because her life suddenly seemed to be spinning out of control and she liked being in control. When she'd been diagnosed with cancer in her teens, she'd lost the ability to control what happened to her. Unless you'd been in a similar situation, you could not understand what that was like.

She pressed his name on her phone as she tried not to chew her lip off while she waited for him to answer. But he didn't answer and it went to voice mail. Relief escaped on a whoosh of breath. For a second she debated not leaving a message, but he'd want to know.

"Hi, Tom. It's me—Kendra. The doctors cleared me to go home. I have mono, the kissing disease. So don't kiss Connor, let Jackie look after him, and if you start to feel unwell… you can blame me. Anyway… Stella is taking me home soon."

She hung up and tears welled. What she wanted to say was she was sorry. But just because she was well didn't mean she suddenly trusted him. This whole thing made her realize she still had issues with the past. This was all happening too soon. It wasn't fair on Tom that she had trust issues. This was her problem and she had to have some space to see if she could get over the fact he only came back into her life because of Connor. Things were moving far too fast and having lost her heart to him once before she was petrified he only wanted her because of Connor. That would never be enough for her.

Did he even know his heart? Was he simply confused about how he felt for her? He loved Connor that was not in doubt but he couldn't have Connor as a family without her.

She changed into her clothes, happy to shed the hospital gown. She hoped she'd never wear one again. She'd just slipped on her brogues when Stella waltzed back in all smiles. "Marcus is over the moon. He said he'd come around to your house tonight to see how you are. What did Tom say?"

"He didn't answer his phone, so I left a message."

"Chicken."

She ignored the truth. "Before we leave, I'd like to visit Tom's father if that's all right?"

Stella nodded. "We just have to wait for your release papers."

* * *

Kendra stood outside the glass window of room 5675. She took in the frail and yellow tinged man lying in the bed, and she could barely see any resemblance to Tom, except perhaps the shape of his eyes.

Her mind couldn't comprehend that this sickly man used to beat his son and make his life a living hell. It was hard to feel any empathy for a man who wasted his life. A man who couldn't love his son enough and a man who left his son in jail. A father who did nothing to shape the wonderful man Tom had become. Why should she bother with him?

With a start, she noted Vince's eyes were open and staring at her. He gave her a tentative smile and she smiled back. He raised a shaking hand and beckoned her into his room. She didn't have the heart to turn away. She turned to a nurse. "Is it all right if I go in? I won't touch him."

"No physical contact and you should be fine."

He motioned her to take the chair by his bed. "I know who you are. I bet you're Tom's girl, Kendra. Connor looks like you and my son."

She nodded. Vince said the words so proudly.

He looked her over. "My Tommie has taste. You're a beautiful woman." He kept staring. "My son said you might have cancer again. He's so scared. You'll have to be brave for him too."

"I don't have cancer I have mono."

Vince's smile could have lit up the whole city. "Tom will be pleased. I couldn't bear to see my son have to deal with my death and yours. Not when he's finally realized how much he loves you."

She looked away and swallowed hard. "He's pissed at me."

"Yeah. He's hurt you didn't want him to be with you. I bet you feel stupid now? You pushed him away for nothing."

Why did the truth always hurt? She looked at Tom's father, and with clarity she wondered if they were alike. They both tried to deal with life and loss their own way. His in a bottle, her by pushing those who cared about her away. "You wouldn't understand." Or would he?

He laughed. Not really a laugh, but the crackling sound of someone who couldn't get enough air. Someone who was dying. "You thought you were dying. I *am* dying." He took a few deep breaths. "Our fears and regrets are private, aren't they? He would have stood with you, fought with you, but I think you know that? I would give anything to have him by my side every minute of the day before I die, so I can tell him how sorry I am for being a terrible father. At least I showed him how to be a better father. He'll never treat Connor the way I treated him."

"People look at you differently when you've been sick. And if I didn't make it, I didn't want him to remember me sick. I didn't want him to fall in love with me and lose me."

"Bullshit. He already loves you." He silently assessed her. "But you don't believe him. Can't see that I blame you, I'm not sure Tom's forgiven me deep down inside. But you hurt him pushing him away like that. You were protecting yourself, but he'll forgive you. I'll tell you something. My son doesn't lie. He never says anything he doesn't mean—good or bad. So if he says he loves you, he bloody well does."

She looked at Tom's father, and the coldness in her heart eased. "Then why did he wait until he learned about Connor to come for me?"

"He is loyal to your brother, that's true, but he also knew you were already struggling with a little boy on your own. He didn't know he was the father. Did you ever stop to think he didn't believe he was good enough to be in your life? That he might think you didn't want him. After all, you had a son with another man—or so he thought. A man whose identity you protected from everyone. He might have thought you loved someone else."

Oh, my, God. She hadn't considered that. "I've made a total mess of everything. Will he forgive me?"

"He's forgiven me a lot worse. He has such a big heart, my son. I don't know where he got it from, not his mother, and certainly not from me. He'll need you more than ever now because he feels guilty about it being too late for me. I blame no one but myself."

Kendra wanted to cry, but not in front of Vince. She'd taken Tom's love and callously chucked it away. She'd walked away like his mother, and his father—when it had taken Tom so long to take a risk and love someone. She hoped he was more forgiving with her than he'd been with his father. "If there is anything I can do for you, just let me know."

He reached for her hand and gave it a squeeze. "Thank you. I want to talk to Tom about taking me home to his place to die, since I know longer have a house. The hospital says I can go if the place is clean, warm, and I have someone to look after me, but I know Tom is busy at work and—"

—"Would you like to come home with me? I would never want to die in a hospital. I would like to be at home. Between Jackie, Connor's nanny, Tom, and me, I'm sure we'd cope and we can hire a nurse too." When she saw a tear form in Vince's eye, she smiled. "Connor would love to get to know his grandad."

"My son picked well. Thank you, that's most kind, but best we check with Tom first. I don't want to cause any more friction between you two. I'll ask him when he visits later."

That didn't bode well. Obviously, Vince thought Tom would hold on to his anger. Not that she blamed him. Kendra stood and moved to the trolley by Vince's bed. She saw a pad and pen, so she wrote her phone number on it. "Ring me and I'll organize everything."

He nodded and closed his eyes as if the conversation had taken all his energy. She stood staring, wishing she could kiss him but best not given her diagnosis. His eyes flickered open. "Don't let Tom use your fear to put those walls back up around his heart."

"I promise I'll try really hard."

"You remind him you gave him a second chance so you deserve one too."

"You're right. I did give him a second chance. Thanks, Vince, I'll see you soon."

She didn't look back as she made her way to where Stella waited outside the room. She didn't know if she wanted a second chance. When she'd been lying in the hospital bed thinking about her life and if she had cancer again, the one thing that became really clear was she didn't trust in Tom's love. She didn't want a relationship with him until she could fully trust him. It wasn't fair on Tom.

His father might think Tom loved her. Maybe he did. But until *she* was sure, things needed to slow down. Since he'd come back into her life, everything had changed. The new house, the nanny, the money he gave her… She struggled with the past. Struggled with the idea that he could suddenly love her when he didn't before. Why had he never contacted her before he knew about Connor? If she was that important to him, why did he barely even know she existed.

That's why she'd pushed him away. She was scared that he could not handle her illness and it would all be too much. He would take Connor and run, because if she died he'd have everything he wanted. He'd have Connor and not be stuck with her. She *was* in self-preservation mode. If he ever left her again… Her heart would be destroyed forever.

This would all end in disaster if she could not put the past behind her. She needed to forgive him for not being there when Connor was born, and she wasn't sure she had. Fear was an insidious evil. She needed to conquer her fear before she destroyed everything.

Chapter Twenty-Two

Tom played the voice message over and over as he drove to Marcus's house. When he'd first played her message and learned she didn't have cancer, he'd collapsed on the living room floor and thanked the lord.

Kendra had mono. She'd live, except if he bloody killed her for being such an ass. She didn't have cancer, and the fear gnawing at his stomach like a jackal over the past few days, eased. He'd buried his fear for Connor's sake, but now the weight of holding everyone together—his father, Sam, Kendra and Connor—the damn burst. He felt tears fall down his cheeks. He wouldn't lose her to the dreaded C, but then he wondered if he'd really ever had her. She didn't trust in his love. Or was it she didn't need him like he needed her? Did she even love him? Had his abandonment cost him the love of his life forever?

You're being unfair. He knew it, but self-preservation was kicking in. How could he expect her to love him the way he loved her, when he'd ignored her for four years? It wasn't fair to her. Would she ever forgive him and love him enough? Was he foolish to want to force her into being a family, when, if Connor wasn't in the picture, she'd probably never want anything to do with him again?

Shit, this love stuff hurt. But he already knew that. A mother who didn't want him. A father who preferred a bottle of Jack Daniels to him, and then to hear Kendra might have her cancer back only to watch as Kendra decided she didn't need him either…

He wondered if love was worth it. No wonder he had always walked away from relationships. Should love be this hard? He'd done everything to convince Kendra he loved her and not just Connor. He'd thought she loved him too, but she didn't love him enough or else she wouldn't have pushed him away.

The messaged played again. Where was the sorry for being a jerk? Where was the invitation to rush round to see her?

His father didn't have much time left, and he needed space to get his head on straight. Could he risk this pain again? He needed to give Kendra time to really think about what she wanted in her life. Did she want him to be a part of it or not? Not just the good times, but every day, the good and the bad. He could not leave his heart in her hands if she could so callously remove him from her life as if he didn't matter.

He pulled into the parking garage at Marcus's apartment complex. He was here to tell his business partner that he would take some time off. Vince wanted his ashes taken and scattered somewhere in the world that was exotic, since he'd never gotten to travel anywhere in his sorry life.

They had settled on the Australian outback. Vince thought the harsh, dangerous beauty suited him.

Marcus answered the door on the first knock, a huge smile on his face and a beer in his hand. He pulled Tom in for a man hug. "Bloody happy day, T. Kendra told me she left you a message. She's fine. She's not ill. Come celebrate."

Tom pushed out of his hold and pushed past him into the living room and said, "Yeah, I knew she'd be all right. She's one tough lady."

Marcus handed him a coke. "What are you going to do, to

celebrate? I could watch Connor so Jackie can have a night off too, since she's been looking after Connor full time."

He glugged down half the bottle; the bubbles making his nerves fizz. He held in a belch. "She hasn't said she wants to see me. I simply got a message telling me she's okay."

"Don't be a dick. Of course she wants to see you. You were the first person she called. I got told by Stella."

His bandaged heart liked that news. "She'll ring me when she's ready to talk." At Marcus's frown he added, "I came to ask if you could spare me for a few weeks. Vince has asked me to take his ashes to Australia when he passes. It's the one place he always wanted to go. I'd like to do that for him. Sam and the family might come too, and we might take a bit of a vacation around the world, head over to NZ and Asia."

"Shit, I'm an arsehole. I forgot about your father. I'm so sorry, man."

He shrugged. "I'm not too cut up about it. I've never been close to him but the last few days seeing him with Connor… I'm so lucky I got off the booze. If not for the booze, Vince might have been a half decent dad."

Marcus ran a hand through his hair. "Listen, I know I gave you shit about Kendra, but I was wrong. If I had known the two of you had such strong feelings—well, I'm sorry that my stupidity cost you the first few years with your son."

Tom simply sighed. "Regrets a terrible thing, isn't it? But it's not your fault. It was mine. I should have read the emails, but I ran scared. I didn't believe a woman like her, beautiful, kind, clever, and from such a wealthy family, could love a man like me —a grease monkey. I used 'not damaging our friendship' as a shield to protect myself. We could've been together all this time. I could've seen my son born, Marcus. Do you know how much it hurts that I wasn't there for any of that?"

"I didn't help. I guess I was a bit overprotective."

That made Tom laugh. "A bit?" Tom said. "I should've opened the emails and she should've told you, so you could've told me. I missed watching Connor grow inside her, I missed the first time he walked, and his first word. But most of all, I missed the joy of loving Kendra all these years. Of having a wonderful woman by my side. I can't get them back and if she'd had cancer again—all of it was too much to lose."

"Train."

Tom's forehead wrinkled in confusion. "What?"

Marcus twisted the cap off another beer. "Connor's first word was 'train'."

"Train?" Tom smiled.

Marcus nodded. "Yeah. From the first time he saw that movie, *Thomas the Tank Engine*, he was hooked. I don't know how many damn times I watched it with him during the off season. I can practically recite it word for word."

The image of Marcus watching the kids' movie over and over made Tom laugh. "I can just see that. Must be hell knowing that he likes trains instead of cars."

Marcus grinned. "One of these days, he'll like cars. You'll help me with that."

Tom's smile faded as he thought of all he'd miss if he was merely a part-time dad.

Not bothering to hide his pain, Tom asked, "Do you think we have a chance if we marry? Do you think she'll ever let me into her life? I'm scared she'll push me away again. Maybe we'd be better as friends who share a wonderful little boy. I never want to end up in a situation where she hates me."

Marcus sighed. "She'd never hate you. She's loved you all her adult life."

"Then she doesn't trust I love her. Why else would she push me away? I can understand why she feels like that. I wasn't there for her and now she thinks I'm only here because of Connor. I'd want her even if there was no Connor. It took Connor to make me realize how unhappy I've been living my life all alone, when I really wanted her."

"You're telling the wrong person. Go to her and make her believe in you."

"Got any great idea on how I do that? You can't make someone trust in your love. They have to have faith in you."

Marcus didn't have any answers. Tom stood. "Can I have the time off once Vince is gone?"

Marcus nodded. "Go and talk to her."

He shook his head. "I'm not the one who walked away. If she really wants me, she'll come find me. I need her to trust in what I feel for her, or it will never work. I don't know what more I can do to make her see I'm a man madly in love with her."

Marcus stood too. "I have faith that you two will work it out, but even if you don't, I'll still have your back and I hope you'll have mine."

They hugged again, both embarrassed by the emotions storming between them.

"Let me know about Vince. I want to come to his funeral. Not for him, for you," Marcus said.

* * *

Tom threw his keys on the side table just inside the door. Stella's car was parked across the road outside Kendra's place, so she must have come home. He had to fight to stop himself from rushing over there, but she had to come to him this time. He had to know she would fight for them.

He moved toward the living room and he scented her fragrance before he saw her. She was sitting on his sofa and she looked so beautiful. The look of despair was gone from her eyes, but they were still shadowed. He hated to think he might be the cause.

He moved towards her and she stood. "No kissing, I have mono. I don't want to make you sick."

He was already sick, love sick. "You should be home resting." His words sounded stilted and a tad gruff.

She bit her top lip and it sent a jolt to his groin. He wanted her so badly. "I'm here to ask if I can stay here and you stay across the road with Connor until I get better. I don't want you, Jackie or Connor to get this. Would you mind?"

"Of course not. I knew it would come in handy living across from each other." He stood waiting for her to say something about how she'd acted in hospital, but she simply kept looking at him. "Can I get you a drink?"

She shook her head. Tom nodded and he too stood there, as mute as a statue. How had it come to this? After everything they'd shared over the last few weeks it felt like they were polite strangers, not hot lovers.

She didn't move from the sofa where she sat rigidly, and said, "Stella's packing some things for me so if you could move across to my place tonight, I can move in here."

Simmering anger reached the boiling point. "What the fuck is going on here, Kendra? Don't treat me as if I'm just one of the mechanics at Bad Boy Autos."

Startled, she flopped back onto the sofa.

"We're lovers. We were talking of building a life together, and now it's a polite conversation about babysitting arrangements. You owe me more than that. At least an apology for being an ass at the hospital."

"I am sorry."

"Sorry for what? For pushing me away or for starting a relationship with me?"

"Both, I suppose."

"Great. Just what I wanted to hear," he added sarcastically.

She looked at him through a sheen of tears. "I owe you an explanation. But I can't think with you standing there glaring at me like the big bad wolf."

"I'm just a man, standing in front of a woman, asking her to love me the way I love her—with all my heart and soul."

"Not very original. Notting Hill if I recall."

"Give me a break. What do you want from me?"

"I want time to recover and think. This has all been too much. Do you know what it's like to think you have cancer—for a second time. I've never been able to think too clearly when it comes to you. You overwhelm my senses."

He sighed and took the chair opposite her not sure he was prepared for what she was about to say.

She licked her lips and he remembered how they felt around his cock. It seemed like a century since he'd last made love to her. God, he wanted her.

"I'm a mess. I'm scared. I do love you. But I also don't fully trust you. Everything is happening too fast, and when I thought I had cancer again, I pushed you away because I thought you'd leave me anyway."

He wanted to say he loved her and he'd never leave her, but he let her talk.

"That night we made Connor meant so much. It was more than a one-night-stand to me. I thought we had made a real connection. I finally thought you cared for me, if not loved me a little. For you to sleep with me and not care what Marcus thought, screamed commitment." She stopped and brushed a lone tear off her cheek. "But then the next morning you left. I knew you had to go back to the circuit, but you simply removed me from your life as if I didn't exist. You would not take my phone calls or answer my emails. It broke my heart."

"I'm so sorry I hurt you like that. I was so scared of the feelings you stirred in me. I had the life I'd always wanted, a successful career, and then that night with you turned my life on its head. I didn't think I was worthy of your love and I didn't really believe in it. I thought you were a young girl infatuated with her brother's best friend."

She smiled through her tears. "I guess that is how I feel now. Can I believe in those three little words from your mouth—'I love you'? In the back of my mind, all I see is your joy at being a father to Connor. I just happen to be part of that package. When I got sick, I thought once you saw how bad cancer gets, you'd simply take Connor and leave me again. I couldn't bear that pain again, so I pushed you away first. And I'm so sorry."

Tom fell from the chair to his knees and crawled to kneel at her feet. He took her hands in his. "I do love you. I love you so much it hurts to be this close and not pull you into my arms and thank God you're not sick. The idea of losing you terrified me. It may have been Connor that pulled us back to each other, but I swear I'd love you even if he no longer existed." He placed her hand over his heart. "Feel how fast my heart is beating. It's beating like that because I'm petrified I'll lose you. And I don't know if I could bear that pain."

"I want to believe you so much."

He rested his lips on her forehead. "What can I do to convince you?"

"Just give me a little space and time. Let me process everything that's happened."

"How much space?"

She smiled and his heart bloomed. "Well, you will only be across the road."

He sat back on his haunches. "I can do that, although I don't want to. We've wasted so much time already. I guess that's why I'm so impatient to make you mine." She simply smiled at him. "Okay, I can do this. I'll give you your space. Just let me know when you're ready. I'll be here waiting with my heart on my sleeve."

"Thank you."

He rose to his feet and with a pain lodged in his chest he said, "I'll go grab a few things and move over the road."

He'd give her the space she needed, but it felt as if someone had placed broken glass under his skin.

Chapter Twenty-Three

A week later and here she was ready for her big audition, but all she could think about was Tom. They'd had dinner together with Connor last night at her house. He'd made such a big deal out of how she would slay everyone with the song she'd written. The boost to her confidence was just what she'd needed, but she also heard the faith and pride he felt for her in his words.

She loved him and her whole body lit up with love when he looked at her. He loved her too. She knew that now. She'd stayed the night with him since her infectious stage was likely over.

As she sat down at the keyboard in the studio, she thought Fate was very cruel indeed since the song she had to play was a heartbreaker. Hard to sing when she was so happy. Not only would she have to play the piano track for it, but then she was supposed to go back and lay down the backup track.

She'd run through it a couple of times yesterday and hadn't made it through the first time because she'd broken down. That's when she'd realized she was being an ass not trusting in Tom.

"Bryce, I will go through it twice," she said. "Let me know when the big-shots get here and are ready to hear me, okay?"

Bryce Scoggins nodded at her from the control booth. "You bet, sweetheart," he said over the speaker system.

Kendra gave him a tight smile and stretched her fingers a little before poising them over the keys. Then she began playing and just concentrated on the instrument instead of hearing the lyrics in her head.

When she finished, Bryce said, "That was good, honey, but seemed a little stiff. Cold. Needs more emotion if you want to impress them."

Kendra sighed. She trusted Bryce's expert opinion. "Okay. I will sing along this time and see if it makes a difference."

"Good idea."

She began the intro and came in at the correct cue. As she sang the sad lyrics, Kendra let the pain come through, remembering how she'd felt about Tom when she'd had Connor on her own. She swayed to the beat as her hands moved gracefully over the keyboard. By the time the song was over, tears rolled down her cheeks.

"Jesus, Kendra," Bryce said. "You got me almost bawling in here."

Kendra wiped away her tears and gave a shaky laugh to cover her inner turmoil. "Is that a good thing?"

"Hell, yeah. You do it that way for Shaina Collins and you're going to nail it," Bryce said. "They'll be here soon. You want to do it again?"

Kendra needed a little time before she played or sang it again. "No. I'm good."

Bryce picked up his cellphone and said something that Kendra couldn't hear through the glass separating them. When he hung up, he turned on the speaker system. "They're here and on their way to the studio."

Kendra felt like a thousand birds had nested in her stomach and they were fighting to get free. She put a hand to her midsection and took a deep breath. Standing up, she went to join Bryce in the control booth. She made sure that her sparkly, flowy black miniskirt, purple mid-drift shirt, and black leather jacket were in place.

"Don't worry, Kendra. You look hot," Bryce said, waggling his eyebrows.

She laughed into his blue eyes. "Shut up. I'll tell your wife you said that."

"Yeah, yeah," he scoffed.

The door opened and Kendra felt faint with nerves as Shaina Collins and her entourage entered the sound booth. The studio manager, Russ Stark, made the introductions and Kendra worked hard not to go all fangirl on Shaina. Shaina had a golden voice that matched the rest of the gorgeous, statuesque blonde.

Russ smiled at Kendra. "Ready to show them your stuff, kid?"

Kendra put a confident smile on her face, even though fear made her heart race. "Definitely."

She left the control booth and entered the studio. Sitting down at the keyboard, she thought of the man she'd almost lost by being so silly, the one who would always hold her heart, and started to play.

A few hours later, she drove home on a high. Shaina had loved her song. She was so excited. This could be her big break.

The only person she wanted to tell was Tom.

She dialed her hands free.

"How'd it go?"

She smiled at the eagerness in his voice. "It was incredible. They loved the song. I wanted you to be the first to know because your pep talk last night and faith in me really helped. I love you, Tom."

There was silence for one moment but then thank God, he said, "I love you too, Kendra. And always will."

The grin on her face was so wide she must look like a clown. "I know. I'll see you soon and we need to talk."

When she hung up, she didn't sing a sad song; she sang her favorite song, A Thousand Years

Heart beats fast
Colors and promises
How to be brave
How can I love when I'm afraid to fall
But watching you standalone
All of my doubt suddenly goes away somehow
One step closer…

Chapter Twenty-Four

That evening, Kendra was on her way to Bad Boy Autos. Marcus had called and invited her to dinner to celebrate her success. She had wanted to talk with Tom and tell him everything she was feeling, but Tom needed to be with his father. For some reason he didn't want her there, which raised her insecurities again until he'd told her Marcus had a huge celebration planned and he would join her there later.

They had bought her song. She would soon be known across USA when Shaina turned it into a hit.

Marcus was taking her to Providence, an upscale restaurant on Melrose Avenue, but she had a stop on the way.

"I don't know why I had to meet him at the shop," she muttered as lightning lit up the sky. "We could've just met at the restaurant."

The first raindrops started peppering the windshield when the van jerked and she heard an ominous, familiar flapping sound.

"Oh, no, no, no!" Kendra quickly pulled over on the side of the road before she ruined another rim. "I don't believe this!" She pounded on the steering wheel. "Shit!"

She sat fuming for several minutes as cars whizzed by her

and then opened her door. Rain immediately battered her, completely soaking her nice dress and ruining her makeup and hair. She saw that the driver's side rear tire was flat. Furious, she stomped as well as she could in high heels around to the hatch and opened it.

"I can do this," she muttered. "I can put this damn donut on it just as Tom taught me."

Her anger gave her strength, and she succeeded in getting the donut out of the well. She leaned it against the bumper and grabbed the lug wrench. Now that she knew how to do it, loosening the lug nuts went fast. She laid them in the van and looked at the jack.

"Where do I put it?" She went over her lesson from Tom, trying to figure it out. They hadn't got to that part in her lesson, but it didn't take a professor to work it out. But as she made to wind up the jack the handle snapped off in her hand. "Goddamn it to hell. I should have let Tom buy me a new car with self-inflating tires. We will pick one out tomorrow—together and I with the money from the sale of my song, I can finally pay for it." She put the donut back in the van, threw the lug wrench into the back and shut it.

Back in the driver's seat, she shoved her soaked hair out of her eyes, and called Marcus' number. "You better pick up." When he didn't, she swore and called everyone else, but no one answered their phone.

At wit's end, Kendra leaned her head against the headrest and let out a primal scream. There was only one final number she hadn't called. Bringing up Tom's number, Kendra looked at his picture and traced it with her finger. He would be with his Dad... but needs must. She hit the call button.

* * *

Tom took his buzzing cellphone out of his pocket and surprise shot through him when he saw that it was Kendra. He hit the answer button. "Hi Kendra?"

"Yes. I'm sorry to bother you as I know you're with your

father, but I called everyone else and no one's picking up. You won't believe this, but I have another flat tire. I tried changing it, but the jack's handle broke. I got the lug nuts off, if that counts. And I must admit I'm feeling pretty exhausted."

Hearing her voice made Tom happy, but hearing that she was stranded again didn't. "Where are you?"

"On Welles Street, a little past Carter Avenue."

"I'll be right there. You get in that fricking clunker and lock your doors."

"I already did."

"I'll be right there."

Tom jammed his cellphone back in his pocket and ran from the shop.

* * *

Kendra's heart kicked into a fast rhythm when she saw a car pull up behind her. A woman alone in a broken-down car on a stormy night; sounded like a good start to a horror flick. When they blinked the lights twice, relief washed through her because she knew that it was Tom.

She watched in her rearview mirror as he got out of his Mustang and walked to the van. Getting out of her car, she met him at the rear. He was already soaked, as was she. Rain ran from his hair down his face and dripped from the suit he wore. He'd never looked better to Kendra.

"Get back in the van," Tom shouted over the growling thunder. "You're sick, remember."

Ignoring his order, she said, "I'm almost fully recovered. I already have the lug nuts off, so it shouldn't take long to fix it. We could use your jack."

"Shit, I forgot to bring one to fit this wagon."

"What do we do now?"

He didn't say anything as his gaze traveled over her. Despite the chilly rain, she heated under his slow perusal. When his eyes returned to hers, she clearly read the desire in them.

"Don't look at me like that."

Tom moved closer. "What?"

She shouted to be heard over the crashing thunder. "Don't look at me like that!"

Just seeing Kendra's beautiful face again filled Tom with hunger, but it was more than just physical. He hungered to always be with her, to share a life, and to be a family with her and Connor.

Maybe it was the storm, but Tom felt a torrent of emotion flood his heart and he couldn't hold back. "Like what?" he yelled back. "Like I want you, and I need you, and love you? Because I do! I've never lied to you, not once Kendra. I may have run from you before, when I was young and stupid, but I'm not running now. Can you trust me? Can you let me into your life and heart?"

The moisture that filled her eyes broke his heart. He wanted to pull her against him and promise that everything would be all right, but he needed her to believe it, to believe in him.

She brushed her wet hair off her face. "I'm so sorry it's taken me this long. I do trust you. I've been miserable without you and I can't believe how wonderful you've been to both Connor and I, even when you thought I didn't want a relationship."

"I feel as if I've waited a lifetime for you Kendra, I'm happy to wait forever if that is what it takes to make you understand I'd never hurt you. I'd never leave you."

She took a tentative step towards him. "I want, need, and love you so much it hurts when you are not around. If you still want me in your life, I'm yours."

He softened his expression. "Do you really mean that? You've forgiven me the past and you trust me with your future? With your heart?"

"Yes. Is it too late? Have we wasted so much time we can't find our way back?"

He grabbed her upper arms. "Do you *want* it to be too late?"

Mustering her courage, Kendra shook her head. "No, I don't

want that! I want to plan a life with you and Connor. I want to have more children with you and I want you there with me."

Cupping her face, Tom asked, "I can live with that."

More thunder crashed overhead and Kendra had to scream to be heard. "You are all I want and I know you'll never hurt me."

"I want to kiss you."

"There's a small chance you might still get mono."

"I don't care." Tom's mouth descended on hers with a hunger borne of all three: need, desire, but mostly love. He didn't care if he caught mono, it was worth the risk.

Fire met fire as she parted her lips and tried to convey all those things back to him.

His arms encircled her in a crushing embrace as they continued kissing while jagged lightning arced across the sky. Neither of them cared about a broken-down van, a dangerous storm, or being buffeted by sheets of rain. All that mattered was that they were together again.

Kendra was left reeling when Tom suddenly drew back from her. He jammed a hand in his suit pants pocket and pulled something out. "What are you doing?" she asked when he kneeled on one knee in a huge puddle.

"What I should've done four years ago." Tom tried to remember the carefully rehearsed proposal that Lexie had helped him with, but only a few phrases came back to him. "Kendra, you're the most amazing, brave, gorgeous woman I've ever met, and I was such an idiot and coward not to admit my love for you back then. I'm sorry that through my cowardice I hurt you so much—"

The sky split, making them flinch.

Tom resumed in a moment, "And wasted so much time because I was too scared to take a chance. But I promise—" More thunder intruded on what was supposed to be the most romantic moment of their lives. "I'll not waste any more time or ever leave you and Connor ag—" The storm just wouldn't give up. Tom yelled up at the heavens, "Shut up! I'm trying to propose to the woman I love here!" In a rush he said, "I loved you then, I love you now, and I'll always love you." He held up a ring box, removed the ring from inside it, and threw the box over his shoulder. "Kendra Black, will you marry me?"

Dumbfounded, Kendra stared at the ring and then into his eyes. He was all she'd ever wanted since she'd been sixteen, and she couldn't believe that she was getting her wish. Love beat through her like the rain on her head. This man loved her and her heart flew free, flew straight to Tom and into his trustworthy hands. Before the next thunder roll, she said, "Yes! Yes, I'll marry you!"

Careful not to drop the ring, Tom slid it on Kendra's finger and swept her into his arms. He twirled her around while they exchanged a damp kiss.

Parting from her, Tom said, "Get your stuff. I'll come get this heap of junk tomorrow and send it to the junkyard. You're getting a new car. Let's get out of this storm."

"Okay. Besides, I've probably made you sick with that kiss. I'm not supposed to be infectious still but..." She smiled sexily. "We should get out of these wet clothes."

"That sounds like a great plan." His eyes sparkled with desire.

Kendra hurried to the front of the van while Tom put the donut in the back and shut it. As soon as they were seated in the Mustang, the storm let up and by the time Tom started the car, there was only a light drizzle.

Tom ran a hand over his face and looked out the windshield. "Really?" he asked the sky. "Really? Now you quit?"

Kendra cracked up and he tried to glare at her, but he couldn't hold back his own laughter.

In a few moments, Kendra said, "I'm all dressed up because I was supposed to be going out with Marcus, but why are you wearing a suit to visit your dad? A suit I can't wait to peel off you, by the way. You should wear suits more often. Or perhaps not, you're way to sexy in them. I'd have to beat the girls off you."

Tom took her left hand and rubbed his thumb lightly over the ring that glittered on her finger. "Well, I didn't have this with me by mistake. I was sick of you being stubborn. I believed in us. I believed in your love for me. The reason he told you to come to the shop was because I was going to propose to you there and we planned a party to celebrate."

Kendra was astounded. "I thought you'd given up on me?"

"Never." He linked his fingers through hers. "Stella told me you just needed time to process everything. What with finding out I never knew about Connor, to being surprised that I wanted a life with you, to thinking you had cancer... It's been one hell of a ride for you the past few weeks."

Tears fell once again. She brushed them away. "The mono makes me weepy." She wanted to move on to happier things. "You planned an engagement party for me?"

"Yeah."

She was deeply touched. "You're unbelievable. How did I get so lucky?"

"Nah. I'm the lucky one," Tom said. "You waited for me."

Kendra squeezed his hand. "We're lucky."

"Okay."

She smiled and shook his hand a little. "Pretty sure of yourself, aren't you?"

"No. I didn't know what you'd say, but I had to be brave and take the chance. I had to know if you still loved me, and still wanted me," he beamed.

"I was living in the past and I of all people know life is short. Trust is a leap of faith, and I have faith in you—in us. I love you and want to share a future with you," Kendra responded.

Just then the sound of a phone ringing fileld the car.

"It's Sam." Tom's scalp tingled with dread.

Kendra sobered as he answered it. She rested her hand on his knee and held her breath while he listened to Sam.

"When? Now?" Tom blew out a breath. "All right. I'll be right there."

He hung up and Kendra was afraid to ask what Sam had said.

Tom looked at her with a strange expression. "That was Sam."

"I know."

"I have to get to the hospital right away," Tom said, pressing his fingers to his eyes.

Tears stung Kendra's eyes and she caressed his shoulder. "I'm so sorry, honey."

Clearing his throat, Tom took calming breaths. "No, Dad's okay. In fact, the surgeon wants to give the transplant a go since he's been improving the last couple of weeks. It's gotta be tonight if there's any hope for it to work, though. He could start getting worse. Dad understands the risks. I'm sor— "

Kendra clapped her hand over his mouth. "Don't be sorry. Just drive. Let's go so you can save your dad's life."

Tom nodded against her hand and kissed her hard when she took it away. Then he turned the ignition and the engine roared to life. At a break in cars, he swung the car onto the road, executed a U-turn on the wet pavement, and put the hammer down.

Epilogue

Three months later, Tom growled and slid the tie from the collar of his tuxedo shirt. "Marcus, tie this thing, will you?"

Marcus snorted. "When was the last time you saw me with a tie on?"

Tom looked at him in the mirror. "You grew up wearing suits so you know how to tie one."

"Nope. Mom or Dad always had to do mine. Or Kendra when she wasn't in the hospital," Marcus said.

"That doesn't help me right now, does it? I can't ask Kendra or your parents. Will you go find Sam? I don't know where the hell he went," Tom said.

"Well, I'm not Sam, but will I do?"

Tom grinned and turned around. "Yeah, you'll do, Dad."

Vincent glanced at Marcus. "Do you mind if I talk to Tommy?"

"Nope," Marcus said. "That'll give me a chance to decide which lucky lady gets to go home with me tonight."

Vincent chuckled and took the tie from Tom as Marcus left the dressing room. "That one's a troublemaker."

Tom raised an eyebrow. "You should talk."

Vincent chuckled. "Takes one to know one, which is why I always knew that you would be our problem child. Sam was easy to raise, but you? You were a hellion from the beginning."

Tom laughed. "Guilty."

"Watch what I'm doing so you know how to do it the next time."

Vincent turned Tom around and started instructing Tom and as he did, Tom's mind went back to his earlier childhood when Vincent had spent hours teaching him and Sam to hit a baseball or how to ride their bikes. He'd been patient and encouraging.

When Vincent finished, he said, "Did you catch that?"

Tom sighed. "No. I doubt I'll ever get it."

Vincent patted his shoulder. "That's okay. We'll keep practicing so that when Connor's older you can show him. You should've picked the pre-tied one like I told you."

Tom turned sheepish. "Kendra liked the look and I didn't want to tell her I didn't know how to work them."

Vincent grinned. "I'm not surprised. We men hate admitting our weaknesses." He patted Tom's tie. "There. You're irresistible."

"Thanks."

"Now, I'll give you some fatherly advice since I'm still around to give it, thanks to you," Vincent said.

"Dad, you don't have to say that."

"Shut up. Your old man's talking."

Tom smiled, but stayed silent.

Vincent collected his thoughts. "Don't be anything like me and you'll be just fine. Don't ever pick up that bottle again, Tommy. I don't care how bad things get, don't do it. If you do, you'll lose everything, just like me. I lost your mother, you, and Sam to a certain extent. I almost lost my life to alcohol and if it wasn't for you, I'd be six feet under."

Tom clenched his teeth against the tears that threatened.

"If you steer clear of booze, you'll be just fine. And don't take it for granted that you'll wake up each morning. I hope you learned that from me and your bride." Vincent grinned. "You sure got yourself a good one, son."

"I know, Dad."

Vincent nodded approvingly. "Now, I need to tell you something else and then I'll quit being sappy. The second time you brought Connor to see me was the day that I started fighting to stay alive.

"I love all my grandkids, but I didn't get to spend any time with *him*. And I wanted to so bad. I also saw how miserable you were without Kendra and I wanted to be there for you, like I should've been when you were a teenager."

Vincent took a deep breath. "After you left that day, I told Dr. Camden to pull out all the stops, to try whatever he could to get me well. I was going to live or die trying."

Tom laughed at his wisecrack.

"I thought I was in hell, but it was worth it to me," Vincent said. "The next thing I know, Dr. Camden said that we have to do the surgery now. I didn't know what the hell he was talking about. I couldn't believe that you agreed to give me a part of your liver." He took Tom's face in his hands. "You're my hero, Tommy, and don't you ever forget that. I love you."

Tom said, "Okay."

"Okay? That's it? Just okay?"

Tom hugged Vincent. "I'm glad you're here, Dad. If you hadn't fought so hard, the surgery would not have worked. I'm really happy that you're getting better. I love you, too, Dad."

"Wow. More than two syllables. That's a record," Vincent teased.

Tom let him go. "Shut up."

Vincent chuckled and clapped Tom's shoulder. "I'll chat up that silver-haired fox I saw earlier."

"You do that." Tom smiled as his dad left the room and turned back to the mirror to study the tie. "Nope. Never gonna get it."

* * *

"Tom's won't be able to keep his hands off you," Stella said. "Fifty bucks says that you guys disappear halfway through the reception."

Kendra laughed. "No, we won't." She cut a sly glance at Stella. "Or maybe we will. I'd much rather start our honeymoon early than stick around with all you degenerates."

Stella pointed at her. "You're lucky it's your wedding day, or I'd smack you for that."

Lexie, who sat in a chair in the ladies dressing room, said, "Now, now, girls. No cat fights on a wedding day. It's bad luck. On second thought, go ahead, because luck doesn't have anything to do with marriage."

Stella said, "Sure it does. I've dodged that bullet so far. If that isn't luck, I don't know what is. Although seeing you and Tom together almost has me thinking I could try monogamy."

Lexie snorted. "Don't. You're a smart girl. Been there, done that. Never going back again."

Kendra said, "Hello. Getting married, here. Quit dissing marriage to the bride, okay?"

Lexie made a dismissive gesture. "Marriage is definitely for you, just not me."

"Yeah, sure," Kendra scoffed.

Lexie smiled and stood up. "I know because you're getting a great guy. Tom might be rough around the edges and all, but he's a good man. Patient, loyal, kind, and smart. And most of all, he loves you and Connor so much. I know you guys will be happy. Me—I always pick the assholes."

Kendra felt bad for Lexie. "You never know, you might meet someone else. A guy who's a lot better for you than Jason Colter ever was."

Lexie smiled. "There ain't no man good enough to ever get me to walk down the aisle again."

Stella grinned. "You could just live together in sin. That sounds like fun. Maybe I'll try it."

Lexie considered that. "If he was the hottest guy in the world, maybe, but I don't know anyone like that."

"You just described, Marcus," Stella said.

Lexie put up a hand and said, "Slow your roll, honey. No way would I ever get tangled up with him."

Kendra frowned at her. "What's so wrong with my brother?"

Lexie said, "Kendra, Marcus blames Jason for his crash and I was married to Jason at the time. I'm guilty by association. He and I argue about everything. We tolerate each other for Tom's sake, but we'll never be buddy-buddy. You better accept that now. Just being honest."

Stella said, "Did you guys have a thing?"

Kendra swung to look at her best-friend. Stella sounded almost like she was jealous. Possession filled her tone. What was that about? Had she and Marcus… no. Stella would have told her—wouldn't she?

Lexie shook her head. "Didn't you hear what I just said? Enough of Marcus. This is a happy day."

Kendra was more than willing to let the subject drop. "Yes, it is. I can't wait to marry Tom. It feels like I've been waiting for him my whole life."

Stella played with Kendra's hair a little, making sure that the updo would stay in place. "You have. I'll never forget the way you gushed about Tom the day you met him. You'd been given the all clear, and at sixteen the hormones were raging. And you've been talking about him ever since."

Kendra swatted at her hand. "Four years ago I didn't speak up, I didn't fight for him, and I lost so much time with Tom. I'll never make that mistake again."

"Which is why you'll be able to tell this little one that they were at your wedding," Stella said, patting Kendra's belly.

Kendra laughed and shrugged. "What can I say? We suck at birth control."

Resting her hand on her stomach, Kendra was thankful that she'd forgotten to get her birth control shot the month before she and Tom had slept together the first time. She couldn't be sure, but based on the timing, she thought she'd conceived on the night they'd admitted their love for each other. She was ecstatic to be marrying him and adding to their family right away.

Which was why she'd turned down Shaina Collins' offer to go on tour with her. Selling songs she could do, but she had no desire to be a back-up singer traveling from town to town. Tom was right; sometimes your dreams change. For the longest time, hers had been having a successful music career, and she would—as a song writer—so she could live out the life that really mattered. A life with her family.

Marcus came into the dressing room. "I hear that there's some crazy woman in here who wants to marry Tom."

Kendra smiled. "Yes, there is."

"God, look at you. You're gorgeous." Marcus kissed her cheek. "Stella, you look hot as always, and Lexie, you clean up pretty good."

Kendra frowned at him. "You be nice to her."

Marcus' eyebrows rose. "What? That was nice."

Lexie said, "Yeah. Trust me, Kendra. That *was* nice."

Marcus ignored her. "Ready to do this?"

Kendra nodded.

"Will you excuse us, ladies," Marcus asked.

"Wow," Lexie said to Stella as they moved towards the door. "He actually called me a lady," as Stella pushed her out the door and shut it behind them.

Kendra giggled as Marcus shot an annoyed look at the door.

Marcus blew out a breath. "I thought this would be easier."

"What? Being around Lexie today?" Kendra teased.

Marcus shook his head. "No. Letting you go. I'll always be here for you, but it's time that I give you to Tom the way I should've—"

"Marcus, don't."

"Please, just let me say this, okay?"

"Okay."

"The only reason I kept you away from Tom was that I didn't feel any guy was good enough, even my best friend." Marcus embraced her. "But I was wrong to keep you guys apart. I'm going to make up for that today by giving you to him. I know he'll take good care of you and Connor, and that's all that matters. So, come on. Let's go get you hitched."

Kendra put a hand on his arm. "I heard you that night, Marcus."

"What night?"

"When I was in the hospital with cancer. When I was sick as a young girl, you held my hand and talked and prayed so much. I held on to your determination to make me well. You made me want to live so we could make more memories together. Thank you for helping me fight. If you hadn't, I would've never met Tom, I wouldn't have Connor, and we wouldn't be getting married now," she said. "So, thank you for always being there for me."

Marcus' eyes were a little too bright and a tear trickled from one. "And I always will be. Okay, let's get out there before Tom comes looking for you."

W alking down the aisle on Marcus' arm, Kendra saw two familiar people near the front of the church on her family's side. She still couldn't believe that Tom had invited her parents, or that they'd accepted. Tom wanted them to work things out. Kendra didn't know if that was possible, but they were all trying. Her father had twisted his knee at golf yesterday or he'd be walking her down the aisle, but somehow having Marcus do it felt right.

Tom looked fantastic in his tux, but she couldn't wait to get it off him so she could see all his rippling muscles and tattoos; especially his newest one. It was the accompaniment of the one that now circled her left ankle. Hers read "Life is too short, so..." and his said, "...let those ponies run."

The closer she came to Tom, the happier Kendra grew, and she couldn't stop smiling. Tom's smile didn't dim, either. When he took her hands, she felt like all the pieces of her life were finally fitting together. She hadn't been completely whole without Tom, and she'd cherish every day with him in the future.

* * *

Looking into Kendra's luminous eyes, Tom could hardly believe this stunning angel in white was his. She was more than he deserved and he would strive to be the kind of man she and their kids could count on. Lowering his gaze to Kendra's stomach, he hoped that they'd give Connor a little sister.

His smile widened as he thought about her new and only tattoo. They'd gotten the new ink together, and he'd held her hand the whole time. With her typical bravery, she'd only whimpered once, but the rest of the time, Kendra had bitten her lip and toughened it out.

Not used to speaking in public, Tom concentrated on not flubbing his vows. Zip was videotaping the ceremony and he didn't want to look like an ass whenever they watched it throughout the coming years

Their gazes barely left each other, even during the ring exchange. The pastor gave them permission to kiss and Tom took her into his arms.

"I love you, Tiger."

"I love you, too."

Their kiss was slow and sensual, a promise of what would come later.

Just as their lips parted, the minister said, "I present to you, Mr. and Mrs. Thomas Vincent Lorde."

Tom tightened his arm around her and sighed. "Ready for pictures, babe?"

She chuckled at his resigned attitude. "Cheer up. We're preserving the memories of the happiest day of our lives."

"You're right. Let's go."

Tom secretly enjoyed the experience, but grumbled the whole time just to see Kendra's emerald eyes shine with laughter. He wanted to always make her that happy. And then there was Connor. Over the last three months, he'd fallen in love with his boy a little more each day.

In one of the pictures, he sat with Kendra leaning back against him with his hand around her waist. He placed his hand over Kendra's stomach and knew that it would be the same with the little life that grew inside her. He'd missed so much with Connor, but it would be different with this baby.

When the pictures were done, Tom picked Connor up and took Kendra's hand. Together they walked outside to the new Porsche Cayenne Wagon that Tom had bought for Kendra. It was decorated with pink streamers and white balloons that said, "Just Married" in silver lettering. She handed Connor off to Vincent and got behind the wheel. She turned the ignition and the purr of the engine thrilled her.

Tom got in and kissed her cheek. "Let's go party."

Kendra put the car in gear and took off.

* * *

Sully pulled Marcus aside just as they were entering the reception. "I took a message from Kade Colter today. He said, he'd be in on Monday with a 1962 Alfa Romeo Spider that needs a complete overall and that you've agreed Lexie would work on it."

At his raised eyebrow Marcus said, "And?"

"Does Tom know about this? I mean, *Kade Colter*—her ex-brother-in-law. What the hell is that about? Lexie will spit like a wildcat when she hears, and Tom's going to have your balls on a plate."

"It's business, that's all. If I can stomach a Colter then so can she. Colter insisted on Lexie working on his car. She is the best mechanic to work on the Italian vehicles. I told him that if he disrespected Lexie, I'd have *his* balls on a plate."

"Let me guess, he's paying good for the privilege." Sully

shook his head. "I want to be around when you find something you care about more than making money. And I'm warning you now. Any funny business from Kade, if he upsets Lexie in any way, I'll make sure he never bothers women again, and you can stick this job where the sun don't shine." With that, Sully stalked into the reception hall.

"Sully seems to be in a bad mood for someone at his boss and best friend's wedding," Stella said as she hooked her arm through Marcus's and led him inside.

Marcus's serious gaze disappeared and his sexy grin that always made her body heat and think of cool satin sheets, replaced it. "I've seen too little of you lately. I've missed you," he whispered as his hand molded her left buttock. "Care to let me take you home and give you wild orgasm's all night?"

Stella usually would have jumped at the chance of taking Marcus home. His body was smoking hot, and he knew his way around a woman's body as well as he could drive fast cars—like a world champion. They'd been FWB (friends with benefits), for years, and she was really proud of the fact that no one even knew. It added to the excitement and eroticism. But watching Tom and Kendra over the past few months had twisted something deep inside.

"Maybe. Catch me later and I'll let you know."

Marcus winked, "I promise not to get thoroughly shit faced then, just in case," and he moved toward the bar.

Just then she caught Kendra starring at her with a frown on her face. The bride made her way across to Stella. "What's going on with you and Marcus?"

Stella laughed. "Going on? Don't be ridiculous. Nothing. Why?"

Kendra tipped her head and looked at her for so long Stella thought she knew. Then Kendra shook her head. "I'm being silly. The idea of the two of you together is ludicrous. Both of you are as bad as the other—relationships are out, hot sex with no ties—is in. It's a wonder you two have never hooked up."

Stella felt her face heat. To take Kendra's mind off her suspicions, she linked her arm with Kendra's and led her back to Tom. "What if I told you I'm re-thinking the whole love'm and leave'm one-night stand thing?"

"I'd say you were overcome by the emotion of the day. I do look good in this wedding dress. You just want a chance to wear one of your own."

"Ah, you know me so well."

Kendra stopped and pulled Stella round to face her. "Are you for real?"

Stella nodded. "I think I want that special person. I want a 'Tom'. You know, the one."

"Well, you don't find 'a Tom' from a one-night stand." Kendra laughed gaily. "Or maybe you do, but only if you've known him for years. You just have to be brave and open to the idea of letting a man into your heart."

"Sigh. Nothing's easy is it?"

"Have you got a man in mind?" the bride asked, not realizing Stella did.

The reason she hadn't been so 'available' to Marcus of late, was she didn't want to just be a FWB to him. She wanted to be important to Marcus. More than just a casual lay. She wanted to be someone he cared about.

She'd hoped by pulling back he'd take note, but so far, he still only viewed her as his little sister's hot, sexy best friend. Somehow, she had to find a way to change his perception and perhaps get under his skin.

Kendra looked around the reception at all the guests. "There's a lot of hot racing car guys here tonight. Maybe we could find one with a heart."

Stella reacted with a pretend shudder. "Lexie would say hell no."

Kendra pulled her in for a hug. "I will make it my mission to find the perfect man for you. Someone who will love you as you deserve."

As they made their way over to the head table, Stella wished Kendra could make her brother grow up and see what was under his nose.

* * *

Once the scrumptious meal was eaten, the DJ announced the 'bride and groom' dance and the newlyweds took the floor.

Taking her in his arms, Tom whispered against her ear, "Ready to shock the shit out of them all?"

Kendra giggled. "I can't wait to see their faces."

"Me, either. Let's do it."

Their song, *A Thousand Years* began playing and Tom waited a few beats before beginning the waltz they'd rehearsed since he'd recovered from surgery. Gliding across the dance floor, Tom couldn't take his eyes from his bride.

He never thought he'd ever be able to live out the dream of marrying the woman who'd captured his heart so long ago. As he twirled her around the dance floor, he vowed to himself that he'd never take her for granted.

Pulling her into his embrace again, Tom said, "I love you, Tiger, and I'll never let you go."

Kendra smiled up at him. "I'll never let you go, either. I love you so much, Tommy."

He kissed her with such feeling he thought his heart would burst.

She pulled back on a sexy grin. "The night I went to your house to tell you about Connor I should have known you were a closet family man." She giggled at his raised eyebrow. "What man, who doesn't want a family, plans to build a big family home." She pressed closer. "Remember the promise you made not long after we became engaged? You promised me our family home would be ready by the time this little one is born," and she pushed her bulging stomach into him.

He twirled her around before adding, "It will be finished. Didn't I promise that I would never, ever lie to you?"

At her look of delight, he secretly hoped his contractor didn't let him down...

"Just as well I told the contractor there would be a big fat bonus if he got the house finished by September. I'd hate for you to have told me your first lie."

He threw back his head and laughed with joy. He had found the woman he could trust with his heart and who would never leave him, even if he was not quite perfect.

Luckily they were perfect together, the perfect family, and that's all that mattered.

The End

Click here to sign up to Bron's Book Club newsletter and receive your FREE eBook.
READ on for the first chapter of Lexie's book - Purr For Me book #2 in the Drive Me Wild Series.

Read other books by Bronwen Evans

Make sure to check out these titles and more on Bron's website.

Excerpt - Wrong Turn

Chapter One

"You've got to be kidding." Lexie glared at her best friend Tom Lorde as she sat on the other side of his desk in the office of Bad Boy Autos. "I can't believe you're doing this to me."

Tom's returning stare was just as direct. "I'm not doing anything to you. You're the best restorer of Italian sports cars here, and that's what this job needs. Besides, Sully is all over this. Do you really think I'd leave you facing this alone? Sully has your back."

Stay cool, don't get angry. The private detective she wanted to hire to find Jason cost more than she ever imagined, and Bad Boy Autos paid the most. She needed this job. Time was running out. Besides, Tom had promised to help her find her ex. If she didn't find Jason Colter and soon, she'd... It was as if the locket hanging against her bare skin around her neck burned.

Lexie lowered her voice to an ominous timber. "That's not what I'm talking about. Kade Colter, Tom. *Kade.* He's my ex-husband's brother. You know, my coke-head husband that beat me, abused me, and then stole all my money."

Guilt and remorse flickered in Tom's blue eyes before his expression hardened. "I know Jason was a real bastard to you, but Kade always treated you decent, right? They're so different I can't believe they have the same parents. Besides, a few months ago we turned his business away for you. We can't do it again. Kade could really damage our reputation if he lets everyone know we keep turning his business down. He's rich and mixes in the right circles to destroy us."

Lexie knew from Tom's tone that he was going to be a real hardass about this. There was no point in wasting her breath with her boss and owner of Bad Boy Autos, but she didn't have to pretend to like it. She rose and left the office without another word.

"Lexie! Come back here!"

Ignoring Tom, Lexie headed for the bay she shared with Jake Sullivan, aka, Sully. Since he was working on a vintage Indian motorcycle that week, there was plenty of room for a car in the bay. An Alfa sat there, looking forlorn with its faded and chipped racing red paint. A couple of scratches ran down the door on the side facing her. They reminded Lexie of the deep wounds gouged in her heart. She wanted to hug the car, it might be damaged like her, but hell, with some tender loving care it would blossom. She took a gulp of air and rubbed her chest. All it needed was a bit of love. Just like her. *No. Never again.* Love sucked. Like this battered car, she'd become bitter and broken and thrown away.

"Can this morning get any worse?" she softly said to herself through gritted teeth. Sweat dripped down her brow as the thermometer inched up to 92 degrees, her temper rising with the mercury. Kade—bloody—Colter leaned against the 'seen better days' 1962 Alfa Romeo Spider. The quintessential sports car was a wreck, but it was a pure diamond in the rough.

What a beauty! She raked her gaze over Colter. Yep, a real beauty. Damn it.

Kade grinned and leaned in, all denim and swagger, smelling

like a male model. Looking like a male model. Hot. She ground her teeth. Handsome wasn't even his middle name. It should be his first—Handsome Colter. And how like him to own the one car her hands itched to work on.

As she walked nearer, she pushed her hair back off her face. All the better to see the car with—*yeah, right.* Her gaze shifted from the car to Kade's dark, mesmerizing eyes. He stepped closer and suddenly the air fled from her lungs. She caught her bottom lip between her teeth to distract him from seeing the pulse pounding hard in the hollow of her throat. Could he see? *Dear God, please no.* Why had she married the wrong brother? Her life would have been completely different if she'd meet Kade first. She hated him for making her think that. Hated him for insisting she work on his car.

"I brought you a present," he nodded his head at the Alfa. "How d'you like to work on my car," Kade's sexy voice added to the headache building behind her eyes.

Placing her hands on her hips, she smiled. Rock and a hard place… This is what it felt like to be trapped. A thought struck. She could tell him to fuck off, but as her fingers trailed over the chassis, she admitted she wanted this job. For the joy of restoring the car, of course. *Only the car.*

A picture of the ATM swallowing her card this morning was all it took to remind her she could not afford to lose this job. Kade stepped closer and he smelled delicious. She should run, leave, but Kade's brother had taken all her choices—taken everything in fact. Money, house and her pride. The other half of Bad Boy Autos, Marcus Black only needed one little reason to show her the door and pissing off Kade was a big reason.

Her eyes narrowed as she took in Kade's stance, leaning over the hood of the Alfa as if he owned this workshop, with a smug look on that handsome face. When did she really ever have a choice?

"She will be amazing when I've finished with her." Her stare dared him to disagree.

"I know," he said as he pushed off the car. "Good—"

"So, what's her story?" Lexie interrupted him. The pleasantries were over. She wanted him gone. She started looking the car over. The hood was in the same sorry state as the passenger side. "Needs a complete new paint job but let's see what's under this battered hood. Keys." She held her hand out to Kade.

He gave her a smile that brought back a lot of memories she wished her brain would forget. "You haven't changed. Still beautiful when you're pissed off."

"Not interested in chitchat. Keys."

"Still tough as nails too."

"Keys."

The warmth in Kade's eyes faded along with his smile. "Look, I know Jason—"

"You don't know shit, Kade, and I'm not discussing anything except this car with you," Lexie said.

Or perhaps not. She eyed Kade and a risky idea swarmed like buzzing bees in her head. Could Kade lead her to Jason? He'd said he had no idea where his brother was. Her eyes narrowed as she waited for him to hand her the keys. Was he lying? Was he protecting his brother?

Only her pride stopped her from asking Kade to cover the debts his brother left her with. This was her fault for being stupid and gullible, so she would fix it. Why should Kade have to pay for his brother's sins? She eyed him slyly. But it wouldn't hurt to have a backup plan. If the worst happened…

Kade slid his Ray-Bans back on and held out a keyring to her. She took it and went around to the driver's side. As she slid into the driver's seat, Lexie spotted Tom standing right behind where she'd just been. His eyes held a steely glint, and he'd crossed his arms over his chest. Their gazes clashed for a moment before she cranked the engine to life.

She smiled at the deep growl that met her ears. However, a moment later, the motor coughed, sputtered, and died. Lexie found the release lever and popped the hood. Kade beat her to the punch and had the hood propped open before she'd shut the driver's door.

"It's a mess," Kade said. "Which is why I had it towed here. Bad Boy Autos is the best at this work. Money's no object."

Tell that to someone who didn't know where her next meal was coming from. Jason was in the wind, hence the detective she now had to pay for too. He'd taken off and left her with debts she could never repay. He'd put the thing she cherished most in this word in jeopardy. *Girls! Never let your husband talk you into mortgaging anything that belongs to you!* She wanted to visit every high school and tell her story.

Jason. Just his name made her stomach fill with acid. Handsome, confident, with a sexy-as-sin-smile, and money to burn, can turn any woman's head, but unlike what she did with cars i.e. check under the hood, she was too young, too desperate for love, and too stupid to look below his surface.

She didn't want to look under another Colter's hood unless it had four wheels, so Kade could take that come to bed smile and try it on a woman stupider than her. But she wasn't opposed to using him to help her get her property back.

She glanced back at Tom, who still stood watching her like a snake about to strike. Tom warned her not to give Marcus cause to fire her. Marcus was not a fan of hers. He tainted her with the same brush as Jason, because on the racing track Jason had caused Marcus to crash, ending his racing career. That meant Marcus was just waiting for a reason to fire Lexie.

She needed this job. Needed the money—lawyers and detectives didn't come cheap. She reached up and fondled the locket she wore round her neck and never took off. She didn't need to open it to see the picture inside. A picture of her mother standing beside their cabin at Clear Lake. The cabin was the only thing her mother had left her, and now she might lose it. She kicked the car's tire. Where the fuck was Jason? Unless she could find him and get her money back, the bank would foreclose on the cabin. She squeezed the locket tighter, wishing she could beat herself black and blue for stupidly mortgaging the property when Jason asked.

Eat, Pray, Love should be required reading for all women.

Back to her conundrum. Pissing Kade off and having him take his business elsewhere would qualify as grounds for termination in Marcus' eyes—*and* Tom's—maybe. Thinking about the sea of debt she was drowning in, Lexie knew this job was the life preserver she needed to keep her head above water and pay for the best detective in California. If he couldn't find Jason… only then would she admit defeat. She still had time. A month. And now she had Plan B.—Kade Colter.

She would work with Kade. What was the saying? Keep your friends close, but your enemies closer? It wouldn't be dangerous at all… She mentally kicked herself. Surely she was immune to men, especially if their last name was Colter?

She choked with the unfairness of it all. Rubbing her pounding forehead, she sighed. Suck it up! She only had to interact with the car. Not sex on legs Kade Colter.

Closing her eyes for a moment, Lexie called on the iron will that had helped her survive all the hell Jason had put her through. She would *not* let Jason win. No, giving up and crumbling wasn't an option, wasn't in her DNA. Pulling in a fortifying breath, Lexie opened her eyes again and started examining the engine with a critical eye that many surgeons would've envied.

Fast Track To Love For Christmas 99c
Novella

Want to see more of Sully? I've a novella of Sully finding his perfect someone in the

BABY IT'S HOT OUTSIDE : A CHRISTMAS DOWN UNDER BOXED SET

It's only 99c on pre-order releasing 25 October 2021

Here's a snippet:
Fast Track To Love This Christmas
By Bronwen Evans

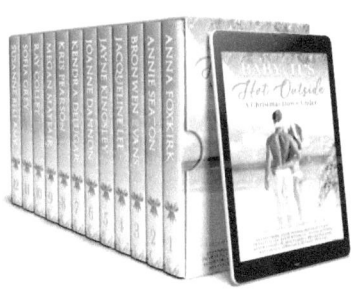

Bronwen set this Christmas romance in her home town of Havelock North, a hero for her heroine, but he's a visitor from the USA... Bron hopes a hero like Sully comes calling soon...

Karla turned and dangled the keys to the Jaguar in her fingers. "She's in good working order, but she's, as you say, vintage. But then you're a mechanic should she get temperamental."

"I can handle temperamental," and he moved closer.

"I'm sure you can."

He moved closer again. "This lunch tomorrow. Shall I pick you up in the Jag? If so what time? And is it casual?"

She swallowed back the desire to run her hand down the muscled chest that was only inches from her. "It's at a winery, outdoors, so it will be hot. A hat and smart casual will do. It's in aid of a charity that raises money for a primary school lunch programme for the lower decile schools in Hawke's Bay."

"That sounds like a good cause. Is primary school little kids? Elementary school we call it in the States. I didn't know NZ had such poverty."

"Most countries do, don't they? Primary school is from five until about ten years of age. How can we expect kids to sit and learn when they're starving. And if they don't learn we can't defeat the poverty cycle."

He reached out and ran a finger down her cheek. "It sounds like you're quite passionate about this. It's a fabulous cause. Anything that can help kids rise out of poverty gets my vote."

She shivered at his touch. This man was turning her insides out with just a smile. *Slow down, girl. Don't go getting real feelings for this man. He's not a keeper.* "I'm on the charity board." She didn't mention the charity was her baby. She'd built it up from nothing with a group of deep pocketed and time rich likeminded people. "Yeah, I am completely passionate about this. Loads of kids didn't have the fortunate upbringing I had, and I want to help even the score." Her ex had said she was wasting her time. She would prove him wrong.

"The world needs more people like you." The warmth in his eyes made her bottom lip tremble. "What time shall I pick you up outside the hotel? Or do you live elsewhere?"

"I live on the top floor of the hotel, the opposite end to your suite. So let's say 11.30am as I need to be there by 12pm and it's about a twenty-minute drive." She really should move away from the car but her feet wouldn't step away from him. Finally, she said keeping her voice light, "Have a good day. Remember to drive on the left," and she skipped round him and headed back to the elevator. Once again she could feel his eyes following her every step.

For one fleeting moment she wished Sully wasn't stirring her senses so much. He was the first man in a long time who affected her this much. She was beginning to hate the fact he would be leaving and that was dangerous. Why did she always fall for the wrong men?

Fall? Nope. No way. Never. Fun was what she wanted.

Only fun.

BUY LINK:

About the Author

USA Today bestselling author, Bronwen Evans grew up loving books. She writes both historical and contemporary sexy romances for the modern woman who likes intelligent, spirited heroines, and compassionate alpha heroes. Evans is a three-time winner of the RomCon Readers' Crown and has been nominated for an *RT* Reviewers' Choice Award. She lives in Hawkes Bay, New Zealand with her dogs, Brandy and Duke.

www.bronwenevans.com

Also by Bronwen Evans

Historical Romances

Wicked Wagers

To Dare the Duke of Dangerfield – book #1

To Wager the Marquis of Wolverstone   book #2

To Challenge the Earl of Cravenswood - book #3

Wicked Wagers, The Complete Trilogy Boxed Set

The Disgraced Lords

A Kiss of Lies – Jan 2014

A Promise of More – April 2014

A Touch of Passion – April 2015

A Whisper of Desire – Dec 2015

A Taste of Seduction – August 2016

A Night of Forever – October 2016

A Love To Remember – August 2017

A Dream Of Redemption – February 2018

Invitation To Series

Invitation to Ruin

(Winner of RomCon Best Historical 2012, RT Best First Historical 2012 Nominee)

Invitation to Scandal

(TRR Best Historical Nominee 2012)

Invitation to Passion

July 2014

(Winner of RomCon Best Historical 2015)

Invitation To Pleasure

Novella July 2020

Imperfect Lords Series

Addicted to the Duke – March 2018

Drawn To the Marquess – September 2018

Attracted To The Earl – February 2019

Contemporaries

The Reluctant Wife

(Winner of RomCon Best Short Contemporary 2014)

Coopers Creek

Love Me – book #1

Heal Me – Book #2

Want Me – book #3

Need Me – book #4

Drive Me Wild

Reckless Curves

Wrong Turn

Slow Ride

Fast Track To Love At Christmas - novella

Other Books

Dukes By The Dozen Anthology Boxed Set

Christmas In Kilts Anthology Boxed Set

Winter Wishes: A Regency Holiday Boxed Set

Highland Wishes And Dream

www.ingramcontent.com/pod-product-compliance
Lightning Source LLC
Chambersburg PA
CBHW020402210626
46816CB00006BB/2083